# DAKOTA HEAT, VOLUME 2

## *Dakota's Cowboys*
## *Dakota Springs*

## Leah Brooke

**MENAGE AMOUR**

**Siren Publishing, Inc.**
www.SirenPublishing.com

**A SIREN PUBLISHING BOOK**
IMPRINT: Ménage Amour

DAKOTA HEAT, VOLUME 2
Dakota's Cowboys
Dakota Springs
Copyright © 2010 by Leah Brooke

ISBN-10: 1-60601-654-7
ISBN-13: 978-1-60601-654-1

First Printing: March 2010

Cover design by Jinger Heaston
All cover art and logo copyright © 2010 by Siren Publishing, Inc.

Printed in the U.S.A.

**PUBLISHER**
Siren Publishing, Inc.
www.SirenPublishing.com

Siren Publishing

Ménage Amour

# Dakota's Cowboys

## DAKOTA HEAT ANTHOLOGY 3

# Leah Brooke

# DAKOTA'S COWBOYS

## *Dakota Heat Anthology 3*

### LEAH BROOKE
Copyright © 2010

## Chapter One

Dakota Wells braced her feet and looked down the barrel of her shotgun. "Get off my land."

The two men who'd just gotten out of their dilapidated truck halted in their tracks. Both lifted their hands, their surprise apparent. They shot a quick glance at each other before the one who'd gotten out on the driver's side spoke. "Ma'am, Mr. Tillman from the feed store told us you might be looking for hands. We were hoping you'd hire us."

His deep, husky tone sent a shiver through her. Dakota fought to ignore it and concentrated on studying them. Both looked to be a couple of inches over six feet tall. The shearling jackets they wore had been left open, giving her a glimpse of their powerful builds. The graceful, controlled way they moved warned her that they could strike out like rattlers. She definitely didn't want them to come any closer.

Their hair hung below their hats, the driver's a deep brown, the other's blonde. Their cowboy hats shaded their faces, preventing her from seeing their eyes. She'd learned to tell a lot about a person by watching their eyes. She tried to ignore the fluttering in her stomach as they both continued to stare at her. Inwardly cursing for allowing herself to be distracted, she forced herself to focus on their faces. The smiles they shot at her looked out of place and forced. Planting her feet more firmly, she narrowed her eyes.

She'd seen enough snakes with fake smiles to last her a lifetime.

When the blonde spoke, she shifted her gaze to him, keeping the gun aimed at the driver. "We know everything there is to know about horses. We also know about cattle, but Tillman said he didn't know if you still had any."

"I don't."

"Well, we can help with the horses and anything else you need help with." He gestured toward the porch she stood on with half the railing missing. "We can fix the porch for you." He pointed to the roof. "You got some shingles missing, and we could chop wood for your fireplace."

"I don't need any hired help, and even if I did, I can't afford to pay you. Goodbye."

The driver of the truck took a step closer and lowered his hands. "Ma'am, we'll be happy to work for room and board. We have no place to stay and can't afford one."

Dakota tightened her grip as the other man also dropped his hands. "I have no place for you to sleep."

The other man took a step toward her. "We'd be happy to sleep in the bunkhouse."

"Burned down."

When the driver started to take another step, Dakota pumped a cartridge into the chamber. "Close enough, cowboy."

He froze, lifting his hands again, looking more frustrated than afraid. "Ma'am, we'd be happy to sleep on the porch or in your stable. We just need meals and a place to shower."

Dakota eyed them warily. They didn't have the cocky attitudes the men Ed Franks usually sent over did. Far from it. These two looked hard and cold, but polite and respectful. Other than frustration, they showed no emotion at having a loaded shotgun pointed at them. The men Ed usually sent over would have already been inching toward their truck and either spurting threats or lewd comments.

It had been a long time since she'd been around a man with any balls. Other than her father and Ben Parson, the town deputy, her neighbor was the only formidable man she'd ever met. But Ed's courage came from his money and the men he constantly surrounded himself with.

In contrast, the two men standing in front of her would have been right at home in the old west. These two looked more than capable of taking care of themselves.

But could she trust them?

She cocked her head, gesturing toward the neighboring ranch. "I saw your truck going up to Ed's place the other day. What were you doing there?"

The driver shrugged. "Looking for work."

"And he didn't hire you?"

"No, ma'am. Said he didn't want any strangers around and to come back next month."

Damn it. That meant Ed didn't want any witnesses around. Now more than ever it would be good to have another set of eyes around. Or two.

"How do I know you didn't take a job with him and he's the one who sent you over here?"

He frowned at her as though confused, making her wish once again that she could see his eyes. "Why would he hire me and send me over here?"

Instead of answering him, she lowered the gun. "Look, I'm sorry you're having a hard time right now, but maybe you'd be better off finding some kind of work in town. Being out here with me could be dangerous."

The blonde flashed her a grin, which did strange things to her insides. "You're a tough woman, ma'am, but I think Joe and I can handle any danger from you."

Dakota narrowed her eyes again as his seductive tone shot heat straight to her slit. She shifted, uneasily. "That's not the kind of danger I'm talking about. But if you're thinking along those lines, then it's best you be on your way."

The driver stepped forward and Dakota raised the shotgun again. "I said that was close enough, cowboy."

He held his hands out again, shooting a look at his friend. "I can't deny you're a fine looking woman, but chasing you around doesn't put food in my belly. My friend doesn't mean anything by what he said. It's kinda hard to see any danger around here, except for falling off a horse, something I haven't done since I was four."

Her daddy had told her to always go with her instincts. She couldn't quite associate these men with Ed Franks. They just didn't seem like the kind of men who would blindly follow orders like the men Ed surrounded himself with.

She lowered the gun again, hoping like hell she wasn't about to make a huge mistake. "Before you decide to stay, you should know that Ed Franks," she gestured toward the ranch next door again, "is doing his best to run me out. Your lives may be in danger, no, make that *will* be in danger when he sends his flunkies over again."

The blonde frowned and pushed his hat back. Getting a good look at his face for the first time, she barely smothered a gasp. Tight features made him look cold and ruthless, but the gentleness in his gaze nearly undid her. "Are you telling us that the men over there are causin' you trouble, ma'am?"

Dakota blinked, trying to remember what they'd been talking about and smiled humorlessly. "You could say that. If you stay here, he's gonna have his men try to scare you off, buy you off, or kill you. Hey, if you can get past the scared, you'll be making money after all. I'm not sure how much he'll offer, but it'll be a helluva lot more than room and board. If you want to work until then, fine."

The blonde stepped forward. "My name's Colt Mason and this is my friend Joe Taylor. You don't have to worry about him buying us off ma'am. We won't leave as long as he's bothering you."

Dakota laughed. "Sure you will. Don't forget about the scaring you off part. You've got to get past that before you get the money."

The driver, Joe, narrowed his eyes. "We won't be taking any money from him and we don't scare easily."

Dakota nodded, not believing him for a minute. "We'll see."

"Yes, ma'am. You will."

\* \* \* \*

Joe came out of the stable and headed around the side of the house as soon as he heard the truck approach. He knew Colt had been out front for a while now looking at the porch, but also to watch out for anyone coming up the drive. He had no idea how far Dakota's neighbor had gone in his threats to her, but he would find out.

He knew how far he and Colt would go to stop him.

His opinion of Dakota had gone up considerably. The horses had been well cared for, and the stable, although old, appeared immaculate. The tack had also been kept in good condition. Dakota Wells knew her horses.

As he turned the corner of the house, he saw the woman who got out of the pickup point a shotgun at Colt. Colt stopped and raised his hands, much as they had earlier with Dakota. What the hell kind of danger had these women faced at the hands of that bastard?

Dakota came out the front door. "It's okay, Jill. These men work for me."

The cute brunette looked reluctant to put away the gun.

Joe stepped forward to stand next to Colt. "Ma'am, if it makes you feel better to hold onto the shotgun, fine, but can you point it away from my friend and me?" They hadn't come this far to get accidentally shot.

Dakota turned to face them, her blonde hair gleaming in the sun. The other woman was cute, but couldn't hold a candle to their employer, who looked like a damned wet dream. With luscious curves and a killer grin, she stirred him up in ways he hadn't been stirred in years.

If things were different, he and Colt would have had a hard time keeping their hands off of her.

Hell, who was he kidding? Already they had a hard time keeping their hands off of her.

But they could do nothing to jeopardize their reason for being here.

"Jill, this is Joe and Colt. I hired them this morning."

The brunette looked them over and apparently liked what she saw because she smiled flirtatiously. "They look tough enough. Did you warn them?"

Looking amused, Dakota smiled at her "How much do I owe you?"

When Dakota reached for one of the bags of groceries, Joe stepped in front of her and gripped her arm without thinking, cursing the thick jacket that kept him from feeling her skin. "We'll get this. Why don't you and your friend get inside out of the cold while we take care of this?"

The stunned look on her face and the way her breath quickened gave him an immediate erection despite the cold weather. Lust slammed into him as he watched her eyes go dark. The slight catch of her breath tightened his groin and brought his cock to full attention.

Surprised to see how tiny she really was, he stared down at her. She'd looked taller as she stood on the porch pointing a gun at him.

Her lips parted, the full bottom one trembling slightly, and it took every ounce of self control he could muster not to bend and claim it for his own.

But he and Colt had come this close to getting their revenge, and he couldn't let himself get side tracked. For a second, a split second, she'd made him doubt his dark intentions for revenge, the need that had driven him for years.

Shocked, he realized she'd done that with just a look.

He stared down at her, wishing things had been different. Wishing that he and Colt had met her after they'd finished their business. Wishing they had the freedom to give her all their time and attention and be what a woman like her would need. His chest tightened as he stared down at her. Her eyes took on a soft, dreamy look that called to every masculine instinct he possessed.

Her eyes, a clear, deep blue, darkened even more. Her long blonde hair, pulled back into a ponytail, looked so silky his hands itched to reach out and touch it. Her skin, clear, smooth and an adorable pink, appeared to be as soft as velvet making him ache to know what it felt like under his lips. Her shoulders looked too narrow to carry the burden she'd handled alone.

They stood that way for what seemed like an eternity. Her friend's tug on her arm had her blinking and pulling away, and only then did he realize the other two stood there watching them.

Dakota gulped. "Oh, uh, fine."

Joe watched her go back into the house, watching her tight ass sway as she took the steps and went inside. Not until she closed the door behind them could he look away.

Colt cursed under his breath. "Of all the fucking times to meet a woman like that, it has to be when we're so close."

"I was just thinking the same thing."

"Fate really has it in for us, huh?"

Joe sighed. "Yeah. What else is new? Let's get the truck unloaded. Tonight I want to find out just exactly what's been going on around here. We have to figure out the best way to get to him."

Colt sighed as he lifted bags of groceries. "Why in hell is she getting things delivered instead of going out to get them for herself?"

Joe hefted a bag of feed. "I don't know. It's another thing we're going to have to ask her tonight."

Colt paused and turned, looking around. "It's a shame we can't stay. This would have been a nice place to settle."

Joe started for the back with the feed. "It's kinda hard to kill a town's most prominent citizen and expect to stick around."

# Chapter Two

In the kitchen with Jill, Dakota tried to keep her attention on their conversation instead of sneaking glances at Colt as he carried in the groceries. She couldn't help but admire his tight butt as he walked back out to get another load.

There hadn't been a man around the house in quite a while, and Lenny had been nothing like the two men she'd just hired on. He would have found something else that needed his attention while she unloaded the truck. Like a beer.

Lenny had been all mouth, talking a mile a minute about his favorite subject. Himself.

These two had spoken no more than necessary since she'd hired them.

She'd always been a sucker for the strong, silent type.

Walking past the sink, she glanced out the window and couldn't look away from the sight of Joe carrying sacks of feed across the yard. Wearing jeans, a shearling jacket and a cowboy hat that had seen better days, he looked so damned sexy she wanted to run out, tackle him to the ground and have her way with him.

"They're really hot, aren't they?"

Dakota spun. "What?"

Jill smiled knowingly. "Your new hands. Damned fine looking cowboys. You going to let one of them in your bed?"

Dakota shushed her when she heard the front door open again. She felt her face burn as Colt walked into the kitchen. She couldn't think of a damned thing to say to break the silence, and Jill just sat there smiling. The uncomfortable silence seemed to last forever.

Colt obviously noticed. He looked at her curiously, and she could have sworn she saw his lips twitch as he put the bags on the table and walked back out again.

"I saw that look the dark haired one gave you outside."

"Joe."

"Yeah, and the other one, what was it? Colt? He eyed you up and down every time he came in. If you hadn't been staring at his chest, you probably would have noticed."

Dakota carefully kept her voice low, glancing at the doorway. "I hired them to help with some things around here. They're drifters, and they needed a place to say. They get room and board. That's it. You know as well as I do they'll be gone within a week. Just because you have a new boyfriend every other week doesn't mean everyone does."

"You're just jealous."

Dakota smiled at her best friend as she put groceries away. "I could never be as carefree as you are, Jill. I tried it once and look where it got me."

"Lenny was an asshole and you know it. These two are nothing like him. Why not have some fun with them? Who knows when you'll get the chance again?" She pulled Dakota to the kitchen window. It had started snowing again as Joe and Colt carried in the last bags of feed. "Those two are real men. I'd bet they have staying power. I'd love to be around when Ed's men tangle with them."

Dakota reluctantly turned away from the window and got the big pot out to start some beef stew. "We'll see."

"Come on, Dakota. Take a chance. You're a beautiful woman, and you don't even have to try to be. If I wasn't your best friend, I might just hate you. Ever since your momma died, your daddy kept you sheltered. All he wanted for you was the ranch."

Jill reached into the cupboard, getting glasses and opening the refrigerator for orange juice as she spoke. "When all that trouble started with Ed, your daddy hovered even more. Then he got sick and died. You never go out, and I'm the only friend you've got. You need to live a little, damn it."

Handing a glass of juice to Dakota, she gestured toward the window with the other. "If the way those men look at you is any indication, I think you're going to be in for a big surprise."

Dakota set her glass on the counter and started cutting the beef into cubes for browning. With the men here, she might get a chance to run into the next town to shop for more food. She hadn't counted on feeding two other people when she placed her order, especially two big men. "Jill, what I know about men could fit on the head of a pin with room left over. Besides, if I start messing around with one of them, it's bound to cause problems. In case you haven't noticed, I've got enough of them. Who cares how they look at me? They've probably been alone for awhile. I'm sure they look at any halfway decent woman the same way."

"Do you think I'm halfway decent looking?"

Dakota laughed at that. Her best friend in the world had had members of the opposite sex chasing her ever since high school. "You're too damned beautiful for your own good and you know it."

"Then why didn't they give me any more than a quick glance? And that was only when I had a gun pointed at them."

Dakota grinned, something inside her warming. "That's the same reception I gave them."

Jill hugged her. "You look sexier handling a gun than I do. I'd better get going, before I get snowed in. Jeff's coming over tonight, and I'm hoping he gets snowed in with me."

Dakota hugged her friend back, holding on longer than usual. "Thanks again, Jill. I don't know what I would have done all these months without you."

"You're the strongest woman I know, Dakota. You would have found a way. Don't forget what I said. Live a little. See ya, honey."

Dakota walked her friend out, waved her off and went back to her stew. Once she had it bubbling, she collected fresh sheets for the beds in the spare bedroom. As cold as it had gotten outside, she couldn't let

Joe and Colt sleep on the porch.

Maybe she should consider letting them sleep in the stable with the horses. At least there would be someone out there watching them. She paced, wondering what the hell she should do. If they worked for Ed, her horses could all be gone by morning.

Why the hell had she hired them when she didn't trust them?

She'd gone with her gut, that's why, she reminded herself. She could almost hear her father's voice telling her to listen to her instincts. She hadn't listened with Lenny and look where it had gotten her.

Besides, her horses were defenseless. She slept with a gun.

Hearing a knock on the back door jerked her back to the present. Dropping the sheets on the bed, she went to answer it. Both men stood on the back porch, which was nothing more than an enclosure for storage.

Joe took off his hat, knocking snow from it. "Ma'am, the horses are down for the night, and we brought up some more firewood."

Dakota stepped back. "Come in. Have some coffee. The stew will be ready soon." She gestured toward the hooks on the wall. "You can hang your coats and hats there to dry." She watched as they hung them and removed their boots. "Have a seat. We have to talk."

She got them each coffee as they sat down, pouring herself one for something to do with her hands. "It's too damned cold for you to sleep outside. I was just getting ready to make up the beds in the spare bedroom. But I'm warning you now, I sleep with a gun."

Both kept their eyes on her as they sipped their coffee. Finally Colt spoke. "Ma'am—"

"Stop calling me ma'am. It's Dakota. If we're going to live in the same house, you can't call me ma'am or knock on doors. But if you step out of line—"

Joe's jaw clenched. "We're not rapists."

Dakota nodded. "Just saying."

She couldn't help but notice their hands as they wrapped them around the thick mugs. They both had the hands of working men, scarred and callused. She couldn't help but wonder what they would feel like stroking her, holding her.

Damn. She couldn't allow herself to think about that.

"Dakota," Colt began again. "What's going on around here? Why did your friend bring supplies instead of you going out to get them? Why do you sleep with a gun?"

She sighed. "I told you. Big Ed next door is giving me a lot of trouble."

Joe leaned forward. "What kind of trouble?"

Dakota pulled out a chair and sat down, wrapping her hands around her own mug. "He burned my barn down. He stole my cattle. He sends his men to threaten me. He tries to steal the horses, or sometimes, just scares them. His men have shot out windows, put sugar in the gas tank of my truck, and cut down fences. Still want to work here?"

Colt's eyes flared. "And nobody stopped him?"

Dakota shrugged. "Well, he practically owns the town. A lot of people owe their livelihoods to him. Those who don't, he threatens. No one in town is allowed to sell me anything, or do business with me. Hell, they're all afraid to talk to me for fear of what Big Ed would do to them. Jill lives in the next town and brings supplies out to me once a week. I'm scared to leave the ranch. I have no idea what I'll find when I come back."

Joe covered her hand with his. "Why is your neighbor doing this to you?"

His touch felt so warm, so *capable*. They were the hands of a strong man, something she hadn't felt in…ever. It had been so long since another man had touched her, and she had to fight the raging need his casual touch aroused. She pulled her hand away. "He wants my land. He bought out or scared off all my neighbors to get the land he has now. But my land is the one he wants the most. It's the one with the pond on it, and he wants the water. He cut down my fence to let his cattle use it."

Colt got up to pour himself another cup of coffee. "Have you ever tried to stop him?"

"Yep. And while I was down at the pond, he had other men busy stealing my cattle. I can't be everywhere at once." She rubbed her arms, suddenly chilled. "They've been in my bedroom."

* * * *

Fury gripped Colt. No longer able to sit, he got up and moved to the window. "How do you know they were in your bedroom? What did they do?" The thought that men had done something so invasive to her brought all of his protective instincts to the surface.

"They messed up my bed, like somebody laid on it. They went through my things, messing them up and emptied my underwear drawer onto the bed and pawed through it."

Standing behind her, Colt couldn't see her face but heard the fear and disgust in her voice. His jaw clenched when she rubbed her arms again. Damn it, wasn't there anyone to protect her? "Did you call the sheriff?"

He shot a glance at Joe, to see his best friend watching Dakota, his own face hard and unyielding. Colt knew that look well, having been witness to it countless times over the years. It didn't bode well for the next man who decided to cause trouble for Dakota. It infuriated both of them when bullies picked on those weaker.

"Big Ed bought the sheriff off a long time ago. The only one who watches out for me is Ben Parson, the sheriff's deputy."

Colt didn't care for the affection in her tone for this unknown deputy and didn't take the time to ask himself why. He took his seat again, wanting to see her face. "Does this deputy have designs on you?" He slid a glance at Joe when Dakota shot out of her chair.

"It's none of your damned business."

Colt blinked as Joe flew out of his chair and was on her in an instant. Joe gripped her arms, his jaw clenched so tight, Colt wondered if he'd crack a tooth. He didn't often see Joe lose control, and it stunned him whenever it happened. Joe shook her once. "Are you fucking this man to help you?"

Dakota paled. "How dare you! Get out of my house."

Joe kept his voice dangerously low. "If you don't want us in the house, fine. We'll sleep in the stable with the horses. But we're not about to leave you here defenseless, and we're not going to stand by and watch this deputy take advantage of you, either."

\* \* \* \*

Dakota fought against Joe's hold and her own reaction to it. "He doesn't take advantage of me. He's a *friend*. I'm not a fucking whore, and I'm not defenseless. Didn't I hold the two of you off earlier?"

The ice in his eyes would have frozen her if it hadn't been for the heat pouring off him in waves. She glanced over to see Colt watching them, frowning.

Joe released her, leaving her feeling both relieved and bereft. "We'll be watching him."

"I told you, he's my friend. If you insult him, you're going to piss me off. He helps me as much as he can." She stepped back, turning away, needing to put some distance between them. Keeping her back to them, she stirred the stew and collected the ingredients for the biscuits. "Neither one of you know what it's been like around here, and you're not going to be here very long. If you start making even more trouble for me, you're gone. Mind your own business and take care of the horses, and we'll get along fine."

She could feel their stares as she started measuring out flour, and resisted the urge to turn around. She didn't care for the way they filled the kitchen with their presence, making the small space feel even smaller.

Her movements stiff, Dakota stirred the buttermilk into the dry ingredients and waited. A touch on her arm made her yelp and jump, flour flying over the countertop.

Colt grimaced. "Sorry. Do you mind if we get cleaned up before dinner? Afterward, we'll go out and bed down in the stable."

Dakota turned back, giving the biscuit dough far more attention than necessary. "No. Yes. I mean—" She drew a shuddering breath. "The towels are in the shelf in the bathroom. And you don't have to sleep in the stable. *Yet.*"

"Thank you," Colt said softly, his breath warm on her ear, making her shiver. He straightened and turned, allowing her to finally breathe. "Joe, if you give me the keys, I'll get our gear from the truck."

She watched through her lashes as he walked out of the kitchen. A minute later she heard the front door close. Rolling out the dough, she could feel Joe's stare. She tried to think of something to say to break the tense silence, but her brain had gone numb. Joe's gaze heated her skin as she heard the front door open again. She glanced over in time to see Colt pass by the doorway on his way to the bathroom.

"How long has Ed Franks been in Fairview?"

Joe's low tone caused an ache, which started at her nipples and worked its way down to her slit. Her mouth went dry. "I guess it's been about ten years now. Why?" She glanced over her shoulder to find him watching her intently, his gaze roaming over her bottom and heightening her awareness of him even more.

"How did he start out?"

Dakota shrugged and turned back to her biscuits. "I don't remember a lot of it. My daddy was sick, and I'd just graduated from high school. I heard Ed was new in town, flashing a lot of money and looking for a place to settle. The Wilsons used to have the property next door and were looking to sell. They wanted to go up north to be close to their daughter and grandbabies. They sold it to him and left."

Using a glass, she began cutting out biscuits and putting them on a baking sheet. She heard the shower start and closed her eyes, trying to fight off the image of Colt standing under the spray, the water making his skin gleam, the trails of soap bubbles traveling—no. She took a deep breath and tried to remember what she'd been saying. Ed Franks.

She cleared her throat. "Big Ed, as he said he liked to be called, hired everybody who needed a job, getting as many people dependent on him as he could. He started building that big house that's there now, and as soon as it was finished, tore down the old one. Then he started taking over."

"Taking over how?"

She shrugged as she finished with the biscuits and washed her hands. "He demanded cheaper prices for anything he bought. He threatened to fire people when they didn't do what he wanted. He made offers for some of the properties bordering his. Two families took his offers, but the rest of us didn't. Fred Tillman, the man who owns the feed store, the one who sent you here, has a son who worked for Ed. He threatened to fire him if Tillman didn't stop selling to those of us who held out."

"So he stopped?"

Dakota stirred the stew, doing anything to avoid looking at him. "Not at first. He said he would sell to anyone who came in. Big Ed fired his son, John. John had a wife and two kids to feed and really needed the money but agreed with his father. So John started working at the feed store but didn't make as much. So Big Ed had the feed store burned down."

Dakota turned when Joe said something under his breath. "What?"

Joe shook his head. "Nothing. So Fred rebuilt and promised not to sell to you anymore?"

Dakota shrugged again and sat back at the table. Picking up her coffee mug, she carefully avoided his eyes. "I can't really blame him. He needs that money to survive. But everyone knew then what Big Ed was capable of. After that, all he had to do was to tell somebody to do something, and they did it."

"What did the sheriff do about him burning down the feed store?"

Dakota shook her head, finally looking up at him. "No proof.

Could have been anything. Called it an accident and went home to eat supper. He and Fred have been friends a long time, and he knew who did it, but it didn't matter. Big Ed controls everything in this town, and nobody can do a damned thing about it."

Joe just stared into his coffee cup for quite some time, while Dakota did her best to ignore the sounds coming from the bathroom. When Joe looked up, she barely smothered a gasp at the ice in his eyes. "We'll take care of Big Ed for you. I don't want you to worry about him anymore."

"Look, I don't want you to do anything. I'm just trying to get by. You don't know him."

Joe shook his head. "He'll do anything to get this place, and with everyone in his pocket, he'll think nothing of having one of his men kill you to get what he wants. I'm amazed that you've lasted this long. Where's your dad now?"

Dakota tried to swallow the sudden lump in her throat. "He passed last summer. He's the one who held Ed off. Ed was scared of daddy. After daddy died, Ed left me alone for a while, I guess because he knew the neighbors would be upset if anything happened while I was still grieving. He didn't start up again until about three months ago. That's when he had his men cut the fence and steal the cattle. What he didn't steal, I sold so he couldn't get it. About two months ago, he burned down the barn." She glanced at him. "If he finds out I hired you on, he's going to send his men to threaten you."

Joe sipped his coffee. "I told you, we don't scare easily."

Dakota nodded. "Then he'll buy you off."

"I won't be bought."

Dakota shook her head. "You don't know Big Ed."

Joe's jaw clenched. "You don't know me."

# Chapter Three

The second she heard the shower turn off, Dakota blinked and rushed to take the biscuits from the oven. Colt had finished making up the beds that he and Joe would use and came back into the kitchen just as she closed the oven. She hadn't done a damned thing since he'd asked where to find the bedding, except to stand there and listen to the sound of the shower running and imagining Joe naked only feet away.

Colt looked around. "Is there anything I can do to help?"

Jolted out of her reverie, she put the hot tray of biscuits on the counter and began to set the table. "No, nothing. Just have a seat." She didn't want to accidentally bump into him as she moved around the kitchen. The highly charged atmosphere made her jumpy already. During the last few months of her father's life, he'd usually been sitting or in bed. She wasn't used to having two virile, healthy males around, and it gave her the jitters.

It also aroused the hell out of her. She found herself wondering what it would feel like to be held against one of those hard bodies and forget about everything else.

She couldn't help but sneak glances at Colt as she set the table. His hair, still damp, had been combed back, highlighting his mesmerizing eyes. The hazel green shot with gold appeared to glitter at times. His expression remained guarded as he watched her, his lips twitching, making her wonder what he'd been thinking.

Not until Joe came back into the room, did she realize she'd been listening for him ever since she'd heard the shower turn off. Without a word, she ladled the stew and served it, nerves making her clumsy.

The men ate heartily, plowing through their food as if they hadn't eaten in weeks, which made her feel guilty as hell.

"I'm sorry. I should have realized how hungry you were earlier and offered you a sandwich. You unloaded all those things for me while you were half starved."

They both stopped eating to look at her, staring at her silently for several long seconds. Finally Colt spoke. "Sorry. I guess we're just used to eating in a hurry. We're fine. We had a burger in town before we got here."

"Oh, uh, okay." Dakota had never considered herself a woman who gave much thought to the opposite sex. She'd worked on the ranch instead of dating and had never owned a hair curler. She'd only been intimate with two men in her life, a boy from high school because she was curious to know what all the fuss was about, and Lenny.

But as she sat there, picking at her stew, she couldn't keep from watching them and wondering. She couldn't help but look at their hands and imagine what they would feel like on her body. Watching their throats work as they ate, she wanted to lean over and put her lips to them. She'd never been turned on by a man's forearms before, but staring at theirs made her hot as hell.

Her insides got all tied up in knots. She had trouble sitting still and popped up out of her seat as soon as their bowls had been emptied. "I'll get you some more."

Joe gripped her arm to keep her in place. "You don't need to wait on us. We'll help ourselves, if you don't mind."

Dakota trembled at his touch. The light contact sent her imagination soaring, wondering what it would feel like to have that firm touch elsewhere. She pulled her arm out of his grip and sat back down before she gave in to the urge to lean into him. "No, I don't mind if you help yourselves."

They did and returned to the table after offering to refill her bowl. Refusing, she ate slowly, not really tasting anything. Finally, with her nerves stretched to the breaking point, she jumped up. "I'm going to go check on the horses."

Colt stood, blocking her exit. "I don't think it's a good idea for you to go out there alone. It's getting dark, and the wind has picked up. If your neighbor decides to come by to test our mettle, we don't want you caught in the middle."

She hadn't expected that. The spurt of anger that he would try to tell her what to do was tempered by admiration at men who acted like men. Because of that, her words didn't come out as harshly as she'd meant them to. "I appreciate that, but this is my ranch, and I'm not going to stay inside because it's dark and cold outside. I've been dealing with Ed and his men for a long time. Like I told you before, you don't know him. I do. I'll be fine."

Aware of their gazes as she donned her boots and jacket, she determinedly kept her own averted, afraid her need for them showed plainly on her face. Damn it. At this rate, she'd be hopping up to run out to the stable constantly just to get some air and cool her lust.

Jesus, she had to get a grip before she did something she might not be able to handle. But then again, maybe Jill was right. Why not take pleasure where she could? As she walked out the back door, she automatically glanced to her left. She could see Ed's men on horseback in the distance, several looking in her direction.

No. Now she had to be more alert than ever, and those two damned cowboys sitting in her kitchen had her distracted at a time when losing her focus could cost her dearly.

She pushed away the niggling suspicion that Ed had sent them. She would have to rely on her instincts. They'd carried her this far.

She just hoped like hell she was right.

\* \* \* \*

Joe stood before the door closed behind her. He and Colt put on their boots, grabbed their hats and coats and started out.

As they followed Dakota's progress to the stable, Colt looked over his shoulder at the neighboring ranch. "She's wrong. We know what he's capable of. If he's going to be bothering her, I don't see the need to scope out his place like we planned. If she's right, he'll be the one to come here. If we're caught, we have no reason to be there."

Joe kept a watchful eye on Dakota as she struggled against the snow and wind ahead of them, careful to keep his voice low. "Agreed. I want to avoid letting too many of them get a good look at us. The men he'll send won't know us, but he still has Buck with him. I don't want to take a chance that either of them will recognize us until it's too late. I also don't want to leave her alone. I'd never forgive myself if they choose to pay her a visit and we're not here. "

Colt nodded. "So we wait. He'll send his flunkies first. See if they can scare us off without him being directly involved. If what Dakota says is true, next they'll try money. When that doesn't work, he'll get curious, especially when we send his men back to him in pieces. He'll want to hire us to do his dirty work. He won't do that until he meets us face to face."

"Exactly. Then we'll kill him."

"It's a shame, huh?"

Joe came to a halt and turned to him, keeping Dakota in his sight. "You change your mind about killing him?"

Colt looked at him incredulously. "Are you crazy? After what we've been through because of that asshole? No. It's a shame we won't be able to stick around and get to know Dakota a little better. She's tough, isn't she? And that body. Jesus."

When Dakota slipped Joe raced forward, but she got up and hurried ahead before he could reach her. He turned to Colt as he caught up. "Looks like she's had to be tough. At least we can make her life easier while we're here and get rid of her biggest problem before we go."

"Yeah, but damned if I wouldn't give a lot for a taste of her."

Depressed now, Joe stepped into the stable, lowering his voice even more. "We'll never have somebody like her, Colt. Just forget it."

"I know, but wouldn't you like to—"

"More than anything."

* * * *

Dakota stumbled into the stable and leaned against the wall to catch her breath. The wind had really picked up. She would have to string a line to the house so none of them got lost if this turned into a blizzard.

She'd seen that Joe and Colt followed her and grimaced. She'd wanted a few minutes away from them to get herself back under control. She sure as hell didn't want to be in the stable with them. Damn it. What the hell was wrong with her? She had enough problems in her life without adding two more. And that's what they would be if she let them.

Shaking her head, she checked the stalls for feed and water. Joe and Colt had already taken care of everything, but she felt better for checking. The door to the stable opened, letting in a gust of frigid air. She turned and saw them walking down the row of stalls, obviously deep in conversation, but their voices were so low, she couldn't make out what they said.

Joe turned abruptly and went out, leaving her alone in the barn with Colt.

She continued down the row, watching him unobtrusively as she checked on each of the horses. Since she only had six left, it didn't take long, and all too soon, she had no choice but to look up at him. "Everything looks great. So you two know a lot about horses, huh?"

Leaning against a post, Colt nodded. "Yes, ma'am. We were both raised around them."

Joe came back through the door, holding onto it as the wind tried to whip it out of his hand. "You ready to go back in?"

Dakota nodded. "Yeah, I should hook up the line—"

"Already done. Ready?"

Getting back to the house turned out to be far more difficult than leaving it. The wind had picked up considerably in the last few minutes and blew against her now, ice stinging as it hit her face. It made walking more difficult, especially with the wind strong enough to knock her off her feet. She slipped and would have fallen if they hadn't each grabbed onto her. Joe pulled her against him, pulling her face into his chest as he half carried, half dragged her back to the house.

They went through the back door to the porch. Colt grabbed the door before it could be ripped out of his hand and pulled it closed, locking it behind him. "Damn, it came in fast, didn't it? On the radio, they said snow, not a fucking blizzard."

With a hand under her chin, Joe studied her face. "Are you all right?"

His cold hand seemed to warm almost instantly against her skin, his touch making her tremble as she looked up into his eyes. They warmed as they searched her features and when his eyes darkened, she felt the pull all the way to her center. Colt came up beside him and touched her arm, overloading her senses.

She pulled away from both of them. "I'm fine, thanks. We'd better get inside." She shook off the snow before she walked into the house and took off her boots and coat. "Have some coffee and warm up. I'm going to go take a bath before we lose electricity."

She left the room without looking at either of them, not wanting them to see the need she knew had to show on her face. Gathering her things, she headed for the bathroom, making sure she locked the door behind her.

Soaking in the hot water, she wondered what the hell she could do about them. She'd been around men her whole life, but had only ever been attracted to two, but neither had ever made her feel as feminine as Joe and Colt did. With them she trembled like a damned little girl and lost focus, feeling the way her friend Jill did with her boyfriends.

It was an entirely new and pleasantly uncomfortable situation for her.

For perhaps the first time in her adult life, she wanted to play.

Dakota sighed and sunk further into the hot water. She wished she could be that carefree, but too much rode on her staying focused. Now that her daddy was gone, she'd learn to rely on only herself. If she didn't have to worry about Ed, she would be on those two in a heartbeat. She deserved it.

Just as Dakota stepped out of the tub, the lights blinked twice and went off. Damn it, she hadn't been quick enough. Now she would have to go out and start the generator. Standing in the dark, she dried her skin briskly, dreading going back out in the cold after finally getting warm.

Hurrying to get dressed, she reached for her clothes and fell as the towel slipped out from under her feet. She yelped in surprise and pain as she landed hard on her hip. Hearing footsteps race down the hall, she groaned. Great. Just what she needed.

"Dakota, are you okay?"

She scrambled for the towel she'd dropped, cursing under her breath when she found her socks instead. "I'm fine, Joe. I'll be out in a minute."

"We heard you fall. Open the damned door."

Dakota couldn't prevent a moan as she stood. In a hurry to cover herself, she hit the same hip on the side of the cabinet she used for storage, knocking bottles of shampoo and bars of soap to the floor. "Damn it."

"Dakota, open this door right now!"

"I'm fine, damn it. Just clumsy. You're making me nervous banging on the damned door. Go away. I just have to get dressed, and I'll be right out."

Another knock on the door and Colt's desperate plea. "Dakota, can you open the door, please before Joe breaks it in?"

"I'm trying to get dressed, Colt. I'm fine. I'll be out in a minute." Where the hell was her underwear? Why the hell hadn't she brought a flashlight with her? Because those two hunks currently standing outside the door had addled her brain, that's why. Wait, didn't she have a flashlight under the sink?

She crawled to the cabinet and of course, hit her head on the corner of it.

"What was that?"

Dakota slumped next to the cabinet, and hissed as she held a hand to her head. Jesus, what else?

"Dakota? Are you close to the door?"

"No, I'm—"

A well placed kick had the door slamming back against the wall. Joe and Colt pushed their way in, each holding a flashlight. Seeing the towel, she grabbed it off of the floor to cover herself. "Why the hell did you do that? I told you I was fine and would be out in a minute."

Joe ignored her. Dead silence filled the room as Colt and Joe ran the flashlights over her bare legs.

Dakota didn't move, afraid she would expose something. She held her breath when the light from the flashlights lingered on her thighs much longer than necessary. "I'm fine."

"Colt, hold the flashlight on her so I can see if she's hurt."

Thankfully, the light moved to her arms. Shivers of delight shot through her when she felt Joe's hands move over her skin. Little tingles of pleasure erupted wherever he touched, and she gripped the towel even tighter in reaction. Trying to keep her voice firm, she did her best to glare at him. "I'm not a child. Just give me one of those flashlights, so I can see to get dressed." Being naked in their presence made her skin hyper sensitive. She could feel the heat from his body as though it reached out and caressed her.

Joe glared back. "If you don't tell me where you're hurt, I'm going to take the towel off and find out for myself."

Shaken by her body's incredible response to his threat, Dakota gulped in air. "Damn you. Get out."

He lifted a brow. "Last chance, Dakota."

Dakota squeezed her thighs closed, trying desperately to relieve her throbbing clit. "Fine. I hit my hip when I fell, and I hit my head while I was looking under the sink for a flashlight. How did you find the flashlights?"

Joe waved that off. "Most people keep one in their kitchen. I found them in the pantry before the lights went out. We have a fire started, too. Which hip?"

Her knees shook, making her grateful that the light stayed higher. "I'm fine. Just leave one of the flashlights so I can get dressed."

"Which hip?"

Colt chuckled. "You'd better tell him. One thing about Joe is when he sets his mind to something, nothing gets in his way."

Dakota sighed. "My left one." She uncovered it just a little as the beam of light focused on it and saw that it had reddened and already started to bruise.

"Shit," Joe muttered and moved the towel to uncover a little more, pulling the towel from her grasp and uncovering her breast in the process. The sudden stillness that came over both of them made her tremble.

Dakota rushed to cover herself but his hold on the towel prevented it.

The silence in the room became deafening, broken only by the pounding of her heart and the howling wind. Dakota swallowed the moan that threatened to escape and forced herself to remain perfectly still.

She sat there, staring down at the dark hand moving over her hip, tightening her thighs as the moisture flowed from her slit. She fought to keep her breathing even as her heart nearly pounded out of her chest.

Mesmerized, she watched his hand trail higher, Joe's finger skimming lightly over her nipple. She jolted at the exquisite sensation, arching into his caress. Enough light reflected that she could see his face. She didn't know which one of them was more surprised.

His eyes widened as they met hers before lowering his gaze again.

Squeezing her eyes closed and holding her breath, she waited expectantly for the next touch on her breast. Thankfully she didn't have to wait long. When a rough finger circled her nipple she couldn't hold back a moan. She tightened her thighs against the throbbing of her clit as Joe lightly teased her nipple.

Colt's voice sounded rougher than usual. "Jesus. Pinch it a little."

Dakota cried out when Joe did just that.

Joe cursed and jerked his hand away, breaking the spell. "Let me see your head."

Dakota fought for composure, covering herself once again. "It's nothing, just a bump. Just leave me a flashlight and let me get dressed, and I'll be right out."

Silence followed and nobody moved for several long seconds. Finally Joe handed her the flashlight, his hand lingering longer than necessary before he released it. "We'll be out in the living room. Come out there when you're done, and we'll put some ice on that hip and the bump on your head."

Dakota shuddered just thinking about it. "No. We won't."

"But it—"

"I just got warmed up, damn it, and I'm not putting ice on anything." As hot as she felt now, it would melt as soon as it touched her.

Colt chuckled. "Hurry up and get dressed, but be careful. If you're not out in a few minutes, we'll be back."

Holding onto the flashlight, Dakota watched them leave. When they disappeared from view, she let out a shaky breath, on the verge of coming. Holy hell.

Trembling, she found her underwear and started dressing, donning a warm sweat suit and thick socks, trying her best to ignore the way the soft material caressed her skin. Taking a deep breath, she stepped out into the hallway, grimacing at the broken lock and splintered frame.

The closer she got to the living room, the warmer it got, thanks to the raging fire they'd started in the fireplace. It burned just as hot as the fire they'd started in her body. Hurrying toward it, she came to an abrupt halt when she saw what they'd done.

The mattresses from their beds and had been placed in front of the fireplace. They'd moved the coffee table and one of her chairs out of the way in order to have enough room. Both had removed their flannel shirts, wearing only jeans and t-shirts and thick socks. They looked up as she entered and Colt smiled at her, a smile she felt all the way to her toes. "There's no point in starting up the generator just to go to sleep. We can all bed down here tonight."

# Chapter Four

She swung her gaze to Colt's, looking for calculation, but finding none. "I'm not sleeping with you." Cursing herself because it had come out sounding breathless instead of the firm tone she'd strived for, she plopped into the chair, curling her legs under her.

Colt frowned at her. "It's warmer out here. Your bedroom's going to be freezing in a little while."

Dakota's gaze kept sliding to the mattresses, already made up with blankets and pillows. An image of lying naked between the two of them in front of the blazing fire emblazoned itself on her mind and sent her pulse racing. She wanted to crawl in so badly she shook. Her damned clit throbbed steadily and her panties dampened even more. She stood, intending to escape before she gave into temptation. "I have blankets. I guess I'll see you in the morning."

Joe came toward her and held out his hand, clearly frustrated. "At least sit here and get warmed up first."

Dakota shook her head and backed away. One touch from either of them would have her begging them to take her. "No. I'm warm enough now. Good night."

She hurried down the hall before she gave in, the difference in temperature making her shiver already. She got an extra blanket out of the closet and crawled into bed, shivering again at the sound of the howling wind. She'd closed and locked her door and now wondered if it would have been better to keep it open and let some of the heat in from the living room.

Crawling back out, she unlocked it and opened it just a few inches. She wanted the heat but didn't want it to look like an invitation. Opening the drawer in her nightstand, she took out her gun, made sure the safety was on, and placed it under her pillow.

Her father had bought it for her before he died because of the trouble Big Ed and his men had been making. He'd wanted to buy her a watch, but they didn't have a lot of money. When it came down to the watch or the gun, he'd bought her the gun.

"A helluva graduation gift for my little girl," he'd told her, shaking his head sadly.

She smiled as she remembered her answer. "It shows you love me, Daddy. This thing just might save my life one day. Besides, what do I need a watch for? When the horses are hungry, they don't care what time it is."

Lying there listening to the sound of the wind and the low murmurs coming from the other room, she realized suddenly that she'd thought about her father a lot today, more so than usual. It had to be because of the arrival of the two men currently stretched out by the fire in her living room.

They reminded her of her dad more than anyone she'd ever met before. Maybe that's why she trusted them on such short acquaintance. They hadn't attacked her in the bathroom when she'd only had a towel for protection. They'd followed her to the stable to make sure she was all right.

But she sensed a darkness in them. She noticed that they always stood braced and alert, and one of them always had their back to the door. They both watched everything, and she couldn't help but notice that every time they walked into a room, their eyes swept over everything as though memorizing it and looking for anything out of place. The way they looked at each other told her they were accustomed to communicating wordlessly. They appeared to carry on entire conversations with just a glance.

The icy sheets gradually warmed from her body heat, and she curled into a ball to get even warmer. Instead of being nervous about the two men in her house, she felt safer, and listening to the blowing wind, drifted off to sleep.

\* \* \* \*

Joe glanced down the hall again. "I wonder if she's asleep yet. I want to open her door all the way so more of the heat can get to her."

Colt yawned and stretched. "We'll give it a couple more minutes and check. She should be damned tired with all the work she does around here and all the sleepless nights I'm sure she's had."

Joe nodded and sat down, careful not to look at the fire. He and Colt kept looking out the windows and didn't want to ruin their night vision by staring into the flames. "I just wished she would have stayed out here. It's not right that we're out here nice and warm, and she's gonna freeze her ass off in there. Go ahead and get some shut eye. I'll take the first watch and open her door when she falls asleep."

Colt nodded and settled down on the mattress and within minutes, his breathing had slowed. They'd both learned to sleep whenever they could, and each knew the other could be trusted to watch his back.

Joe waited ten minutes before he crept down the hall to Dakota's bedroom, avoiding the spot in the hallway that creaked. He slowly slid her door open, grimacing when it groaned. At first he didn't see more than a lump in the middle of the bed. Because of the bright moonlight shining through the window, he could see her blonde hair fanned out on the pillow as he stepped closer. His groin tightened, and he wished like hell he had the right to crawl into bed with her and warm her body with his.

He stood staring down at her for several minutes, just listening to the sound of her breathing.

*He could hear her breathing.*

He crept to the window and looked out. The wind had finally died down, and it had stopped snowing. The clouds had cleared, and the moon reflected on the snow, making everything appear much brighter than it should have.

Hearing a low moan, he glanced over his shoulder, frowning as he watched Dakota snuggle into a tighter ball. A fist tightened around his heart. One day, some lucky man would have the right to lie next to her and pillow her head with his shoulder as she snuggled against him trying to get warm. If she belonged to them, he and Colt would surround her with their warmth, and she could snuggle all she wanted to. Damn. He had to stop thinking of her in that way. Right now she was a means to an end. He adjusted his jeans, grimacing at the raging hard-on he got every time he got anywhere near her.

Sex had become something he and Colt engaged in to fill a need and nothing more. This need he had just to hold her didn't sit comfortably with him. He and Colt couldn't stay, and he had the unpleasant feeling that he would be leaving a piece of his heart behind when he left here.

Not that it mattered. He doubted he'd ever need it. When he and Colt finished what they had to do, they'd get a ranch of their own and spend their lives doing the only thing they knew how.

They eventually wanted a wife and kids but he didn't hold out much hope. It would take a strong woman to deal with all the emotional baggage he and Colt would bring to a relationship.

Dakota was the strongest woman he'd ever met. He smiled to himself when he thought of how she looked holding them both off with a shotgun. He wondered what she'd think of him if she knew the sight of her holding that shotgun on them, her eyes full of fire, had given him an erection.

Jesus, to think that she'd held off that bastard on her own enraged him. From what he'd heard in town and from Dakota, the whole fucking town had abandoned her. And still she'd survived.

Well, they wouldn't abandon her. At least not until they got rid of her troublesome neighbor.

*Big Ed* had owned another town once. He and Joe hadn't been as lucky as Dakota had been so far.

Colt's parents hadn't lasted long after he and Colt had been arrested. His father had suffered a stroke, and his mother's heart had given out as she tried to care for him. Colt hadn't even been able to say goodbye.

Joe's own plans for the future had been destroyed. The girl he'd loved hadn't even come to the trial, and his letters to her went unanswered.

His father, knowing Joe's temper, had believed them guilty from the start and had written him off. His mother and sister had stood by him at first until pressure from his father made their lives unbearable. Their visits came further and further apart until he'd finally asked them to stop coming.

He and Colt had both lost their families and dreams for their future because of the man next door. Hate had burned inside him hotter and hotter every day.

Until it became ice cold.

That's when he and Colt had made a new plan for the future.

Killing the man responsible.

A movement caught his attention. He pulled the curtain back a little more, confident that with the bright moon and the absolute darkness inside that no one could see him. He saw two, no three men heading for the stable, creeping slowly and looking toward the house. They could probably see the smoke coming from the chimney and if they were that bastard's men, they would know that the electricity had gone off. They probably assumed Dakota had huddled next to the fire and therefore would be in the front of the house.

Dakota shifted again, drawing his gaze. She got to him more than he'd like to admit and he'd gotten distracted, something that he couldn't afford.

He leaned over her and put his hand over her mouth, silencing her cry and gripping her hand as she reached under the pillow.

\* \* \* \*

Dakota came awake abruptly, terrified. *Calm down. Think.* The hand over her mouth silenced her cry while the other kept her for reaching for her gun. Oh God! Somehow, someone had gotten into her house.

"Shh, Dakota, it's me. Joe. I didn't want you to make noise or shoot me. There are some men going into the stable, and I wanted you to know that Colt and I will be out there. Get up. Be quiet and go into the kitchen. Take your gun if you want but don't shoot us by accident." He released her and moved silently out of the room.

Her heart pounding, Dakota grabbed her gun and fought the pile of blankets to follow. She ran into the kitchen just in time to see both of them pulling on their boots. They reached for their coats, speaking softly under their breath.

Dakota ran up to them. "Here, take my gun."

Colt shook his head. "You keep it. We have the shotgun. Stay in the kitchen."

"Why not the living room?"

"They'll see your shadow. Stay in the kitchen so we know where you are."

"I'm coming with you."

Joe unlocked the door, and pulled it open, not even turning. "No."

A gust of cold air came in as they slipped through the door and closed it behind them.

Dakota stayed low and looked out the kitchen window, watching them work their way to the stable. To hell with this. This was her ranch, and she wasn't about to sit here inside while Joe and Colt confronted Ed's men. They had no idea just how ruthless he could be to men who failed him. So none ever did.

She ran for her own boots, slid them on and shrugged into her coat. With the gun in her hand she started out, trying to be as quiet as possible. She stepped outside just in time to watch Joe and Colt enter the stable.

She had no idea how many men Ed had sent this time. Scanning the yard carefully she continued to move cautiously forward. She didn't hear anything coming from the stable and remembered Ed's foreman, Buck, and his penchant for knives. If Buck or any of his men had attacked Joe or Colt, she might not have heard it. Her panic rose as she imagined Joe and Colt lying on the stable floor bleeding. Moving as silently as she could, she stayed in the men's footsteps, as she headed for the stable. The sky had cleared, the bright moon reflecting off the snow making her even more cautious. Standing out in the middle of the yard, anyone who looked this way would see her.

Just as she got to the stable door, all hell broke loose.

She heard the sounds of a scuffle and what sounded like a fist connecting. A second later a man came flying through the air out the stable door, slamming into her and knocking her to the ground. The gun flew out of her hand. Landing hard, his considerable weight on top of her, she had the wind knocked out of her. Struggling for air, she pushed at him, fighting to get his weight off of her. She finally managed to move out from under him and scrambled to find the gun.

Seeing it in the snow, she scurried toward it, crying out when the man behind her pulled her up by the hair. She turned and kicked him in the kneecap, getting pulled down with him when he fell. Fighting, she kicked and twisted, trying to break his grip. "Let go of my hair, you asshole. You fight like a girl."

The sound of a shotgun shell being pumped into the chamber made both of them freeze. She looked up to see Joe leading two men out by the back of their collars, both looking a little worse for wear. They looked a little dazed and fell, only to have Joe lift them back to their feet again. One had a bloody nose, the other a bloody lip.

Colt stood to the side and had the shotgun pointed at the man holding onto her hair. "Let go of her right now. Nice and easy."

As soon as he released her, Dakota scrambled for the gun and moved to stand next to Colt. Turning, she got a good look at the men. "The one on the ground is Bart. Eli has the bloody nose and Jasper's the one with the bloody lip. They're Ed's men. What the hell were they doing in the stable? Are the horses all right?"

Joe shoved the two men he'd been holding on to, and stood over where they lay sprawled in the snow. Eli and Jasper scrambled to their feet, alternately cursing and groaning. Joe stood with his hands on his hips, as though waiting for them to come at him, but both apparently decided against it.

Looking at his face, she didn't blame them. Joe's features appeared to be carved from granite as he moved to stand on the other side of her. "Are you okay?" He reached for her arm to pull her slightly behind them.

Eyeing him with new respect, Dakota stood her ground. "I'm the one with the gun. I can handle them."

Joe disarmed her easily, startling her with just how adeptly he'd accomplished it. "Get inside, Dakota."

Dakota clenched her teeth. That tough guy persona was a hell of a turn on, but she had never been a damsel in distress and had no intention of starting now. "Have you forgotten that *I'm* the boss?"

"No, Dakota. Not for a minute. Now get inside. We'll be right in." He moved like a snake, striking out at Bart.

Something flew through the air as Bart went back on his ass. Bart lunged at him, but Colt snapped the butt of the shotgun out in a move so fast, she barely saw it, and hit Bart in the temple, knocking him unconscious. Her admiration for both men went up considerably, and she couldn't help but look from one to the other as she walked over to retrieve whatever had flown from Bart's hand.

Dakota picked it up, turning it in her hand and came back to stand between Joe and Colt, more than a little stunned. "It's a knife. He was actually going to cut you with this." Shaking her head, she looked at Ed's three men. "They've never gone this far before. They've never actually grabbed me before or pulled out a weapon."

Colt spared her a glance, his expression hard. "Get in the house, Dakota."

Ignoring them, she faced Eli. "What the hell did you plan to do with my horses?"

He shrugged and if she didn't know better, she'd think he looked a little embarrassed. "We were supposed to let 'em loose."

"And since you must be the geniuses who put sugar in my tank, I would have no way to catch them, no transportation at all. Does Big Ed have plans to kill me now, too?"

Eli held a handkerchief to his nose to stop the bleeding and stepped forward, only to step back again when Joe shifted his weight. "Miz Wells, why don't you just sell to Big Ed and be done with it. You can take the money and get yourself a fancy apartment in the city."

Dakota blinked. "What the hell would I do in a city? And who the hell do you or your sleazy boss think you are to try to make me leave my home? I'm not going anywhere."

Jasper opened his mouth to say something, but a glance at Colt had him snapping it shut.

* * * *

Joe had seen and heard enough. His blood boiled at what had been done to Dakota and by what he knew would have happened tonight if they hadn't been around. He spared a glance at her to see that she looked shaken to realize that Big Ed had just stepped up his game.

"Get inside, Dakota." Joe ordered over his shoulder. When she hesitated, he took a step back and lowered his voice. "If you don't move right now, I'm tanning your backside."

She blinked up at him and he met her gaze coolly, watching as her eyes lit with anger. Good. It was a hell of a lot better than the way she'd looked before. If he could piss her off long enough to get her into the house, it was worth it. She moved closer to whisper to him.

He had to bend to hear her, simultaneously taking the knife from her.

She glared at him, glancing quickly at Ed's men. "I'm only going in so you're not distracted, but don't ever think to boss me around again."

When she stomped back to the house, it took tremendous effort not to turn and watch her tight ass. Not hearing the porch door open, he shot a warning glance over his shoulder. He couldn't see her face clearly at this distance, but her jerky movements as she turned and went in, letting the door slam behind her, told him just how pissed she was. Good.

Assuming Bart to be the leader of the three, he turned his attention to him. "We're letting the three of you leave in one piece because we want you to deliver a message to your boss for us. The next man he sends to cause Dakota Wells any trouble is going to have to get through us to do it. We're a lot meaner than the men in town he's steamrolled and aren't going to go down easily. I want you to tell him that." Joe folded the knife and stuck it in his pocket with his own.

Colt lowered the shotgun slightly, his grin lethal. "Oh yeah, and tell him we can't wait to meet him."

\* \* \* \*

Dakota stood just inside the porch as Ed's men ran back to their horses like their asses were on fire. Joe and Colt stood with their hands on their hips and watched them until they disappeared from view. Only then did they turn toward the house and start for the back door, where she waited.

Joe grabbed her arm and hustled her through the porch and into the house. "You don't listen worth a damn. We told you we would take care of them." Releasing her, he yanked her coat off and hung it before removing his own.

Dakota glared at him before bending to remove her boots. "I've been taking care of myself for a long time. I'm not a little girl who needs somebody to take care of her."

Colt gripped her arm and pulled her through to the living room. It infuriated her that her struggles didn't even slow him down. "Get by the fire. You could have been hurt out there or distracted us enough that one of us got hurt. Face it, we're bigger and stronger than you are and a hell of a lot meaner. And you can't stay awake twenty-four hours a day to watch the house."

Joe had followed them into the room and stood with his hands on his hips. "You're soaking wet. Get out of those wet clothes and get in front of the fire. Now, Dakota, or I'll strip you myself."

Dakota blinked at his bossiness, but he didn't seem to notice as he continued.

"I woke you up so you would know what was going on and not rush outside if you heard something. I didn't want you to be lying in bed if one of those men got past us. Next time do what you're told. Now get those wet things off and get under the blankets."

Dakota poked a finger at his rock hard stomach. "Don't tell me what to do. I run this ranch, and you work for me. I'm going back to bed."

Colt blocked her. "You hired us to handle things. That's what we're doing. We're going to take care of you, whether you like it or not. We're not about to let Ed get to you, and we're not going to allow you to do anything to hurt yourself. Including getting sick. Your bedroom is freezing by now. If you go in there, we're just going to carry you back out here." He pulled a flannel shirt out of his bag and tossed it to her. "We'll go into the kitchen while you change and get under the covers. If you try to get past us, we'll just haul you back."

Stunned, angry, and somehow touched, Dakota watched them walk away, shouting after them. "What did you say to Ed's men?"

Joe kept walking, glancing over his shoulder. "Get those wet clothes off. Call us when you're under the blankets, and we'll tell you."

Since she'd started shivering, she threw off her wet clothes as soon as they left the room and donned the flannel shirt. She wrapped her arms around herself, pulling the warmth and softness of the shirt closer to her skin.

Crawling beneath the covers, she moaned softly as the warmth from the fire and the warm blankets touched her skin.

Throwing caution to the wind, Dakota stretched out, laying her head on the pillow. "I'm ready."

# Chapter Five

Dakota settled the blankets around her as both men walked back into the room. Feeling too vulnerable lying down, she sat up, making sure she stayed completely covered. "So what did you say to them?"

Joe sat in the chair at her feet. "I told them to give their boss a message for me. If he sends any more of his men back over here, we'll send them back looking a lot worse than they did."

A shower of sparks from the fireplace made her jump.

Colt poked at the fire and straightened, replacing the poker before turning to her. "We also told them if we saw them around again, they'd get more of the same. We didn't break any bones this time, but will if they come back. Their boss isn't going to get much work done if his hands are all beat up."

Dakota wrapped her arms around her blanket covered legs. "He's got about fifty hands. If he decides to send more than three at a time, we're going to be in big trouble. In the past, he hasn't because he didn't need to. Now he will."

Joe stood and pulled off his socks, leaving only his t-shirt and jeans. Lying flat on his back next to her, he closed his eyes. "Don't worry about it. Go to sleep. I'm beat."

Colt sat in the chair Joe had just vacated. "I don't think anyone will be back tonight, but I'll keep watch for the next couple of hours."

Dakota's body came to life as his gaze swept over her. Wearing nothing but a pair of panties under the flannel shirt, her breasts had been left free, allowing her pebbled nipples to brush against the flannel as she shifted. Already sensitive, they became even more so.

Joe hadn't bothered with the blankets, affording her a good close up look at his body. The huge bulge in his jeans, only inches away, captured her attention and seemed to grow even larger under her gaze. "Go to sleep, Dakota."

Dakota's gaze flew to his face, meeting his heavy lidded gaze. Knowing she'd been caught, her face burned as she glanced over to see that Colt still watched her steadily. "I, uh, goodnight." She turned her back to Joe and lay down facing the fire. Closing her eyes, she willed herself to sleep. Extremely aware of the two men so close, she held herself stiffly. When neither did or said anything, she began to relax. The heat from the fire and Joe's body soon warmed her completely and she drifted off.

* * * *

Moaning, she snuggled into the warmth surrounding her. A light touch on her breast made her arch, seeking more of the delicious contact. The thudding beneath her head both comforted and excited her, and she shifted to get even closer. The touch on her nipple made her moan. It felt so good. Incredible. She moved against it, wanting more. Rubbing her thighs together, she tried unsuccessfully to ease the ache that had settled there.

Something hard and warm touched her bottom and she pushed back until it pressed more firmly against her. Something firm and warm settled around her waist, pulling her back against even more heat. The heat at her waist moved lower, smoothing over her abdomen, slowly moving downward and inside her panties. It kept moving lower, forcing her thighs to part as it worked its way between them. She parted them eagerly, needing more and moaned as it grazed over her clit.

A series of bit off curses woke her abruptly from her erotic dream to find it hadn't been a dream at all. Opening her eyes, she looked up to see Joe watching her, his eyes blazing with need. With her head pillowed on his chest, she could hear his heart beat even faster. His hand had worked its way under her shirt and covered her breast.

Colt, obviously awakened as she'd been by Joe's cursing, remained motionless, with his hand down her panties and his finger on her clit. Pressed firmly against her back, his breath warm on her neck, he leaned down to kiss her shoulder. "This wasn't planned, Dakota. I was asleep when I reached for you. If you want us to stop, we will."

His sleep roughened voice caused her juices to flow freely. More aroused than she'd ever been, Dakota couldn't lie still. Shifting restlessly, her hips tilted of their own volition. "I don't have any condoms." She groaned, arching to push her breast further into Joe's palm.

Joe leaned over her, pushing her onto her back. "We do. Do you want this?"

Dakota shuddered as his hard body covered hers. She couldn't believe this was really happening. If it was a dream, she didn't want to wake up. "God yes."

Colt touched her cheek, sliding his hand from between her legs to make room for Joe. "We didn't intend to get you aroused, honey, but we can satisfy you without taking you if you don't want to do this."

In answer, Dakota reached up and grabbed fistfuls of Joe's hair and pulled him down. His kiss made her soar, so hot and possessive it took her breath away. His arms came around her, pulling her close. She kicked out, fighting the blankets that kept her from putting her legs around him. She couldn't get close enough.

Still kissing her, Joe moved back to the side and she felt the blankets being pulled down to her feet. Joe held her slightly away from him as Colt reached between them to unbutton the shirt she wore and part the sides.

Joe lifted his head, his eyes glittering darkly as he looked down at what Colt had exposed.

Dakota trembled as Joe used the tip of his finger to trace a nipple, gasping at the arrow of pleasure that shot straight to her pussy.

He smiled faintly. "I haven't been able to get the sight of your beautiful breasts out of my mind."

Colt touched her cheek, turning her toward him and swallowing her moan when he covered her mouth with his own.

Hands moved over her breasts, tweaking and lightly pinching her nipples and sending her into a frenzy of need. Colt's hair felt silky under her hands as she tangled her fingers in it to pull him even closer. He ran his tongue over the seam of her lips, nibbling teasingly, chuckling when she groaned in frustration. "You're greedy. I like that in a woman."

Her stomach quivered when she felt her panties being removed. Colt had to have felt it.

He lifted his head as he ran a hand over her belly. "Do you have any idea what we're going to do to you?"

Joe tossed her panties aside and looked down at her slit hungrily.

Dakota parted her trembling thighs, gulping in air. "Do your worst."

Joe's eyes flared as he ripped off his t-shirt and lowered his head.

Colt leaned over her, grinning. "Yes, ma'am."

She cried out at the first touch of Joe's mouth, gripping Colt's shoulders as hot tingles radiated from her slit outward. Joe ate at her hungrily and she tightened her hold on Colt as her defenses crumbled all around her. Holding her buttocks in his hands, Joe lifted her to get better access and simply devoured her, robbing her of all reason.

Colt's mouth moved over hers, brushing his lips against hers and down her jaw to her throat while his hand stayed busy on her breasts. Suddenly, a large swell of pleasure washed over her, stealing her breath as she arched, her body tight.

Joe held onto her, his mouth gentle as he brought her down so slowly she thought it would kill her.

"Damn, you're beautiful," Colt told her against her lips as he took them again.

Joe released her and she heard the sound of their duffle bag being unzipped and then the rip of foil. When Colt lifted his head, she looked down to see Joe rolling on a condom.

Joe's jaw clenched as he ran his hands from her knees to her thighs. "I've never wanted a woman as much as I want you."

Dakota lifting her hips in invitation. Her entire body had gone up in flames and she wanted more. Wanted it all. "Take me."

Colt lay next to her, watching her face and running his hands over her thigh as it wrapped around Joe. It felt so erotic and naughty to look into one man's eyes as another man began to fill her.

Dakota turned her face to watch Joe's eyes as he slowly began to enter her, so slowly she didn't know if she would survive it. She struggled to accept him. His size and the fact that she had been celibate for some time made his possession deliciously snug. She lifted her hips higher, trying to take even more of his thick heat into her.

Joe brushed her hair back and tilted her face to his. "Easy, Dakota. I don't want to hurt you."

"Please. You're killing me. More." His thick length burned inside her, each bump and ridge of his cock delighting her.

"She's so fucking tight," he told Colt through clenched teeth. "Dakota, look at me, honey."

Dakota lifted her gaze, rocking her hips to take even more. "God you feel so good. Stop treating me like a baby, damn it. Show me how much you want me."

His eyes flared. A heartbeat later his lips covered hers again, taking her mouth with none of the finesse he'd used earlier. His strokes came faster now, each pressing more of his cock into her. He ended the kiss to stare down at her.

Her breath caught at the heat in his eyes. It erased any inhibitions she may have had. She couldn't believe how good it felt, each stroke taking her higher and higher. Her body began tightening again and she thrashed on the pillow to fight it, not wanting the magnificent feeling to end. He relentlessly dug at a spot inside her that gave her no choice but to surrender.

Braced on his elbows above her, Joe kept his eyes on her the entire time. "Go over, Dakota. Don't you dare fight it."

He spoke through clenched teeth, and she could see he was barely hanging onto his own control. Leaning to one side, he slid a hand under her bottom and lifted her into his thrusts. "You're so damned hot."

Colt's hand slid over her hip and thigh before he reached up to cover a breast, running a rough thumb over her nipple. "We won't let you fight it, Dakota. You're gonna come, honey. Let go. Let us make you feel good."

Joe thrust to the hilt inside her and she couldn't help but cry out at the pleasure. She tried to pump her hips but he held onto her, controlling her movements. Those little sparks got stronger and started to spread far too soon.

"No. Not yet." She moaned, thrashing on the mattress. She dug her heels into his taut buttocks, lifting herself even more. "It's too good."

Joe groaned harshly. "Incredible."

Dakota gripped him tighter as the wave of pleasure crested, washing over her so completely she felt it in her toes. Her body bucked and jolted helplessly as Joe thrust harder. She gloried in his possession, losing herself to the pleasure as his control finally snapped.

He covered her body with his, burying his face in her hair as he thrust, stroking his hot length deep inside her. Groaning, he slid his arms under her, pulling her even closer as he found his own release.

Colt's hands ran over her, firm but gentle.

Running one hand over Joe's back, she reached for Colt with the other one, gasping for air. "Why doesn't it feel wrong to have Colt touch me while you're still inside me?"

Joe lifted onto his elbows again and gave her one of those rare smiles. "Because he's as crazy about you as I am."

Dakota cupped his cheek, thrilled that she had the freedom to do so, at least at this moment.

Colt leaned down to brush his lips over her shoulder.

Joe kissed her again and withdrew, moving away and allowing Colt to take his place.

Covering her body with his own, Colt bent to kiss her, all teasing gone as he claimed her mouth possessively. Lifting his head slightly, he murmured against her lips. "You are so fucking beautiful."

He'd already undressed and rolled on a condom, so she lifted her hips in invitation.

Instead of entering her, he slid his hands beneath her, lifting her to lie over his arm and closing his lips over a nipple. Joe came back to join them, lying next to her and reached out to lightly pinch the other.

The combined sensations drove her wild and she gripped them both tightly, whimpering at the exquisite pleasure. Joe's hand slid over her stomach and down to her slit, which dripped with her juices.

Colt lifted his head. "She's so fucking responsive. As soon as we touch her, she goes up in flames. Look at her."

Joe lifted his head to look down at her, smiling indulgently. "Wait until you get inside her."

Their words sent a thrill through her and she cried out as Joe gave his attention to her clit. "Take me, damn it."

Colt bent to nibble at her lips, chuckling and deftly avoiding her as she tried to deepen the kiss. "Greedy little thing, aren't you. Do you want more?"

"Yes, damn you." Dakota groaned as Joe teased her clit, giving her enough friction there to keep her climbing, but just when she thought she'd go over, he slid his hand up to rub her stomach again. "Stop teasing me."

Colt scraped his teeth over a nipple, making her gasp. "How would you like to have your ass stretched so we can both take you next time?"

"No, Colt." Joe's tone was adamant. "I don't want to hurt her."

Dakota trembled as a combination of fear and lust went through her. She'd heard about anal sex but she'd never experienced it before. With them she wanted to experience it all. "Yes, anything. Everything."

Colt cupped her face, running a thumb over her lips as he gradually began to press his hot length into her. "I saw some oil in the bathroom."

Joe slid his hand away from her clit again as Colt continued to press forward. Her entire body shook with need, anticipating the pleasure to come.

She panted, breathless as Colt filled her with his cock. It felt long and thick, hot as it stretched her. She rocked her hips, crying out hoarsely as he slid into her all the way. "Oh God, it feels so good."

"You're so tight and hot, Dakota. Jesus. Joe, go get the oil."

Joe bent over her and dropped a quick kiss on her shoulder before standing. "If you don't like what we do to you, Dakota, just say so and we'll stop."

Dakota groaned, crying out as Colt filled her again. He moved so slowly, she thought she would die. "Faster."

The head of his cock rubbed along that place inside her that Joe had found and she gripped him on every thrust to intensify the sensation.

Colt chuckled. "No you don't. Not yet."

Dakota's breath caught as he shifted their positions until she lay sprawled on his chest. Tightening her thighs on his hips, she sat up to ride him, groaning when he pulled her back down and held her tightly to his chest to stop her. "Damn it, Colt." She struggled, but he only tightened his grip.

"Easy, honey. You can ride me cowgirl, just as soon as Joe works his finger up your ass."

"Oh God." Dakota groaned and buried her face in his chest. "I've never done this."

He smoothed a hand over her hair. "You'll love it, I promise."

She couldn't prevent a shiver when Joe's hand ran over her bottom.

"Just relax, honey. I'll go nice and slow."

Dakota clenched on the cock inside her, drawing a groan from Colt.

Colt looked over her shoulder at Joe. "Not too fucking slow. Neither one of us can stay still much longer."

Held firmly against Colt's chest and straddling his hips, Dakota was wide open for Joe's ministrations. She jolted at the first touch of his oiled finger at her puckered opening. She panted as he pressed slowly into her, adding even more oil. The oil dripped to her slit and she moaned at the unfamiliar feel of having something push into her bottom. The completely alien sensation startled her, and she couldn't prevent the whimper that escaped.

Joe crooned to her, speaking so softly she couldn't make out his words, but just his tone reassured her. He rubbed her bottom with his other hand as he continued to work a thick finger into her.

Dakota drew several unsteady breaths as she struggled to adjust to such an erotic feeling. With both openings filled, she couldn't stop clenching her inner muscles, which made it feel even tighter.

Colt continued to stroke her as he held her against him. "You like that, don't you, honey? Just think how good it's going to feel when Joe and I take you together, one cock in your sweet cunt and another in your ass."

Dakota couldn't think. Joe's strokes and the feel of a hard cock filling her made her wild. The image Colt created in her head made it even worse. "I'm going to come. I have to—I need to—Ohh!"

Colt released her and helped her to sit up. "Ride me, Dakota." He gripped her hips tightly to help her, lifting his hips to thrust into her.

The finger pressing deep into her bottom, and the devastating strokes of Colt's cock turned her into a mass of mindless need. Her coordination gone, she let the men guide her, each downward stroke driving Colt's cock into her pussy and Joe's finger into her ass.

Within only a few strokes she felt that wonderful tingling feeling, and then that glorious pleasure that swept through her system. Her body jolted and bucked, and she rode Colt even harder. Her cries and Colt's deep groans filled the room.

Sparks raced through her, touching her everywhere and she clenched repeatedly on both men. The too full feeling, the delicious forbidden sensation of having her bottom invaded set her off again. She screamed her release, her body bowing as Colt surged into her one last time, pulling her hips down to fill her completely.

They froze that way for several moments, reveling in the pleasure, both trembling and moaning, the tortured sounds coming from both of them making it all the more erotic.

Joe kissed her shoulder, wrapping an arm around her waist to steady her as he withdrew, before lowering her gently onto Colt's chest. Patting her bottom, he bent to place a kiss on her back. "You're incredible, honey."

Struggling to catch her breath, she lay collapsed on Colt, watching Joe's naked butt as he walked down the hallway.

Colt ran a hand over her back soothingly as they both struggled to catch their breath.

She'd never had this kind of attention after sex before. It gave her a warm fuzzy inside, and she smiled as she snuggled closer.

Colt tightened his arms and rolled her onto her back. "Joe and I will go take care of the horses and start the generator. I'll put another log on the fire as soon as I get dressed. Why don't you stay here and keep warm?"

Dakota smiled up at him and pushed back the lock of hair that hung rakishly over his forehead. "Why don't we all go back to sleep?"

Colt chuckled. "It's morning, sleepyhead."

Dakota arched her neck to look at the window to see that the sky had started to lighten.

Joe came back into the room. "Before you get dressed, let me see that hip."

Colt cursed and jumped up. "Shit, I forgot about it. I'm sorry, honey. I hope I didn't hurt you."

Dakota grinned and sat up. "I never even felt it. It's fine." She reached for her clothes. "I'll get dressed and start the coffee."

Joe held her down easily and ran a hand over her hip, inspecting it before frowning. "I still think you need to put ice on it."

Dakota shuddered, just thinking about it. "No way. I'm nice and warm, and I'm not putting ice anywhere."

Colt chuckled. "I can make you change your mind about that."

Joe smiled and kissed her hair. "Why don't you stay where you are while Colt and I go take care of the horses and start—"

"The generator," Dakota finished for him. "Colt just said the same thing. I have a great idea. Why don't the two of you go do what you have to do while I stay here by the fire naked and warm? Then whenever you're ready, here I am."

Colt laughed as he fastened his jeans. "Great idea."

Dakota shook her head, smiling. "Idiot. I have a ranch to run. I *did* manage to do it all by myself until you two came along."

Colt pulled on his t-shirt. "Does that mean you're not going to stay naked and wait for us?"

Joe chuckled softly. "Dakota, all teasing aside, what just happened meant a lot to both of us. I don't want you to think it was just a lay. But I want you to know that we can't stay here forever. We've got some things to do, though, before we leave. But I promise you we'll take care of you while we're here and make sure you won't have any more problems with your neighbor before we go."

Dakota forced a smile. "I know you'll leave. I guess we've all been lonely too long—"

"Don't." Joe's face tightened. "Don't diminish what we just did. I'd do anything to be able to stay. You're a helluva woman, Dakota."

Joe bent, kissing her forehead before handing her the panties he'd removed earlier.

She watched them dress as she pulled her panties and sweatpants on, warmed by the way they watched her.

Colt finished dressing and turned her toward him to button her shirt. "All day I'm going to be thinking about how great it felt to be inside you." After kissing her softly, he and Joe turned to leave.

Rooted in place, she listened to their low murmurs as they donned their boots and coats. Hearing the back door open and close, she raced to the kitchen window.

Dakota watched them walk across the yard with a sinking feeling in her stomach. She knew they'd eventually leave. She'd told them so herself yesterday, but she thought it would be because of a payoff. She no longer thought that and wondered why they felt as though they still had to go.

She couldn't regret what they'd just done. She'd never experienced anything like that before, and she would make love to them as often as she could as long as they stayed.

Something about both of them drew her as no man ever had, and she promised herself that she would enjoy it to the fullest for the time they were here.

# Chapter Six

Since the men started the generator first, Dakota had time to have a hot breakfast ready by the time they came back in. Hearing them come into the porch, her body reacted immediately. By the time they walked into the kitchen, her heart raced, and she felt flushed and tongue-tied.

Both men had red faces from the cold, their hair windblown and both looked good enough to eat. Setting the table, her eyes kept shifting to them as they hung their coats and pulled off their boots, speaking to each other under their breath. Neither said a word as they washed up at the sink, but both kept glancing at her, their eyes possessive as they moved over her.

Taking the bacon out of the pan and putting it on paper towels to drain, her eyes were drawn to their hands and forearms as they soaped them, remembering far too clearly just what those sturdy hands had done to her earlier. Her nipples tingled and beaded when she remembered how they'd touched her. Eyeing the way Joe's shirt pulled across his broad shoulders, she couldn't help but remember what it had felt like to hold onto them as he gave her pleasure like she'd never known before.

Joe finished and went into the living room, glancing at her unsmilingly as he passed. He seemed to be deep in thought about something, and she wished she could ask him what bothered him. It seemed strange to have been intimate with both men but still be virtual strangers.

She turned her attention to Colt as he washed up. Neither acted as though they were angry with her, just distant. She wondered if they regretted this morning. Although she didn't have a lot of experience, she'd never known of a man regretting getting laid.

Maybe this was their way of showing her that it hadn't meant any more to them than that and didn't want her to get any ideas.

She couldn't hold it against them. What could she expect after having known them for only a day?

She usually had no problem dealing with men. She just didn't know how to deal with men like them. Their presence made her uncomfortable and clumsy, a sensation she didn't have much experience with. She could talk cattle and horses, but when it came to anything intimate, she had a little more trouble.

Her ex-boyfriend, Lenny, had been nothing like them. He'd always been upbeat and happy go lucky. Lenny's life's mission had always been to have a good time, and she never had to worry about talking. He did enough for both of them.

He'd taken Ed's money and gone to work for him in a heartbeat. The payoff and steady paycheck from Ed meant he could go into town and get drunk every weekend, and with a pocketful of money, he always had women surrounding him.

Joe and Colt were the exact opposite, and she really didn't know how to handle them. She would be more comfortable facing Ed's men than trying to figure out these two. She poured two cups of coffee and set them on the table, glancing at Colt warily. His continued silence made her uneasy.

By the time Joe came back into the room and joined Colt at the table their cool demeanor had started to worry her.

"Is something wrong? Are the horses okay?"

They both glanced at her and nodded. Colt smiled faintly. "Everything's fine. Joe and I just have a lot on our minds."

Joe continued to stare into his coffee cup as though looking for something. Or trying to avoid looking at her.

Mentally shrugging, she finished the pancakes and placed the big platter of them on the table along with the plate of bacon.

Joe and Colt ate in silence. Like the night before, they shoveled food in as though it would be their last meal and finished before she had even finished half of hers.

There were a few more pancakes on the plate in the center of the table. "Would you like some more?"

They shook their heads, their faces red when they looked at her plate. Colt got up to get more coffee. "No. We're just used to eating fast. Sorry about that."

The phone rang before she could reply, and she got up to answer it. "Hello?"

"Dakota, Sam and I are on our way. Coupla hunters got themselves lost."

"Sure, Bob, no problem. How many horses do you need? Are just you and Sam going out?"

"Yeah. The guy at the lodge is letting us handle it."

Dakota smiled at the sarcasm in his voice. "He usually does."

"We'll need four. They went out on foot, and they'll need a ride back."

"Make sure they know what they're doing. If they hurt my horses—"

Bob laughed. "We always take care of your precious horses, darlin'. We'll be there in about an hour."

"Okay, Bob. Thanks."

She hung up and turned to find both men watching her, their eyes narrowed.

Joe stood and moved to the window, looking out at the stable. "Who do you think is going to hurt the horses?"

Dakota smiled, shaking her head and went back to her breakfast. "That was Bob Miller. He and Sam Jackson are trackers, and there's a lodge across the ridge." She gestured toward the ridge behind the stables. "They cater to hunters and some of them are always getting lost. Bob and Sam are going out to find two more. They use my horses instead of bringing their own because it's easier and it gives me an income. Plus, they were friends of my dad. The lodge pays me."

Joe nodded. "This Sam and Bob, they can be trusted with the horses?"

Dakota smiled again. "Of course. They do this all the time. And they *hate* Big Ed. I think they started using my horses just to make him mad, but it works out."

She wanted so much to go up to him and put her arms around him, but he and Colt once again had assumed that cold, solemn look. If not for the way her body still hummed and the sensitivity between her legs, she could almost believe their lovemaking this morning hadn't happened.

Colt reached for his boots. "How long before he gets here?"

Dakota couldn't help but admire the way his shirt pulled over his big shoulders. She thought about how those muscles had bunched and moved under her hands as she bent over him, riding his cock to completion.

"Dakota?"

Snapping back to the present, she jumped up, moved to the sink and squirted soap onto the dishes. "He'll be here in about an hour. I'll take care of the horses. Both of you lost a lot of sleep last night. Why don't you catch some sleep now, while I'm awake to watch things? Besides, if Big Ed's men see Bob's truck here, they won't do anything. They like to make trouble when they're sure no one is around. They can't afford any witnesses." She snapped her mouth closed when she realized she was rambling.

Joe leaned back against the counter, watching her again. "We're not about to go to sleep while you're expecting someone. We'll sleep later. How many horses does he need?"

"Four." She wiped her hands and started for her boots when Colt stopped her, blocking her path. "What?"

"We'll take care of it. Isn't that what you hired us for?"

Dakota sighed and plopped into a chair. "I hired you because I felt bad for you and because I thought it would be nice to get a couple of nights sleep before Ed buys you off. I figured once he gave you the money, you'd at least be able to afford a place to stay."

Colt came closer and knelt in front of her, lightly gripping her arms. It was the first time either of them had touched her since they came in. "We're not taking Ed's money. We'll get rid of him for you, and then you can live in peace."

"What do you mean 'get rid of him'?"

Colt shook his head. "Nothing. We'll just make sure he doesn't bother you anymore. Joe, let's go get the horses ready."

Dakota went to the window to watch them cross to the stable. For the first time since she hired them, she felt uneasy and it scared her.

He father's advice about following her instincts went through her mind yet again.

"Daddy, what the hell should I do when my instincts tell me they're the best thing that ever happened to me, but at the same time, they're hiding something from me?"

* * * *

Joe waited until they walked some distance from the house before he turned to Colt. "What the hell are you thinking?"

Colt scraped a hand over his face. "I know. I know. She's got my brain scrambled. I haven't felt like this since before—"

"We can't afford to get attached to her." Joe tried to ignore the heavy weight that settled in his stomach. He already had.

"You're already attached to her, the same as I am. Don't try to deny it. I was there with you, remember? I saw the way you looked at her."

Joe walked into the stable without answering. That was the problem with having a friend who knew you as well as Colt knew him. They'd been friends ever since they could remember, and circumstances had led to them spending far more time together than most friends did. They'd been able to read each other perfectly for so long he couldn't remember a time when they hadn't.

They prepared the horses with little conversation. None was necessary.

He thought about the way Dakota had looked in the early morning light as he made love to her. Christ, she made him as horny as a teenager, and somehow he'd turned to her in his sleep. He'd been dreaming, fantasizing actually, about touching her, gathering her close and palming the breast he hadn't been able to get out of his mind.

In his dream, her breast had fit his palm as though it had been made for his hand. She'd felt so soft there, so delicate and he'd moved his hand over her gently so as not to hurt her. When she pushed into his touch, the pebbled nipple poking into his hand, he'd used his callused palm to give her the friction he knew would take her higher. Her moan had awakened him and ended one dream only to begin another.

God, she was so sweet. Under that hard shell she used to protect herself, Dakota was so soft and feminine it blew him away. She'd done a fine job in taking care of herself, but he knew it couldn't last. The only reason she'd lasted this long was because for some reason, her neighbor had decided to play with her. Now that Big Ed knew she had company, he would realize his mistake and would become more determined.

When Ed found out the identity of her company, he would get desperate.

He and Colt had to keep her inside and safe as much as possible until they took care of her bullying neighbor.

"Do you think she'd be willing to go with us?"

Joe sighed. The same question had been going through his mind all morning. "I wish I knew. But she seems to really love it here. She told us herself that she hasn't lived anywhere else."

Colt sighed. "And you don't think we'll be able to stay?"

Joe grimaced. "The people here would never accept us. Besides, can you really picture her tying herself to not one, but two killers?"

"Fuck."

"Yeah."

\* \* \* \*

Dakota walked Bob and Sam out to the stable, chatting about the hunters that had gotten lost and where they thought they might find them. She'd already told them about Joe and Colt, who stood waiting with the horses. The older men had questioned her about them, having become protective of her while her daddy was ill, one of the reasons she hadn't told them what Ed had been doing.

Even though both men had reached their sixties, they still acted as though they were twenty years younger. Although both stayed in good shape, she was scared to death that either one of them would get hurt if they faced off with Ed. They were both hard-headed and would waste no time confronting Ed if they found out. When her daddy died, they'd assumed that it had all blown over, and she continued to let them think that.

She walked with them to where Joe and Colt had let the horses out into the small fenced area, the only area she could keep fenced because of Ed.

After introducing them she watched, amused as the men all gave each other a once over before Sam and Bob loaded their bags onto the horses and started out.

None of them spoke as they headed back to the house. When the men went into the living room, she avoided temptation and stayed in the kitchen. She put a roast and potatoes in the oven and went out to the living room with the intention of asking for their clothes so she could start the laundry.

She stopped in the doorway, leaning against it and smiling when she saw they'd both fallen asleep. They'd put another log on the fire, making the living room toasty. Colt slept on the mattress on the floor, while Joe lay sprawled on the sofa. The laundry could wait until later. Both had to be tired, having taken turns all night watching for Ed's men.

For the thousandth time she thought about leaving Fairview. Why the hell did she stay in a place like this? But where the hell would she go?

She went back out to the kitchen and sat at the table with a cup of coffee, her head spinning with possibilities. She'd been in this town all her life. She'd never seriously contemplated leaving, even when Ed burned down the barn. The people who lived here were plain, hardworking people. She didn't expect them to try to fight a man like Ed Franks, but she had thought they would have stood up to him a little more than they had. But even when the state police had been called in, no one would say a word against him.

But still…this was her home.

Restless, she slipped on her boots and coat and went out the back door. Circling the house, she looked over the place wondering just how much longer she'd be able to hold out. Ed could send a bunch of his men and drive her out at any time, and it made her nervous as hell.

Hearing a truck, she looked up in time to see Ben Parsons coming up the lane. She shaded her eyes against the bright sunshine reflecting off of the snow, smiling as she waited for him to get out. He was gorgeous as all get out, and she'd wished more than once that she felt more than a brotherly affection toward him.

"Heard you hired two hands. Those two men that have been asking questions around town. I want you to get in my truck and stay there."

Dakota blinked. "Hello to you, too. What the hell are you talking about? Why should I get in your truck?"

He gripped her arms, his expression hard as he studied her face. "Are you okay?"

Dakota frowned. "Yes. Why? Ed's men came out here last night and tried to cause some trouble but—"

Ben's jaw clenched. "What happened?"

"Joe and Colt took care of them. Beat the crap out of them and sent them back to Ed."

He shook her. "Damn it, Dakota. Why didn't you call me?"

"Get your fucking hands off of her."

Dakota twisted to see Joe standing on the porch, Colt right behind him pointing the shotgun at Ben. "No! It's Ben Parsons, the deputy I told you about." She turned to Ben, placing her hand over the gun he'd drawn. "They thought you were one of Ed's men. You don't need this."

Ben pushed her behind him and faced Joe, keeping his gun pointed at him. "Pack your things and get the hell out of here."

Dakota fought off Ben's attempt to keep her behind him and came around to face him, standing between him and the coldly furious men on the porch. "Ben! What are you doing?"

Cursing, he lowered the gun. "Do you know who these men are? I followed them in town and got their license plate number. They've been in town for a week, and I never could get a good look at them." He gripped her arm again. "They're killers, Dakota. Convicted murderers. They served twelve years for killing a man. They got out of a maximum security prison three years ago."

Stunned, Dakota turned to the men on her porch, the men she'd had sex with only hours before. A lead weight settled in her stomach as she faced them. She swallowed the sudden lump in her throat. "Is this true?"

Colt lowered the shotgun to his side as Joe stood there staring at her, the vulnerability in his eyes a sharp contrast to the hard lines of his taut frame.

Dakota slowly moved forward, shaking off Ben's restraining hand. Staring up at Joe, she caught the softening of his gaze before it became hardened once again, his jaw clenching. She couldn't believe they'd ever kill anyone. When Ed's men had shown up, they could have easily hurt them a lot more than they had. But their concern had been for her. Still, she had to hear them say it. "Is it true?"

Several seconds passed, and she'd begun to think he wouldn't answer her. She glanced at Colt who took a step toward her and stopped abruptly. The look on his face was terrible to see and with a sinking heart, she knew she already had her answer.

"Yes."

Joe bit the word out, his jaw clenched tight. His face looked as though it had been carved from granite, his eyes bleak as he stared down at her. "I haven't lied to you, Dakota."

His tone had been so low, his words barely carried.

She couldn't help but notice that both men stood braced, as if for a blow. They never even glanced at Ben, so she knew they expected the blow to come from her. A verbal blow.

They might not say it, but if they had to brace themselves for her rejection, they had to feel something for her. Maybe it was just wishful thinking on her part, but she would have to follow her instincts. She wanted to know what had happened. She couldn't imagine Joe and Colt killing someone in cold blood. She couldn't believe it.

She wouldn't believe it.

She couldn't feel this strongly about them if they were truly evil.

If her instincts were wrong…

Ben came forward, his hand resting on the gun he'd holstered. "You two get out of here and get the hell out of Fairview."

Neither man moved other than shifting their eyes to Ben and then back to her. Colt's brow went up. "Your call, Dakota. We'll do whatever you want. No hard feelings."

Ben gripped her arm to stop her as she started toward Joe. "Stay back, Dakota. I'll handle this."

Dakota had just about had enough of bossy men, and she didn't trust the icy look in Joe and Colt's gaze as they sliced to where Ben gripped her arm. "Let go of me, Ben. I'm fine, I promise." Shaking him off, she ignored his curses as she went up the porch steps and stood toe to toe with them. She let out a shuddering breath and braced herself. She had to know. She didn't know what she would do if they had killed someone. "Did you do it?"

They froze, appearing stunned. Colt finally answered. "No, ma'am."

Dakota kept her face blank, as relief weakened her knees. She believed him. "You plan on killing me?"

Colt's eyes softened and his lips twitched. "No, ma'am."

Joe's eyes glittered as he reached out to touch her cheek, pulling his hand back at the last moment. "I would die to keep you safe."

Filled with such joy she thought her heart might burst, Dakota smiled. "Let's hope it doesn't come to that." She turned back to Ben to try to calm him down. She knew he'd never leave until he could be sure of her safety. "Come on, Ben. Let's walk."

* * * *

Joe forced himself not to move, when everything inside him wanted to run after them, pull Dakota away from the deputy and carry her back into the house.

"She asked if we did it." Colt looked incredulous as he watched them disappear from view.

Joe had a hard time assimilating that fact himself. No one ever had. The sheriff had come and arrested them, pulled them out of his house in the middle of the night, and that had been the end of it. The court appointed attorney had never even asked them if they'd done it, just nodded disbelievingly every time they'd proclaimed their innocence. His own family hadn't believed him.

In their ignorance, he and Colt had believed that they'd be found not guilty and justice would prevail. It hadn't. Neither one of them had believed in anything but each other and their need for revenge for a long time.

Until now. Now they also believed in Dakota.

She really believed them. He could see it in her eyes. Incredible. Love for her washed over him, making him feel cleaner than he had in years.

He believed what he felt for her even if he couldn't stick around.

They would both do whatever they could to keep Dakota safe. But nothing would sway them from killing the man she knew as Ed Franks. He and Colt had made up their minds to it years ago, and it had been the only thing that kept them going. They both knew they could live with murder.

But Dakota never could.

They couldn't ask her to.

So they would have to live without her.

# Chapter Seven

The electricity came back on during the day, making it unnecessary for anyone to sleep in the living room. Colt dragged the mattresses back to the bedroom, hoping like hell it would go off again.

After he finished, he sat on the edge of the bed and sighed. Would killing Dakota's neighbor really be worth it? He'd been all for it until he'd met Dakota and had the wind knocked out of his sails. He didn't know yet if they could have a future with her, but the possibility unsettled him. Right now they had a chance to explore what they'd both begun to feel for her, but once they committed murder…

"Can you tell me about it?"

Colt looked up, startled that she'd been able to sneak up on him. Bitterness weighed heavy in his stomach as he thought about how much he could tell her. He couldn't tell her everything. If he did, she would either be forced to report them or would become an accessory.

So he began with the basics. "Joe and I grew up in the same town. We've been friends so long that I don't ever remember not being his friend. I'm an only child, but Joe has a baby sister. I was one of those late in life babies."

Not being able to sit any longer, he got up and started out to the kitchen with Dakota right behind him. He poured them each coffee, needing to wash the bitter taste from his mouth. He looked out the window to see Joe outside with the horses. Without turning, he began again.

"My dad was getting up in years and wanted to sell the ranch to buy a little house in town. I told him I'd take care of it, but he didn't want me to be tied to the ranch the way he'd been. I told him that's all I ever wanted, but he wanted me to get out and see the world before I settled down."

Bile rose in his throat. It had been one of the last things his father had ever said to him. "My dad never believed in lawyers. While I was out of town he sold the place to a con man and it wasn't until afterward that my father realized the check he'd gotten wasn't a down payment, but the full amount of the sale price. The bastard had bought my dad's ranch and all the horses for ten thousand dollars. Hell, mom and dad didn't even have enough to buy a little house and were out on the streets right away. When I came home and found out, I was in a rage and tracked the guy down. Joe saw me in town and came after me to find out what was wrong."

His chest tightened as he thought about that day. It was a day he'd never forget. He remembered the hot sun beating down on him as he told Joe what Frank had done. He remembered Joe's own anger as he went with him to confront Frank.

He shook his head at his own naiveté. "I was only nineteen years old. Joe was twenty-one. We tracked the man who'd cheated my parents to the feed store. Arrogant and cocky, I walked up to him, demanding that he either gave my parents back the ranch or paid what he owed."

He couldn't turn to face her but from the scrape of the chair, he knew she sat right behind him. "The lawyer in town had gotten paid to write the contract the way F—the bastard wanted it, and since my dad signed it, there was nothing we could do. I went into a rage and started swinging and before I knew it, Joe and I were fighting him and his men. The sheriff was called and broke it up, and Joe and I left. We went to the house my mom and dad were staying in, with one of her friends. He'd made them move right away. I told my mom that I'd go and find a lawyer in the next town and we'd get everything fixed. My dad gave me the money they'd gotten to pay for the lawyer, and Joe and I left. We made an appointment for early the next morning. We left that night so we could spend the night there so we wouldn't be late."

"What happened?"

He scraped a hand over his face and took another sip of coffee as a lead weight settled in his stomach. "The damned truck broke down in the middle of nowhere, and Joe and I had to walk back to town. We'd just crashed at Joe's when the sheriff broke the door down and hauled us out to his car, asking why we did it. We didn't know what the hell he was talking about. Then he asked why we'd killed F—the bastard that had bought the ranch from my parents."

The surge of rage he felt when he thought of that time nearly choked him. He hadn't been able to help his parents after all. They'd blamed themselves for being conned and for him going to prison. They'd both died feeling like failures, feeling like they'd ruined their only child's life.

Colt could never forgive that.

Locked in prison, he'd been unable to help them. It had been torture knowing what they were going through and of their illnesses and unable to be with them.

His hand tightened, gripping the mug so hard, it surprised him that he hadn't broken it. He carefully loosened his grip and placed the mug on the counter before turning to face her.

Surprised to see her tears, he went forward and knelt at her feet, running his thumbs over her wet cheeks. "Don't cry. I couldn't stand it."

Dakota wiped her cheeks and nodded. "What happened to the man who cheated your parents?"

"They found the ranch house I grew up in burned to the ground. There was a body inside, burned so badly they could only identify him by the ring on his finger. It was the ring that bastard wore. We were charged with setting the fire that killed him."

Dakota laid her hands on his cheeks, and he wanted nothing more than to bury his face against her breasts and hold onto her. "That's awful! How can that happen?"

Colt laughed humorlessly. "We lived in a backwards town with a sheriff who could be bought. Sound familiar? All of a sudden there were all kinds of people testifying that we'd had a fight with him and that I'd threatened to kill him."

"Yeah, but you weren't even there!"

"We couldn't prove a damned thing. The only alibi we had was each other. And nobody believed us. So they found us guilty and sent us to prison. We served twelve years for murder."

"Oh, Colt." Tears streamed down her face as she leaned into him. Humbled and terrified that her little body shook with sobs, he gathered her close and pulled her from the chair to sit with her in his lap.

"Shh, baby. It's over. We're fine." He cupped her head, rocking her as she buried her face in his neck.

"You must have been so scared. You were so young."

Acid churned in Colt's stomach when he remembered the paralyzing fear that had gripped him when the jury found them guilty. He hadn't thought it would be possible, had hoped that something would happen at the last minute, that the jury would somehow know the truth. He and Joe had been scared shitless, with good reason as it turned out. "Yeah, we were scared."

When Dakota lifted her head, he struggled to keep his face bland. "Did they hurt you in prison?"

Colt stood and placed her on her feet, walking away to look back out the window. "Two kids in a maximum security prison with a bunch of hardened criminals. We were small town boys, and didn't know any more than horses and cattle. In prison, you become cattle. The less you know, the better. Joe and I don't talk about it. But we started lifting weights and soon got strong enough to fight back. Fight dirty. We got mean. And we survived."

Fuck. Thinking about prison made it feel as though the walls were closing in on him. "I need some air."

"Colt?"

He paused with his hand on the doorknob, but didn't turn, not wanting her to see what the memories did to him. "What?"

"I'm so sorry."

\* \* \* \*

Dakota wiped her eyes as Colt walked out the door, moving to the sink to watch him walk across the yard to Joe. She felt as though she understood them both a little better now. Learning what they'd been through broke her heart.

Clapping a hand over her mouth, she gasped remembering Joe's initial refusal to touch her bottom and his gentleness when he did.

*I don't want to hurt her.*

Had they been raped in prison?

What had been done to them astounded her. She wanted, more than anything, to see them happy. Wanted them to have some joy in their lives.

She just plain wanted them.

Learning the truth left her in no doubt of her feelings. She would do everything in her power to make them happy and hoped like hell she could convince them that the three of them had a future.

But what the hell did she know about what it took to make a man happy?

\* \* \* \*

After dinner that night, she watched the men get up from the table to go out to sit on the front porch. An idea to cheer them a little formed. After gathering what she'd need, she went out to the front porch. "How about a game of poker?"

It had gotten too dark to be able to see their expressions clearly, but she was relieved when both nodded and stood.

Dakota divided up the poker chips and began shuffling the cards. She gave Joe and Colt her best smile. "Do you gentlemen know how to play this game, or do you need me to teach you?"

Joe's lips twitched, but he only nodded, staring into his coffee cup.

Dakota sighed inwardly. "Twos, threes and one-eyed Jacks are wild."

Colt smiled, giving her hope. "Is that all?"

About to deal, Dakota paused. "I heard sarcasm. When it's your turn to deal, you can do whatever you want. Right now, I'm the dealer."

Colt flashed a grin. "Yes, ma'am."

Dakota won the hand but she knew the reason. Neither man paid much attention to the game. They seemed to be lost in their own thoughts, and Dakota was determined to snap them out of it. "You know, I never gave much thought to big muscles before, but yours turn me on."

Joe jerked, spilling coffee. Grabbing napkins, he cleaned up the mess and began dealing. "Working out was necessary in prison. Fours are wild."

Colt shot Joe a look before turning to her, smiling faintly. "I'm glad. We feel the same way about your soft curves."

Dakota nodded and looked down at her cards. Taken aback by Joe's abrupt attitude, she remained silent for several minutes, working up her courage to try again. Damn it. What did she have to do to get Joe to smile?

Not looking up, she sorted the cards in her hand. "Maybe next time we should play strip poker."

Colt chuckled softly. "There's an idea."

Encouraged, Dakota looked up at Joe. "What do you think?"

Joe threw down his discard and picked up the deck. "You'd get cold. Colt, how many cards do you want?"

Dakota waited until Colt took one card before laying down her four discards. "Maybe you'd be the one getting cold. But if it would make you feel better, we could play in the living room with a big fire going."

Joe raised a brow at the four discards but dealt her four more. "I don't think so. Colt and I would have you naked in no time."

Dakota sat back, elated to finally have him talking. "Nope. As soon as the two of you saw my breasts, you wouldn't be able to concentrate on the cards, and I'd win." Her nipples pebbled just imagining it.

Colt's gaze flew to her breasts. "Good point. But you have very sensitive nipples. If Joe and I played with them, you'd forget all about your cards."

Dakota shook her head, tightening her thighs against the rush of warmth. "There would be no touching during the game."

Colt frowned. "Then what's the point?"

"Anticipation."

Joe and Colt glanced at each other and shifted in their seats.

Dakota hid a smile. "We'd all just sit here playing cards with clothes coming off here and there."

Joe turned to her and opened his mouth, only to snap it shut again. His gaze dropped to her breasts, making them burn. Turning back, he threw two chips into the pot. "Twenty."

Through her lashes she watched both Joe and Colt sneak glances at her breasts. Her nipples poked at the front of her shirt and she did nothing to hide it. Laying her cards face down on the table, she stretched her arms over her head, arching her back. Her lips curved when Colt accidentally knocked over his chips.

"Damn it, Dakota."

Lowering her arms, she did her best to look innocent. "Something wrong?"

Colt began to restack his chips. "I ought to turn you over my knee."

Joe's head shot up. "Shut up, Colt."

Dakota struggled to hide her grin. She'd learned a little about them by now. Their rigid posture and glittering eyes told her just how much her playfulness affected them. "You wouldn't be threatening to spank me, would you?"

If possible, Colt's eyes grew hotter. "Let's just play cards."

"You have something against talking while we play?"

"No. Just talk about something else."

Dakota arched a brow as she placed her own bet. "You don't think I have a right to know if you have plans to spank me?"

Joe remained silent, not looking up, but she could see the muscle in his jaw work and he clenched his teeth.

Colt narrowed his eyes at her. "I didn't threaten to spank you, but I will if you keep it up. Somebody needs to take you in hand. You don't listen worth a damn, and you're too ornery for your own good."

Amused, Dakota leaned forward. "And you think you can 'take me in hand'?"

"I know damned well I can."

"Don't bite off more than you can chew, cowboy."

"I have strong teeth." Colt laid down his cards. "Four nines."

Dakota stared down at her straight and stuck out her bottom lip. "I think you're cheating."

Raking in his chips, Colt glanced at her. "Little thing like you can get herself into some big trouble making accusations like that."

Intrigued, Dakota propped her chin on her hand and stared up at him. This had turned out to be a lot of fun. "Really? What kind of trouble?"

Joe's chair scraped back as he stood. "I'm going to go get some sleep. Colt, wake me in a couple of hours."

The game forgotten, Dakota watched him leave, feeling a lead weight settle in the pit of her stomach. Turning back to Colt, she rubbed her arms, suddenly chilled. "What's wrong with him?"

Colt sighed. "You remind us of what we've missed. Joe and I have a lot of bitterness inside us, Dakota. You make us wish for things we can't have."

Dakota blinked back tears and had to swallow the lump in her throat before speaking. "Prison is in the past. You can both put that behind you and get on with your lives."

Colt nodded. "We're trying. We have something to do before we can do that."

"What happens after that?"

"We leave, Dakota. And never look back."

Hours later, lying in her bed, she replayed the conversation over and over in her mind. She twisted restlessly, still wanting them. Her traitorous body remembered all too well how much pleasure they could give her and demanded more.

But it wasn't only physical. She wanted to be close to them, fall asleep to the sounds of their heartbeats and steady breathing. She wanted to be in their arms and sleep surrounded by their warmth.

Oh God, she'd really fallen for them. Knowing they would break her heart when they left didn't seem to matter.

She leaned up and punched her pillow again, which was possible only because she'd left her gun in the drawer of the nightstand. With Joe and Colt in the house, she didn't need it. Knowing one of them would still be awake, she tried to be as quiet as possible as she settled back, closing her eyes and willing herself to sleep.

* * * *

The day had warmed considerably, melting a lot of the snow and in some places, she could see the grass again. She'd just finished cleaning up from breakfast when she saw Bob and Sam coming across the ridge. She turned to Joe and Colt still sitting at the table, drinking their coffee. "Looks like Bob and Sam found their hunters."

Joe stood and moved in behind her, looking out the window himself. "Yeah, it looks like you're right. We'll go take care of the horses."

Dakota had been holding her breath since he'd come up behind her. The heat of his chest against her shoulder and the erection pressing into her hip caused a flutter in her stomach. Without thinking, she leaned into him, closing her eyes as his arms came around her. Breathing in his scent, she sighed. She hadn't known just how much she'd needed this.

His lips brushed her hair as his hand slid over her bottom. His other hand slid up to cup a breast, running his thumb over her pebbled nipple. "The next time you can't sleep because you're aroused, or because you're lonely, come to us and we'll take care of you."

At her gasp, he lightly pinched her nipple. "You tossed and turned all night. We'll go see to the horses. Then we'll be back to take care of you."

When he moved away, Colt came up behind her and slid his arms around her waist, pressing his erection into the small of her back. His warm breath on her ear caused a shiver. "My dick was hard all night, missing your tight pussy. Now that I've been inside you, I want more. And I sleep better with you cuddled against me." He smacked her ass as he walked away, throwing a wink over his shoulder as he followed Joe outside.

Dakota watched them go out, dragging air into her lungs. Damn, they could get to her like no man ever had. She had it bad. Slipping on her boots and coat, she started to follow them out when the phone rang. Backtracking, she went to answer it, glancing out the window, smiling as she watched them cross the yard.

"Hello?"

"Dakota, this is John. John Tillman, from the feed store."

Dakota blinked. Why the hell would Fred's son call her? "What can I do for you, John?"

"My father and I are worried about you. Word is around town that the men he sent up there to look for work are convicted murderers. I want you to know that he didn't know anything about that when he sent them up. We just wanted to help—look, we all feel bad about the way that Big Ed's been treating you and—hell. Look, we're really sorry. About everything. And we wanted to make sure that you're all right. I can get a couple of men to come up there with me and get rid of them for you if you want."

The thought of John, or any of the other men in town trying to get rid of Joe and Colt made her smile. "That's not necessary, John. Joe and Colt are working out just fine."

"Are you sure? If you're just saying that—"

"I'm positive." Looking out the window again, she watched them deal with the horses. She saw Bob and Sam introduce them to the two hunters, who moved lethargically, obviously exhausted. "They're working out just fine."

"Have Ed's men been harassing you?"

"Of course, John. They've never stopped. If that's all, I've got work to do."

"Dakota, listen. We're all real sorry about the way we've abandoned you." He lowered his voice conspiratorially. "I've called a friend of mine, who knows somebody in the FBI. I told him what's been happening around here. He said that somebody's already taking care of it. I don't know when they're going to send somebody, but I'll keep you posted."

Dakota opened and closed her mouth several times, not knowing what to say. It had been a long time, since her daddy died, that she'd even heard from most of the people in town. "What the hell is bringing on this sudden attack of caring about your neighbor? What's going on that I don't know about? Did you hear that Big Ed's going to try to kill me today or something?"

"Damn it, Dakota. No. It's nothing like that. We're just worried about you, that's all."

The last several months of not sleeping and fear for herself and her animals, and the worry her father had endured, had her fury spewing like hot lava. "Since when the hell did you start worrying about me? You and your father won't even sell me feed. I have to get it delivered. The whole damned town has cut me off because I'm the only one here with enough balls to stand up to Ed. I could have been hurt any number of times already, and not a damned one of you would have cared. Do you know he stole my cattle? Burned down the barn? Tried to steal the horses? Put sugar in my gas tank to strand me here? He sends his men over to bug me at all hours of the night, so I can't even sleep. You and the rest of your pussy friends can go fuck yourselves."

She slammed down the phone and had just started for the back door again when the phone rang again.

Dakota snatched up the receiver. "What the hell do you want now?"

"Well isn't that a fine way to talk to your best friend?"

Dakota smiled at Jill's amused tone. "Hell, Jill, I'm sorry. John Tillman just called." She told her about it and about Ben's visit. She also explained that Joe and Colt had been in prison.

Jill remained silent as she told her everything. When she finished, Jill finally spoke. "Are you sure you can trust them? Listen, what if I come to get you and—"

"No, Jill. They've been nothing but kind to me and if anything, they're overprotective. They explained some of it to me. I know there's more to it, but they're not ready to talk about it yet. When they are, they'll tell me. I trust them. I promise you, if I need you, I'll call."

"I'm coming out there."

"Don't. Ed's already sent a couple of men. This time they had knives. I want you to stay away from here until I tell you it's safe. Promise me."

Jill sighed, and Dakota could well imagine her friend pacing back and forth in her kitchen. "Okay. Okay. But only if you promise me something. You promise to call me if you get the tiniest feeling that something's wrong."

Dakota smiled. "I promise. Thanks, Jill. I love you, you know."

"I love you, too. I mean it. You call me. You know what? I'm going to call every day to check on you. Oh, and Dakota?"

"What?"

"If John Tillman decides to get some men together and come out there to kick Joe and Colt off the place, you call me."

Dakota frowned into the phone. "Why?"

"Are you kidding? I'd pay big money to see that. I'll call you tomorrow."

Shaking her head, Dakota replaced the receiver. She just hoped Jill kept her promise and stayed away. Starting for the back door again, she heard a noise from out front.

*What now?*

A glance at the window over the kitchen sink showed her that the six men were all still talking. Joe and Colt took the horses into the stable as soon as Bob and Sam unloaded their gear. Walking through the living room, she looked out to see Lenny and Buck get out of Lenny's new truck. She headed out, in the perfect mood to deal with them.

\* \* \* \*

Hearing the sound of a vehicle pulling in out front, Joe gave the reins of the last horse to Colt. "Take care of him. I'm going out front. We have company."

He started for the front of the house, aware of the men behind him, but ignoring them. His main concern was for Dakota. He heard her voice raised in anger and started to run. At the crack of a blow, he put on a burst of speed and heard a muffled cry as he raced around the corner of the house. Seeing red that someone would dare hit her, he ran to her, looking for injuries, keeping an eye on the other two men.

He came to an abrupt halt between her and the men, one of whom lay on the ground with a bloody nose. He shot her a glance. "You okay?"

She nodded. "Fine. Get out of my way."

Joe had recognized Buck as soon as he'd turned the corner and now turned to face him fully. He didn't say a word, just raised a brow as Buck continued to stare at him.

The years hadn't been kind to Big Ed's foreman and right hand man. Buck's stomach hung over his belt buckle and his face had gone soft and flabby from too much drink and not enough work. He'd taken a step toward Dakota but had backed off when Joe stepped between them.

Buck tried his best to look tough, but failed miserably. "You one of them convicts everybody's talkin' about?"

Joe allowed his lips to curve slightly. "Yes." He looked at the other man who scrambled to his feet, holding a handkerchief to his bloody nose. He purposely kept his tone cool, his expression amused, hiding his burning rage. "Looks like you have everything under control, Dakota."

The man got up and swiped at his nose again and tried, unsuccessfully, to sidestep Joe. "You hit me! What the fuck is this Dakota? You're my woman. What are you doing, letting two ex-cons live here with you? Get rid of them, Dakota. I mean it."

Dakota laughed. "I'm not your woman, you slimy worm. When Ed bought you off, you were in such a hurry to run over to him, you left a trail of dust. Get off my property before I pop you again."

"What the hell's going on here?"

Joe didn't even turn at Bob's question. "Nothing much. Just a couple of bullies trying to bother Dakota."

Out of the corner of his eye, Joe saw Bob share a look with Sam, drop his gear and start toward them. "Is that a fact?"

Joe kept his gaze on the two men standing in front of him, shifting his weight as Dakota squared off with the younger man. He put out a hand to keep the older men back. "We've got it, Bob. Thanks."

Neither Bob nor Sam paid any attention and stepped closer. Sam gestured toward Buck. "Ain't that Big Ed's foreman?"

Joe nodded. "I believe so." Out of the corner of his eye, he saw

Colt approach. Buck's eyes widened when he saw Colt, who moved past them to stand on the other side of Dakota. Joe bared his teeth. "Who's this guy, Dakota? The one that thinks you're his woman."

Dakota shook her head in disgust. "I was. He took Ed's payoff and went to work for him. His name's Lenny."

Joe looked over the younger man and wondered what the hell Dakota had seen in him. Except for the blood covering the front of his shirt, he looked crisp and pressed. Even his boots had a shine to them. Lenny was obviously no working cowboy. The green fist of jealousy grabbed him by the throat, and he fought to breathe normally as his blood boiled.

It was none of his business, he reminded himself.

Like hell.

Lenny moved forward, only to back off when Dakota balled her hand into a fist. "Dakota, honey, it's not like that." He glanced at Buck, frowning, obviously confused at the way Buck kept staring at both him and Colt. "Why don't you just sell to Big Ed? We can buy a house in Dallas or Houston, you know, the city."

Dakota laughed. "Let me get this straight. You want to use *my* money to buy a house for us in the city? I hate cities and I hate you."

Colt grinned. "That pretty much shoots that plan out of the water. Besides, if you want Dakota, you're going to have to go through us to get her."

Lenny looked from one to the other and then back at Dakota. "Both of them, Dakota? No wonder you never liked sex. You need two men. You're a fucking whore."

The word had barely left his mouth before Joe's fist shot out, clipping him in the jaw and knocking him cold. He turned to Buck. "Get this piece of shit off Dakota's land."

Buck didn't even glance at Lenny. "What's your names?"

Joe bared his teeth. "You know our names, Buck. Tell *Big Ed* we said 'Hi'."

# Chapter Eight

Dakota waited until Bob, Sam and the bedraggled hunters left before turning to Colt. She knew it would be easier to get an answer from him than from Joe. "Buck looked like he was surprised as hell to see both of you. How do you know him?"

Colt slid a glance at Joe, who had already turned away to walk back to the stable. "Just a ghost from the past, Dakota. Let it go. We have to go take care of the horses."

Dakota started after him, his long strides eating up the ground and forcing her to practically run to keep up with him. "Damn it. I want to know what's going on."

Colt didn't even glance at her. "You hired us to take care of things around here. I've already told you too much, but I didn't want you to be afraid either of us would hurt you. Just let it go, Dakota."

"But I—"

Colt stopped and whirled on her. "No!" He stopped and scrubbed a hand over his face and took several calming breaths. "Look, Joe and I appreciate that you've given us a place to stay. We're attracted to you. A lot. We really like you. A lot. We want you. A hell of a lot. But we can't tell you anything else. We'll do what we can to help you around here. That's it. Leave it alone."

The misery on his face startled her. Without thinking, she reached out to cup his cheek. "Why? What aren't you telling me?"

Colt stared at her for several long moments, his eyes bleak. He reached out to tuck a wayward strand of hair behind her ear before shaking his head and turning away. "Let it go, Dakota."

Dakota followed him into the stable and went to deal with her own horse, glaring at Joe as he unsaddled Stunner. "Why don't I let both of *you* go? If you're going to leave, leave!"

Turning her back to both of them, she took care of settling her horse as Joe fed all of them. Beauty, sensing her mood, grew restless, so she forced herself to calm down. By the time they finished, Dakota's mood had turned from angry and hurt to just depressed. She couldn't help but follow their movements as they finished and walked out of the stable. Her stomach knotted. Were they, right now, going inside to pack their things?

It didn't matter. She'd done fine without them before, and she would do fine without them again.

But as she wandered the stable, dreading walking back to the empty house, she knew she lied to herself. She'd never met men who she could respect, who stood tall and behaved like men, not like little boys who only thought about themselves. Not like Lenny, who only thought about the next good time to be had.

Her heart bled for the boys they'd been and yearned for the men they'd become. Fate must be laughing its ass off at her right now. She doesn't fall for one man, oh no, not her. She falls for two. And she can't have either one of them.

She had to stop thinking about them. So what if they were the type of men she thought no longer existed. So what if they turned her inside out. She didn't need any more complications in her life, and if they wanted to leave, it would be better if they did it now before she could fall even harder for them.

Walking back to the house, she looked up toward Big Ed's place. Shading her eyes, she watched as two men sat on their horses, looking over in her direction. From this distance she couldn't be sure, but it looked like Buck and Big Ed himself. She raised her hand high and gave them the finger.

Walking to the house, she sped up when she heard the phone ring. Racing inside, she answered, "Hello."

"Dakota, it's Ben. Be careful. Something's going on between Ed and the sheriff. A lot of hush hush phone calls. The sheriff finally left to go out there. Do you know what's going on?"

Hearing sounds from out front, Dakota went to the window to see Joe and Colt working on the front porch. She grinned, not realizing how tense she'd been until then. "I have no idea, Ben. All I can tell you is that when Lenny and Buck came over a little while ago, Bob and Sam were still here. Also, it looked like maybe Buck knew Joe and Colt, but neither one of them would tell me anything."

"Damn it, Dakota! Why don't you kick them out? They're trouble, Dakota. I mean it. Get rid of them."

Dakota's temper snapped. "I'm tired of people trying to tell me what to do. They're helping me out, Ben, when everyone else turned their backs on me. And I don't need you or anyone else to try to tell me how to run my ranch." She slammed the phone down and began to pace the kitchen.

She'd had enough of this. Enough of Ed. Enough of the worry about her ranch. Enough of doing nothing about it except surviving and worrying. Enough of those damned cowboys out front turning her inside out. She wouldn't cower. She would take care of Ed on her own. If Joe and Colt wanted to leave, they could leave. She didn't need anybody.

Grabbing her pistol and her shotgun, Dakota went back out to the stable. She saddled her own horse, her movements jerky, and she found herself apologizing to Beauty more than once.

"What are you doing?"

Dakota spun at the Joe's cool tone. "None of your business. I thought I told you to leave." She gathered the reins, ignoring him.

Joe stepped forward and took the reins out of her hands. "I asked you a question."

Dakota tried unsuccessfully to get the reins back. Furious, she shoved him, and it only pissed her off even more when he didn't budge at all. "I'm doing what I should have done a long time ago. I'm going to Ed's and having it out with him."

Joe dropped the reins and moved toward her. "No. You're not."

A red haze filled her vision. She couldn't remember ever being so enraged. "What? You're not going to tell me what to do! Who the hell do you think you are?"

Colt walked into the stable. His brows went up but he didn't say a word as he took the reins, led her horse away, and calmly began to unsaddle her.

"Don't you dare. Leave Beauty alone. I'm going over there, and you two are leaving."

Joe shook his head. "Wrong on both counts."

Dakota saw the dark intent in his eyes as he closed in on her but couldn't move fast enough to avoid him. He bent and put his shoulder into her stomach and lifted her as easily as he lifted the feed.

"Damn you. Put me down."

She kicked. She punched his back. She wiggled. But she couldn't get away. When a hard slap landed on her ass, it surprised her enough to render her immobile. "You hit me."

"I slapped your ass. Stop fighting me. You're not going anywhere. You're going to stay right here where Colt and I can keep an eye on you."

"Keep an eye on me? Put me down, you jerk. I'm the boss here, and don't you forget it."

"Yes ma'am, you are. And it's our responsibility to make sure that you don't get hurt."

Dakota punched his ass, both irritated and intrigued to find it firm and muscular. "I didn't hire a bodyguard, damn it. Put me down." A firm hand over her legs kept her from doing the damage she wanted to do. Bouncing on his shoulder, she got a firm grip on his belt and bit his back.

Several sharp slaps landed and she bit him harder as he walked into the house. Walking straight to her bedroom, he pushed a hand between her thighs, making her gasp in surprise. As soon as she released him, he tossed her onto her bed and rolled her to her stomach.

"What do you think you're doing? Let me up!"

Lying half on top of her, he held her down by half lying on her back and throwing a heavy leg over hers.

Then he started spanking her.

"What are you doing? You can't spank me. Ow. Stop it. Even my daddy never spanked me."

"That's obvious," Joe replied dryly and smacked her ass again. "Are you going to stay on the ranch until we can deal with your neighbor?"

Furious at both his high handedness and the fact that having her ass spanked was turning her on, she fought him with everything she had. "You have no fucking right to tell me, ow, damn you. Let me up. You're fired. Get out."

"No. Are you going to be a good girl and let Colt and I deal with Ed?"

Dakota railed at him. She screamed. She threatened. She tried to escape but couldn't move at all. Her ass burned, but not altogether unpleasantly, and the heat rapidly spread to her pussy. Her panties had become soaked and she found herself lifting into his heated smacks and trying to rub herself on the bed to get relief.

When she heard Colt walk into the room, it only got worse.

"Well, well, what do we have here?"

Joe paused, running his hand over her bottom. "She wants to go to Ed's and fight it out. I'm convincing her that it might not be such a good idea."

"The horses are taken care of, and the doors are locked. How about if I help you?"

Dakota panicked at the dark intention in Joe's voice and the almost playful threat in Colt's. Joe's legs moved off of hers as Colt straddled her and she began to fight again. Lust gripped her by the throat when she felt Colt reach under her to undo her jeans. "Get off of me. Get out. You're both fired. I don't want you here anymore."

Colt chuckled and shifted down her body to remove her boots. "Wound up some, isn't she?"

Dakota struggled as Colt began lowering her jeans. "Stop it. Leave me alone."

He didn't stop until her jeans and panties had been lowered to her knees. "There. That's much better."

Joe rolled toward her, his lips warm against her ear. "You're not going to go to Ed's. You're going to let us handle it and when we do, you're going to stay out of it. Right?"

Dakota shuddered when he ran a threatening hand over her now naked bottom. "Joe, I can take care of it myself. I should have gone over there before. I'm mad at myself because I didn't."

His hand slid between her thighs. "You don't know what you're getting into. Just stay out of it, and let Colt and me handle it."

Because of the jeans twisted around her knees, she couldn't spread her legs the way she wanted to. "Joe, please."

"Please what? Please don't spank you anymore. Ahh, you're all wet, Dakota. I think you like having your ass spanked."

Dakota couldn't lie still as the heat from her bottom spread, and Joe's talented fingers slid through her juices. When he rolled her onto her back, she pulled his head down until their lips touched.

Heat rolled through her, sending her head spinning.

He lifted his head to look down at her, his eyes dark. "I want you. Do you want this?"

She was already pulling her shirt over her head. "God. Yes."

Joe got rid of her bra while Colt slid her jeans and panties down her legs and off. She moaned, arching when Joe slid a hand over her breasts. The way he watched her as he made love to her heated her blood even more.

Her pussy clenched as Colt spread her thighs and moved between them. His hands slid under her bottom, heating it even more as he raised her slightly and lowered his mouth to her slit. The first swipe of his tongue had her crying out. Her cries and moans mingled as Joe's hand slid under her hair and lifted her, covering her mouth with his as he cupped a breast.

He pinched her nipple between strokes, lightly at first, his pinches growing steadily more forceful. When he lifted his head to stare down at her, his eyes glittered with dark intent as he pinched both nipples none too gently. "You like it a little rough, don't you, baby?"

Dakota couldn't answer as Colt slid a thick finger inside her at the same time he sucked her clit. Hard. She screamed, the overwhelming pleasure tightening her body and making her arch off of the bed. The mouth on her slit eased its torment, changing to soft little licks as she fought to drag air into her lungs.

Joe brushed his lips over her jaw. "I'll take that as a yes." Cupping a hand around the back of her head, he lifted her again, watching her face as she began to come down. "I love watching you come. I'll have to paddle your ass more often."

Dakota's breathing still came out raggedly when she fisted a hand in his shirt. "Try it, cowboy and I'll—"

Colt moved and flipped her before she could finish and another sharp slap landed. "You were saying?"

Dakota writhed under their hands. Shivers ran through her as Joe fisted her hair and pulled her head aside to nibble at her neck. "Damn you both. If you think you can get your way with, ah, oh God, with, um, sex, hell, I can't think when you do that."

Joe chuckled as his finger slipped into her pussy. "You still have a lot of mad to get rid of, don't you, honey? Let's see what Colt and I can do about that. Colt, go get that oil." He covered her legs again with his own when Colt released them, rendering her struggles useless. "If you want it a little rough, we'll have to see what we can do to give it to you. If it hurts, we'll stop, Dakota."

With his weight holding her down, Dakota couldn't move. But instead of panicking, her struggles against his superior strength turned her on even more. She shuddered when oil drizzled down the crease of her bottom. "I can take anything you can dish out, cowboy."

Joe nipped her shoulder. "Yes, ma'am. I'm sure you can." With that, a thick finger pressed against her most forbidden opening, and with the oil easing the way, it slid deep.

Dakota gripped handfuls of the bedding as she panted. Shivers ran through her as every nerve ending surrounding the thick finger came to life. She froze, struggling to adapt to the feelings his far too intimate touch inspired.

Lust. Trepidation. Curiosity. Uncertainty. And to her tremendous amazement, submission.

Her need to submit to their demands, her need to experience the sensations their touch created, her need to surrender to their strength stunned her. She wanted desperately to belong to them, even for a little while. The promise of pleasure in giving herself over to not one, but two strong men, made the decision easy.

She would take whatever they would give her for as long as they stayed.

Colt, now naked, lay next to her as Joe moved between her thighs, parting them.

Sliding a hand beneath her abdomen, Joe lifted her slightly and began stroking her anus, slow, deep strokes that wiped away all inhibitions. Trembling helplessly now, she found herself rising into them. Her entire focus came down to Joe's invasion of her bottom.

Colt ran his fingers over her back, leaving a trail of fire in their wake. Reaching beneath her, he caught a nipple between his thumb and forefinger. "You are so incredibly hot," he murmured, pinching her nipple more firmly.

Dakota gasped and rose even more, giving both men better access. "What are you doing to me?"

Colt shifted on the bed. He lifted her to slide under her, lifting her arms over his thighs as he settled her on top of him until her face was now only inches from his cock. Mesmerized by the sight of the large, plum-sized head, she traced her finger over it. When a drop appeared, she stuck out her tongue to lick it off, moaning as the finger in her bottom withdrew. Colt's groan rumbled through her, traveling all the way to her pussy. It clenched desperately, empty and needing to be filled.

Joe chuckled, a sound that was like music to her ears. In the bedroom at least, they both relaxed their guard with her, and she felt closer to them than ever. "Now I'm going to work two fingers into you, Dakota, then three. You're awfully tight, honey. It's going to hurt a little. Whenever you want me to stop, just say the word, okay."

Dakota shivered as more of the oil drizzled over her. "I want this, but I'm scared. Will it hurt a lot?"

Colt fisted her hair with one hand, and with the other began stroking his cock. When she tried to open her mouth over it, he tightened his grip to pull her back, sending a flare of heat through her. "It will pinch as he stretches that pretty little rosebud, then it will burn. Joe's going to use a lot of oil. But I promise you, you're going to come like never before."

Dakota believed him. Already her body was on its way to another release.

Colt loosened his grip on her hair. "Honey, I'm dying to feel your tongue on my cock."

"Let go of my hair, damn you, and let me have it then."

Colt's short laugh sounded tortured. "You were about to dive on it and I want this to last. Nice and easy."

Dakota tried to sneer at him but knew she failed miserably. Joe had poised two fingers now at her tight opening, working more of the oil into her. "Pussy."

With the grip he had on her hair, Colt turned her head, forcing her to look up at him. "Did you call me a pussy? You really want it rougher, don't you honey?"

Almost mindless with need, Dakota leaned down and bit his thigh. "Stop babying me. Are you going to fuck me or not?"

A sharp slap landed on her bottom and a split second later, two large fingers pushed into her anus. Joe rubbed her ass, spreading the heat once again. "Let's see how tough you are, little girl."

Dakota's cries became muffled when Colt lowered her head onto his cock. She opened wide immediately, wanting to make him as wild as she felt. Her cries mingled with moans, hers and Colt's. Colt pinched her nipple again as Joe continued his demonic stroking. The burn, the feeling of being stretched and invaded like never before made her clench on him, making the burn even hotter.

Needing to learn every bump and texture, every spot that drove him wild, Dakota tried hard to concentrate on Colt, but Joe's tight grip on her hip and his erotic invasion drove every other thought from her mind. Instinct and need controlled her actions as she took Colt's thick shaft as far into her throat as she could. Sucking him deep, she ran her tongue over the underside, thrilling at the groans she drew from him.

"Now three fingers, Dakota," Joe warned, his voice deep and tight, as though he spoke through clenched teeth.

She moaned around the cock in her mouth as Joe pressed his fingers inside her, the burn stealing her breath. Colt caressed her hair and released her nipple to stroke her jaw. "Let go, Dakota. I don't want to come until Joe works his cock up your ass."

The hand on her cheek moved to his cock and pulled it away from her lips. "You're too fucking good at that. Damn."

Joe ran his hand over her bottom, delivering small slaps all over it. "She took three fingers. She still tight, but I've got her oiled up good. Hang onto her."

His slaps had effectively reignited the heat on her bottom, which spread quickly. When Joe slid his fingers from her bottom, she clenched uselessly, crying out in protest. "Oh God. What have you done to me? I need it."

Colt turned her face back up again from where she'd buried it against his thigh. "I want to watch your face while Joe takes your ass."

He continued to stroke her jaw as Joe began to press into her. It felt different, the invasion more penetrating, the act more dominant than just using his fingers.

Dakota felt as though she'd been drugged, her senses struggling to catch up as she tried to accommodate him, needing him to fill her. His cock pressed forward, and she cried out when the head broke through the tight ring of muscle at her entrance. "Joe, oh it feels so, ahh, it burns."

He froze, not pressing any further. "Do you need me to stop?"

Colt touched his finger to her lips. "It's going to feel so good, baby. I promise."

Joe started to withdraw. "If it hurts her—"

Dakota pressed back onto him. "I want you to take me, damn you. I have to come. I'm just scared. It's too much."

Joe's hands tightened on her hips. "You want your ass filled, honey?"

She writhed, trying to move on him and at the same time trying to pull away. "Don't let me stop. Help me do this. Oh God, I can't wait. I have to come." Letting Colt take her weight, she reached for her clit, cursing like a ranch hand when Colt grabbed her hand to stop her.

"No, you don't, darlin'. You're not coming until Joe's inside that ass."

Dakota fought him, desperate to reach her clit, even as Joe pushed forward, inch by inch, stroking shallowly. Each stroke took him further inside her, burning her and sending a riot of sensation throughout her lower body. Pulse after pulse of mini orgasms shot through her, making her clench on Joe's thickness and burning her even more.

"Oh God. Oh God. It's too big. Help me. I want it."

Joe's grip on her hips tightened. "You can take me, Dakota. Suck Colt's cock and I'll make you come real good."

Dakota eagerly reached for Colt's thick shaft only inches away. Already she craved the taste of him again and wanted to hear those deep groans and bit off curses that told her just how strongly she affected him. When those delicious noises came from both of them, it worked like an aphrodisiac, taking her even higher.

They bombarded her senses with so many erotic sensations at once, she simply had no defenses left. Joe's strokes worked his length deep inside her, finally burying himself to the hilt in her bottom.

She felt taken as never before. Submitting to them had somehow given her a feeling of power. The sounds coming from both men became louder and increasingly more desperate, thrilling her even more.

"That mouth, Jesus. I'm gonna come, Dakota. Let go."

Dakota gripped Colt's thighs more firmly to stop him from pulling away. Her bottom clenched on Joe's cock, and she felt the intense wave of release hit her just as Colt's cock pulsed, splashing his seed down her throat.

She barely remembered to swallow as the intensity of her own orgasm stole her breath. She'd never felt anything like it before. Joe held himself deep inside her, his hand covering her mound as his fingers moved on her clit.

Colt withdrew from her mouth, his hands running over her back as she came yet again. This orgasm, though not as intense, proved more devastating on her already battered system.

Minutes later, they dropped on the bed on either side of her. Drowsily, she snuggled into them. Joe got up and she protested when he wiped a damp cloth over her bottom and Colt lifted her into his arms. "I don't wanna go anywhere."

Colt kissed her softly. "Joe's just pulling down the quilt. Go to sleep, baby."

That was the last thing she heard.

When she woke an hour later, both men had gathered supplies from the storage room in the back and were in the process of repairing her front porch. As she prepared dinner, her mind kept replaying the feeling of incredible closeness she'd had with them earlier.

She'd never felt so close to anyone before and was determined to make the most of the time she had left with them.

* * * *

As they sat down to a dinner of fried chicken and mashed potatoes, Dakota watched both men from beneath her lashes. Although they both seemed a little too quiet, they looked more relaxed since their lovemaking.

She hadn't been able to play for years before they'd arrived. She'd had a lot of responsibility thrust on her and took it seriously. When her daddy died, she'd turned to Lenny. His reluctance to take things seriously meant that she'd had to.

With Joe and Colt it was very different. They took everything too seriously. It freed her from some of the worry and induced her to play, to make them forget about everything else and just have some fun.

Watching as they ate, slower now in deference to her, she smiled to herself. Knowing they'd been in prison, she now understood why they'd eaten so fast. Now they took their time. "How do you two know Buck?"

Both tensed and glanced at each other before looking back down at their plates. Colt shook his head. "Leave it alone, Dakota."

She didn't push, not wanting them to retreat again. Lifting a chicken leg, she tried to appear innocent. "You two are eating like you've worked up an appetite. Did you do anything special?"

Colt's grin nearly stole her breath. "Yes, ma'am. A filly gave us a little trouble."

Dakota nearly choked on her chicken. "Really? What kind of trouble?"

Joe's eyes twinkled playfully. "She's spirited and headstrong. Had to rein her in for her own good."

Dakota took a sip of iced tea. "You break her?"

Joe shook his head. "Don't want her broken. I like spirit."

Dakota's insides quivered at the playful look on their faces.

Placing the chicken leg back on her plate, she slowly began to lick her fingers. "If you can handle spirit, why'd you have so much trouble? Hmm, maybe more spirit than you guys can handle?"

Colt paused with a forkful of mashed potatoes halfway to his mouth. "Oh, she wasn't that much trouble. We just worked up an appetite reining her in."

Both Joe and Colt stared at her mouth when she continued to lick her fingers.

She took her time, licking her lips repeatedly. "Reining her in, huh? What if she doesn't like being reined in?"

Joe reached over and gripped her wrist, bringing her hand to his mouth. Taking her index finger inside, he circled his tongue all around it.

Dakota's breathing grew harsher as he caressed it with short flicks of his tongue. Remembering what that same action felt like on her clit had it throbbing in response.

Colt leaned forward. "She has to be reined in sometimes for her own good. And I think she liked it just fine."

Dakota struggled to remember what they'd been talking about. Pulling her hand away from Joe, she reached for her iced tea. "Just because I had an orgasm doesn't mean you reined me in. You got lucky. Don't think it'll be so easy next time."

Joe picked up his piece of chicken. "We definitely got lucky. Every time we get you naked, we learn more of your sensitive spots. It'll get easier every time."

Dakota pouted, more than a little turned on by their playful banter. "That's not fair. You don't give me a chance to find yours. One of these days I'm going to get you helpless and torture you. Slowly."

Both men grinned. Colt wrapped a hand around her neck and pulled her close for a kiss. "I can't wait. Then maybe Joe and I will do the same to you."

Dakota tangled her fingers in his hair. "You already do. Two against one is not fair."

Colt grinned, releasing her. "Life's a bitch, huh?"

Later that night, she lay cuddled against Joe, his arms wrapped around her and holding her close. Colt had been with her until just a little while ago, but had gotten up to relieve Joe. Smiling into the darkness, she cuddled closer. Colt had also held her close while he'd lain next to her. She wondered what would happen when she finally got a chance to sleep with both of them.

Smiling at the thought of being the object of a tug-of-war, she drifted off to sleep.

# Chapter Nine

Dakota smiled as she looked out the window. Joe had taken off his shirt to chop wood, and she stood there enjoying the show. Watching the play of muscle as he worked, she felt the spark of need ignite inside her. She'd been surprised at how muscular they both were. Since she'd learned that they'd started lifting weights in prison in order to survive, she'd quickly dropped the subject.

She hadn't mentioned it again, except to tell them both just how much she got turned on watching their incredible muscles bunch and shift as they moved. She bit into them during sex and held onto them tightly. Hopefully now, they thought of the pleasure she got from their strength and not the necessity for it. Watching Joe chop wood, her eyes slid to where Colt walked back to get another load. He too, had removed his shirt in deference to the warm day and the physical labor. Her nipples tightened in anticipation and little butterflies made her stomach quiver. Hmm, perhaps it was time to check out those muscles again.

It had been more than two weeks since any of Ed's men had come over. Jill called every day, chomping at the bit to visit, but so far Dakota had held her off. Joe and Colt had taken turns taking her to the next town for supplies, with one of them always standing guard at the ranch. Over her protests, they'd bought supplies themselves. She had no idea where they got the money, and when she mentioned it, they'd clammed up.

Each day she felt a little closer to them than the day before, but there were still shadows in their eyes and a lot of things they wouldn't discuss with her. She got a bad feeling in the pit of her stomach every time she thought about it. One day it would all come to a head, and she would have to deal with whatever secrets they hid.

She knew they couldn't go on this way much longer and wondered what it would take to get them to open up to her. She didn't press. She finally admitted to herself that fear kept her from asking too many questions. Knowing what they had was still too fragile to withstand it, she'd backed off. She knew damned well she acted cowardly by putting it off, but fear of losing them kept her silent, hoping they would one day feel they could tell her.

Drying her hands, she walked out the back door and toward them. At least they no longer spoke about leaving. At times when they became distant, she knew they thought about it.

She left the house, not even glancing next door. All of her attention remained focused on the prime specimens in front of her. Colt passed her on the way to stack firewood, bending down to give her a light kiss as he went by. "Hey, honey."

Joe paused in his chopping when he saw her approach and smiled at her. His smiles came more frequently now, but they were still rare enough to bring tears to her eyes. "Hi."

"Hi yourself. I've been watching out the window."

Joe sobered and gestured toward her neighbor's ranch. "I haven't seen Ed or any of his men staring over this way. The sheriff just went up again."

Dakota raised a brow. "What's that, six times in the last two weeks? Something must be going on. And how do you know you haven't seen Ed? Do you know what he looks like?"

Joe turned away to pick up another log. "I haven't seen anyone except the men we see every day."

Ice formed in her stomach at how deftly he avoided the question. Neither one of them lied to her but both could be evasive as hell. The fact that they wouldn't come right out and lie to her though, told her that her instincts about them had been right after all. Men like Joe and Colt had become rare in her world.

Noticing how quiet he'd become, Dakota circled around him, enjoying the close up view of all those rippling muscles. "Don't you think it's a little strange that nobody's been over for two weeks now? Do you think he's given up?"

The axe came down, chopping the log in two. Joe picked up both pieces and threw them aside. "Nope."

Dakota glanced over at Ed's to see several of the ranch hands working with the horses, but she didn't see Ed at all. "What do you think he's doing then?"

The axe came down on another log. "Planning."

Damn it. Every mention of Big Ed made him distant again. Dakota vowed to fix that. She sauntered over to him and waited for him to bend to pick up another log. When he did, she patted his ass. "I wasn't looking out the window to see what Ed was up to. I happened to glance outside and saw two fine looking cowboys cutting firewood. No shirts. Nice rippling muscles." She walked back and forth behind him, running a hand over his back and shoulders with each pass.

He'd straightened, glancing at her over his shoulder. "Did you now?"

"I did. Couldn't look away. But then I thought, why am I standing there at the window when I could come out and see them both close up? Maybe get a little feel." With that, she squeezed a bicep. "Yes, all those muscles sure do turn a girl's head. Gives her crazy ideas."

Joe's lips twitched. "What sort of ideas?"

Pleased to see that the bulge in his jeans grew as she moved to stand in front of him, she struggled to keep her face bland. "I don't know. All sorts of ideas. Like, what it feels like to mount a cowboy with muscles like that and hold onto them as you go for a ride. Or what it feels like to bite down on them when he's stroking his big, thick cock inside you. Or—Oof."

Dakota's breath left her lungs as he bent, hauled her over his shoulder and headed for the house. She started laughing as he strode across the yard with her, his hand possessively over her bottom. "Put me down, you big oaf. I haven't finished telling you my ideas."

Joe slid his hand over her bottom again. "That's all right. I have a few of my own."

She heard Colt's chuckle, but couldn't see him.

"What's up?"

Joe kept walking. "Dakota saw us out here working and has some ideas, something about muscles and riding thick cocks."

Colt came around Joe's back and pulled the hair away from her face. "Is that a fact? Well, I guess we'd better keep the boss happy."

Dakota's heart leapt. She felt almost dizzy, not just from being over Joe's shoulder, but from the lighthearted banter. It was fun to play, something she'd almost forgotten how to do. The satisfaction she got at pulling them out of their remoteness, even for little spurts, made it even better.

Joe walked into the house with her and didn't stop until he reached the bedroom. Tossing her onto the bed, he stood with his hands on his hips and looked down at her. "Now, let's see. Where should we start?" He'd just bent to reach for her when there was a loud banging at the front door.

Dakota scrambled off the bed and automatically reached for the gun in her nightstand. "Who the hell could that be?"

Joe and Colt had already started out of the room, all trace of amusement gone. Colt looked over his shoulder. "Stay here."

"Like hell." She started out after them. If someone wanted to cause trouble, she doubted they'd knock at the door, but her stomach tightened as the banging continued.

"Dakota, damn it, open the fucking door!"

Dakota walked into the living room just in time to see Joe open the door. Ben ran into the house and started toward her, brought up short when Joe and Colt grabbed his arms.

"Let go of me, damn it. I've got to talk to Dakota."

Dakota looked on, shocked as Ben broke their hold and started toward her. The look of surprise on both men's faces might have been funny in other circumstances. She put out a hand to hold Joe and Colt off when they both started toward Ben again. "What is it, Ben? What's got you so worked up?"

He gripped her arms, his face harder than she'd ever seen it before. "Listen, I don't know what the hell's going on, but there's a lot you don't know. Ed and the sheriff are planning something, and it's going down today. I don't know what it is, but you need to get the hell out of here. Trust me, Dakota. All of this will be over today. Then you can have your life back."

To her utter amazement, he reached out to stroke her cheek, his eyes fierce with emotion. "I promise nothing will happen to you. After today you'll know everything. Just come with me. I'll take you to my place. I'll come and get you when it's over."

Joe grabbed his arm and jerked him away from her. "Like hell."

Ben shook off his hold. "You're only going to make more trouble for her, and she's had enough."

Dakota jumped between them as Colt raised his fist. "Stop it right now. All of you." She turned to Ben. "I'm not going anywhere. This is my ranch, and I'm not about to leave it. What the hell makes you think I would? If I wanted to leave, I would have done it before now. What the hell's going on? What makes you think something's going to happen today?"

Ben kept one eye on Joe and Colt. "The sheriff tried to send me on some lame errand to get rid of me today. He thinks I've left town. I put my truck around the side of the house so no one would see it. I've called in some people and they're going to surround the house, if they're not there already. You probably won't see them. But I want you to know that you're not alone in this."

Seeing the rage in Joe and Colt's eyes, she shook off Ben's hand. "I've got my guns, and my aim is real good. I can take care of Ed and his men if they show up."

"I don't want you shooting anybody. You'll probably hit one of my men by mistake."

Dakota went to the window and looked out but couldn't see anyone. "Ben, you're not making any sense. What men? Where are they from?"

Ben sighed and moved to stand in front of her. Reaching into his pocket, he pulled out his wallet and flipped it open to show her. "I'm FBI, Dakota. We've been watching Fairview for almost two years, trying to get proof. Ed and the sheriff along with several of Ed's men will be arrested today."

Dakota spun and jabbed Ben in the chest. "Are you fucking kidding me? All this time I've been dealing with Ed with no help, and the FBI knew about it all along and did nothing? The stress from dealing with him killed my father. And you did nothing!"

Ben ran a hand through his hair. "Damn it, Dakota. I couldn't tell you."

Furious, Dakota moved away from him. "That's why you came here, isn't it? You took the job to watch Ed. How did you know? Even the state police wouldn't believe me. Everyone they questioned called me a liar."

Ben shot a look at Joe and Colt. "They hired a private detective when they got out of prison. He called us when they left town. Evidently, he was intrigued enough to keep digging. When we heard his story, so were we. The deputy that was here before has been relocated so that I could take his position. The bureau made sure no one else applied for the job. We've been building a case against Ed ever since but haven't been able to get close enough. Fred and John Tillman also started feeding the bureau information several months ago. But these two are the key. Ed's been in a panic ever since they got here."

Dakota's gaze shifted to Joe and Colt, a knot forming in her stomach when she got a good look at their expressions. She'd never seen them looking so hard, so completely cold. Their eyes had darkened and glittered like ice. "What's going on? What haven't you told me, damn it. Why would you hire a private detective to investigate Ed?"

Joe looked away. "None of it concerns you."

She gasped at the kick to her gut. A chill went down her spine at the jagged edge in his tone. She struggled to hide the wave of hurt that washed over her, cursing herself when she felt the prick of tears. She would not fucking cry in front of them. Their expressions and tone told her more than anything else that what they'd had was over. Whatever was going on, they had their own agenda, and it didn't include her.

Ben faced them squarely. "So you didn't tell her? Well, that's something, at least."

Dakota took a deep breath, hoping to loosen the knots that had formed in her belly. So angry and hurt she could barely speak, she gritted her teeth. "Tell. Me. What?"

Before he could answer, all hell broke loose. The living room window exploded, glass flying everywhere. She found herself shoved to the floor, a hard body covering hers. Joe. Even now she knew the feel of her lover as gunfire rang out from all directions.

# Chapter Ten

Dakota fought to get out from under Joe, but he held onto her firmly. "Let me up, damn it. Get the hell off me."

"Be still and shut up."

The shooting stopped almost as quickly as it began. Buried under Joe, she couldn't see a damned thing, but she heard a lot of yelling. "Get off of me, damn it."

To her surprise, he did and took off toward the kitchen. Ben grabbed her wrist and helped her to stand. "Are you okay?"

Dakota shook off the glass that covered her arms. Except for a few small nicks on her hands, she'd come away unscathed. "I'm fine. What the hell happened?" She looked out the jagged glass where her front window used to be to see Ed's men being disarmed and handcuffed.

She started out the front door, and came to an abrupt halt. Joe and Colt had gone out the back. Where the hell would they have gone?

Changing direction, she headed to the kitchen and through the back door. Two men with jackets marked FBI held their guns pointed at someone around the side of her house.

"Drop your weapon."

"Not a chance."

Dakota felt nausea rise up in her throat when she heard Joe's refusal. "Joe? Oh God."

Ignoring the agent's demand that she stay back, she ran around the side of the house and straight into Colt.

Grabbing her arm, he pulled her to the other side as he stood next to Joe. "Stay back, Dakota."

Big Ed didn't look so tough at the moment. Standing with his hands up in surrender, he looked scared to death as he faced the shotgun Joe had pointed at him.

Out of the corner of her eye, she watched the agents move closer. Breaking free of Colt's grip, she ran behind Joe and faced the agents, their blurred images the first hint that she was crying. "Please don't shoot him. Please. He won't hurt anyone, I swear. Please don't shoot."

"Ma'am, get out of the way."

She turned to face Joe's back, plastering herself against him and standing on her toes to see his face. "Joe, please don't do this. You're not a killer. Let the police deal with him."

"Colt, get her out of here. Hello, Frank. Tell her, Frank. Tell her I *am* a killer."

Ed's eyes nearly bugged out of his head. "It *is* you!" He glanced at Colt. "How did you find me? I covered all my tracks."

Colt tried to pull her away from Joe, but she held on fast. Giving up, he bared his teeth at Ed. "You covered yours, but not Buck's. We found him and there you were. Sloppy, Frank."

Still standing on her toes, Dakota watched everything from over Joe's shoulder, more scared than she'd ever been in her life. Agents, including Ben stood behind Ed, their guns drawn.

Ben took a step forward. "Frank Phillips, you're under arrest."

Dakota slid a glance at Colt. "What's he talking about? His name is Ed. Ed Franks."

Joe tensed under her hands. "Get away from him, Ben. He dies today."

Dakota wiped her eyes, struggling to keep her voice calm. Oh God. She had to get through to him. He couldn't do this. The pieces of the puzzle fell into place, and she knew how much Joe wanted to kill Ed. No matter what he believed, she knew he'd never be able to live with it. And everything they'd begun to build would be over, damaged beyond repair. "Please, Joe. Don't do this. You'll go back to prison."

Joe laughed humorlessly. "They can't even arrest me, can you, Ben? You see, Dakota, Colt and I already served our sentence for killing him. Twelve long fucking years behind bars when he faked his own death. We've spent all our adult lives in prison because of him. We paid for it. Now we want what's owed to us. We can kill him, and they can't do a fucking thing about it."

Dakota fought to remain calm while her insides twisted in agony. At least Colt had stopped trying to pull her away from Joe. But a quick glance at his features made her stomach drop. Amusement curled his lips as he watched Ed fall apart.

Tears rolled down Ed's face as he begged Joe not to kill him. "I didn't mean for you to go to jail. I just wanted to get away. You two were on to me and so were the McAffertys. I couldn't hang around anymore. I had to get out and didn't want anyone coming after me. I've been careful since then, got myself a fortune. Name your price. I'll give you anything."

Dakota looked at Ben pleadingly, tears running down her face. He gave a short nod and signaled to the other agents to wait.

"I want you dead."

Dakota shivered at Joe's tone and hoped like hell she could get through to him. She remembered what Colt had said. Once Joe made up his mind about something, there was no changing it. He'd proven that over and over in the last couple of weeks. Moving to his side, she never even glanced at Ed. "Joe, baby. Please don't do this. Let Ben arrest him. He'll go to jail for a long, long time. Make him suffer what you suffered. He's not as strong as you. He'll never survive it."

Joe never took his eyes from Ed. "He can't possibly suffer what we suffered, Dakota. He's had a chance to live his life. We didn't."

Dakota ran a hand down his chest. "Live one now. You and Colt. Stay here with me. Let's build a life together, the three of us. I love you, Joe. Both you and Colt. I think you're both starting to love me, too. Don't let Ed ruin what we have. Please don't do this. You'll never be able to live with it."

Colt moved up behind her and touched her hair. "We care for you, too. But we've dreamed about this day for twelve years, Dakota. Do you really think we'll be able to hang around after he's dead? The folks in this town won't allow it."

She looked up at him, gripping the hand that lay heavy on her shoulder. "Do you think I care about them, after the way they've treated me? Let's go away. Let's leave here and start all over somewhere else. A new beginning for all of us."

Joe's gaze slid to hers, his eyes moist. "He deserves to die."

Dakota shook her head. "He deserves to suffer. Make him suffer." With tears running down her face, she gripped both of them. "Do you remember when you came here, you said that you would do anything to be able to stay with me?"

Colt gripped her hand and looked at Joe. "Joe? I know we said— Hell, whatever you decide, I'm with you."

Joe looked down at where Dakota gripped his arm and slid his gaze to Colt, before looking back at Frank. "Do you know how it is in prison, Frank? Can you imagine what it was like for two young boys who'd never been out of the small town they were born in?"

Ed cried pitifully now. "I'm sorry. I didn't mean—"

Colt stiffened. "Shut the fuck up, Frank." he turned to Joe. "Joe?"

Dakota gripped Joe desperately, shaking so hard her teeth chattered. "Joe, please don't do this. Please, baby. Stay with me. Don't let him ruin this for us."

No one spoke or moved for several long moments as Dakota's heart nearly pounded out of her chest. Tears continued to pour down her face, but she never let go of either of them and she never took her eyes off of Joe. Her entire life depended on what happened now.

When he finally lowered the gun, the wave of relief turned her knees to rubber, and she would have fallen if Colt hadn't caught her.

Joe watched Ben handcuff the sobbing man, his eyes full of both pain and pity. They hardened when they slid to Ben. "You'd better make sure he goes to prison for a long time."

Colt moved away from her, pushing her into Joe's embrace, and moved to stand in front of Ed. "If you ever get out of prison and come anywhere near us, remember that we've already paid for killing you. I like to get what I've paid for."

Ed crumbled. "You'll never see me again, I swear."

Dakota kept her face buried against Joe's chest, gripping him tightly as she tried to stop crying. He held her lightly, running his hands up and down her back as Ben and the others gathered Ed's men. She ignored all the conversations going on around her and focused on Joe.

Joe hadn't killed him. He'd listened to her and hadn't killed him.

When he held her slightly away from him, she looked up at him in wonder.

The look on his face froze her tremulous smile before it could fully form. His eyes looked wild and the tortured look on his face scared the hell out of her.

"Joe? I can't believe—"

"Colt, take care of her."

Dakota spun to look at Colt. The surprise on his face shook her. She looked back at Joe. "What is it? What's wrong?"

Joe clenched his jaw and walked away. A moment later, they heard the roar of his pickup and watched as he sped away.

Dakota spun to face Colt. "Where's he going? What's wrong?"

Colt sighed and raked a hand through his hair. "Ben said he wanted to talk to us. I'll bet Joe goes there but then he's going to want to be alone. Letting Frank go cost him dearly, Dakota. He's lived on his hate for that man for fifteen years. That and me are all that's kept him going." He pulled her against his chest, burying his fingers in her hair. "He'll be back. He won't leave me."

Dakota opened her mouth but closed it again. Colt had said he wouldn't leave him, but said nothing about Joe not leaving her.

"Dakota?"

Dakota turned at the sound of Ben's voice. "Thanks, Ben. They would have—" Her voice wobbled, and she had to swallow before continuing. "They would have shot him if you hadn't stopped them."

Some kind of silent communication passed between Colt and Ben. Colt turned his gaze to her, staring down at her for several long seconds. Without saying a word, he bent and kissed her forehead before moving several feet away.

Afraid that he would leave too, she started toward him, only to be stopped by Ben.

"Colt's not going anywhere. He knows I want a minute with you."

Dakota looked up at his handsome face wondering why she'd never felt anything more for him than friendship. Ben was a good man and, for a long time, had been the only one to help her. "What did you want to talk to me about?"

Ben sighed. Waving off an agent who approached, he smiled faintly. "I wish things had turned out differently for us, Dakota. I think you know how I feel about you."

Dakota nodded sadly. "I'm sorry, Ben. You've been a good friend, especially since daddy died. I wish I could have..." She shrugged, not knowing what to say.

Ben smiled humourlessly. "So do I."

Dakota's gaze kept sliding to where Colt stood several feet away. Although he spoke to one of the agents, his eyes never left her. The emotion in them did nothing to calm her fears. Joe had looked at her that same way several times and yet had stilled walked away.

Turning away, she faced Ben again. "You're a good man. A wonderful man. What will you do now that this assignment is over?"

Ben nodded to another agent and pointed at his truck. "As soon as all the paperwork's done, I'll go back to the field office and onto the next assignment." Gripping her shoulders lightly, he bent and kissed her forehead. "Be happy, Dakota. You deserve it."

Dakota smiled through her tears. "You, too, Ben. I'm going to miss you." Watching him walk away, she felt like she'd just closed a chapter in her life. Not knowing how the next chapter would turn out, she rubbed her arms, suddenly chilled. When Colt approached and put an arm around her, she snuggled close, staring at the spot where Joe's truck used to be and shivered.

# Chapter Eleven

"Why don't you go to bed, Dakota?"

Dakota turned from where she'd curled up in the chair, leaning over the back and looked out the window Colt had replaced. She'd dressed in one of Joe's t-shirts after her bath, and with a blanket wrapped around her, had sat there waiting for Joe for hours. "I don't want to miss him."

Colt sighed, lifting her into his arms and sat in the chair, settling her onto his lap. "Neither one of us will leave without saying goodbye." Tilting her head back over his arm, he lowered his mouth to hers.

Dakota cuddled into him, trying to absorb as much of his heat as she could. She found the hard planes of his body unyielding as she pressed into him, trying to get closer. It helped but she knew the chill she felt came from inside, and she wouldn't be warm until Joe came back. The hand at her nape held her firmly in place for his kiss while the other roamed over her hip. She squirmed on his lap, desperate in her attempt to get even closer. Not knowing how much time they had left, she wanted to make the most out of every second.

Colt lifted his head, studying her thoughtfully, his eyes moving over every inch of her face. "I'm going to talk to Joe. But if you want us to stay, you know you'll be taking on both of us."

Dakota blinked back tears, trying to smile. "I hope so. I can't choose one of you over the other. If that makes me selfish, I don't care. It would break my heart to lose either one of you."

Colt nuzzled her jaw. "I'll talk to Joe, honey. Not having Joe around would be like losing an arm, but I don't think I'm going to be able to walk away from you. I love you too damned much."

Dakota choked back a sob. She sat up to straddle him, touching her forehead to his. "Oh, Colt. I love you, too. But I'm scared. What if we can't make Joe stay?"

She hadn't worn panties so the rough denim of his jeans rasped against her slit. Leaning back slightly, she pulled the shirt over her head and tossed it away. Rocking her hips against him, she tangled her fingers into his long hair, pulling him closer, desperate for him now. "Take me like I belong to you."

Colt pulled her hands away from his hair and pulled her own head back to look down at her. "If you belonged to me, I would take you in every way. All the time. I can't get enough of you. I can't even fucking sleep without you next to me anymore."

She almost came on the spot as her heart filled with joy. She tried to lean toward him, but the hand in her hair prevented it. "Do it. Take me. I need you so much."

When he looked over her shoulder and smiled, she tried to turn her head but couldn't. Before she could react, two rough hands captured her nipples and squeezed.

"If you ever fucking stand between me and an enemy again, I'm going to paddle your ass so hard you won't sit for a month."

"Joe!" Dakota tried to turn to face him, but the hold both men had on her didn't allow it. "You're back. What—" The tug on her nipples made her gasp.

"Be quiet. If Colt and I stay, you *are* going to belong to both of us. Are you willing to do that? No matter what the neighbors say?"

"Yes. Oh God, yes. I don't care about anything else." Happiness like she'd never known consumed her, making her giddy.

Colt released her hair to grab her buttocks, his fingers moving close to her puckered opening, tightening his hold enough to make her opening sting. "Be sure, Dakota. No changing your mind later on."

Dakota's breath caught, not daring to believe. "You're staying? You promise?"

Joe chuckled and lightly bit her earlobe. "Everybody in town is talking about Dakota's cowboys. How Dakota Wells tamed two hardened convicts and has them eating out of her hand. How anybody who messes with Dakota is gonna have their ass handed to them. We wouldn't want to disappoint them, now would we?"

Tears of joy rolled down Dakota's face as her body trembled with need for her lovers. The smile on Colt's face as he tightened his grip on her melted her heart.

Colt chuckled, bringing one of his hands back around to part her folds while the other traced the crease of her ass. "Is that a fact? You gonna try to tame us, Dakota?"

She grinned at him through her tears, leaning back against Joe. "Hell no. I want you just the way you are. Wild and hard."

Joe lifted her and pulled her back against him. "Yes, ma'am. Wild and hard it is." He ran his teeth over her shoulder while Colt reached into his pocket and grabbed a condom before pushing his jeans and underwear out of the way.

She couldn't look away from his thick cock as he exposed it, her pussy clenching in anticipation of the pleasure only they could give her. When Joe settled her back onto Colt's lap, she couldn't help but rub her slit against his hardness, moaning at the friction of it against her clit.

Colt's hands on her hips aided her movements. "Damn, somebody's soaking wet. You in a hurry, darlin'?"

Gripping his shoulders, Dakota arched and rocked her hips more frantically. "God yes!" Aware that Joe undressed behind her, she shook as she took the condom from Colt to roll it on him.

Joe pulled her back with an arm around her waist, giving her room. His cock pressed against her buttocks and she couldn't help but wiggle against it. He waved a tube in front of her face. "When I went for a drive, I stopped in a town about two hours from here. Look what I found in the drugstore there."

Dakota looked down as Colt whooped. "You bought lubrication?

Holy hell."

Joe chuckled in her ear and opened the tube.

She watched as he squeezed some out onto his fingers, her bottom tightening involuntarily.

Recapping the tube, he tossed it aside. He used his lips on the sensitive spot on the back of her neck as he showed her his lube-coated fingers. "Guess where this goes."

Thrown off kilter by this new, playfully wicked Joe, Dakota's arousal grew until she shook with it. The hard edge was still apparent in both of them, something she would work on smoothing, but she knew it would always be a part of them.

Need hardened Colt's face as he lifted her and poised her over his cock. His eyes flared as he slowly lowered her onto it.

Dakota moaned as he filled her, as he stretched her inner walls inch by inch with his delicious heat. She held onto Colt's shoulders as he filled her completely, arching as Joe's hand came around to cup her breast. She clenched on the thickness inside her, the myriad of emotions racing through her already taking her to the brink of orgasm.

When she would have moved on Colt, Joe wrapped his arm around her from behind to stop her. "No. Not yet. Not until we both fill you, Dakota."

When a thick lubed finger pressed steadily into her bottom, Dakota couldn't hold back her cry of pleasure. Without warning, her first orgasm hit her and she screamed, gripping Colt even tighter.

Colt pulled her against his chest as Joe worked more lube into her. "Already, baby? You *do* like it hard and wild, don't you?"

Joe held onto her shoulder as he began to press the head of his cock through the tight ring of muscle. "We've only just started, honey. Let's see how hard we can make you come when you're filled everywhere."

Dakota whimpered as Joe pushed forward, the burning, too stretched feeling much more intense than before.

"So fucking tight," Joe groaned, as he pressed another inch of his cock into her anus. "You okay, baby?"

Dakota squeezed her eyes closed and tried her best to relax her bottom. "Don't you dare stop. I can take anything you, uh, ahh God, dish out, c-cowboy."

Colt caressed her bottom, pulling her more firmly onto him.

Dakota rocked her hips as much as she could in time with Joe's shallow strokes. Joe's steady stream of curses and erotic promises and Colt's praise and encouragement poured over her.

Joe groaned. "Her ass is milking my cock already. Colt, hold her still, damn it."

Colt's arms tightened around her. "Try to be still, baby. Christ, we're all going to come before Joe can even get inside you."

Dakota whimpered in her throat, fighting to move. "I'm coming again. Oh God. Oh God. Take me. Hurry. Ahh!"

Joe slid a little farther into her as she shuddered in release. He started moving again before she had the chance to come down completely. His strokes got deeper. "Fuck, you're tight. Come on, baby. You can take me. That's it. That's my girl. So fucking tight. Your ass is perfect, baby. Just a little more. That's it. I'm in. Fuck."

Colt lifted her slightly, his eyes glittering wildly. "Ready darlin'? Come on, cowgirl. Just hang onto me and let Joe and me do all the work."

Dakota threw her head back in ecstasy as Joe's hands covered her breasts. After a few strokes, they established a rhythm and took her like she'd never been taken. With her ass and her pussy full of hard, thick cocks, and her heart full of love, she felt as though she might burst at any moment. Their strokes intensified, quickly driving her over the edge yet again.

Their strokes stopped abruptly, their breathing harsh as they both held onto her, cursing ripely.

Joe buried his face in her neck, his voice sounding tortured. "Don't you fucking move. Fuck. Dakota, if you move I won't last. Stay still, baby. I want you to come again."

Dakota opened her eyes and looked down to see that Colt had squeezed his shut, the agonized look on his face telling her just how close he'd come to losing control. "I'm so full. It feels so good. I want to move."

Colt tightened his grip. "So fucking tight. Give us just a minute, honey, and we'll start again. Then we'll all come together."

Held securely by both of them, Dakota tried to concentrate on breathing. Moaning in frustration, her focus remained on the two cocks inside her. She couldn't stop clenching on them, the incredible fullness and the strength of their grips as they held her immobile keeping her on the edge of release.

She couldn't believe she'd survived her entire life never knowing this feeling. Vulnerable, yet powerful. Taken completely, while demanding everything.

Joe lightly bit her shoulder as the stroking resumed. "Come hard, baby. Take us with you."

Their strokes were more demanding this time, harder, faster and her cries filled the room. Nothing existed but the hot shafts filling and stroking her pussy and anus. Fire raced through her as they groaned and cursed, caught up the tremendous pleasure.

Those warning tingles had barely begun when a wave of the most indescribable bliss washed over her, making her scream and tighten on both of them. Her skin tingled everywhere. She became so lost in sensation she couldn't even scream.

Startled at the whimpering moans that came from her, she held on tighter to Colt as her body shook with the force of it. Everything splintered around her, and if not for the hold the men had on her, she feared she would have shattered into a thousand pieces.

Hearing their harsh groans, she gasped as they surged deep inside her as they followed. She could feel every bump and ridge on their cocks as they pulsed their own releases.

Completely spent, she collapsed against Colt's chest, snuggling into him as his hard arms came around her. Groaning as Joe withdrew from her, she panicked and jerked herself up, grabbing for him when he started to move away. "Joe."

Pulling her back against him, he nuzzled her neck. "I'm not going anywhere. Come take a shower with me."

Relief weakened her knees. She nodded and leaned forward to kiss a grinning Colt before Joe lifted her from his lap and carried her to the shower. As much as the sight of his naked body drew her attention, she couldn't keep her eyes from his face as they stood under the spray. "You left."

Joe nodded and pulled her lightly against him, stroking her hip. "I needed some time alone. I've spent most of my adult life planning my revenge and when it was gone—" He released her and shrugged, turning away to face the spray.

Dakota's stomach knotted. "It was the right thing to do. You know that. You couldn't have lived with the fact that you killed him in cold blood that way."

Joe turned to face her, wiping the water from his eyes and pushing his long hair back. "Yes, I could have. But you couldn't." Leaning over her, he braced his hands on the wall behind her. "And I don't want to live without you. You're the best thing that ever happened to me. Frank already cost me most of my life. I couldn't let him take you from me, too."

Dakota's eyes welled with tears as she took his face in her hands. Although she opened her mouth, sobs clogged her throat, preventing her from speaking. Her breath caught when he smiled as he wiped her tears away. Finally she managed a shuddering breath. "You'll really stay?"

"If you'll have us."

Dakota grabbed handfuls of his hair and kissed him deeply, putting everything she felt for him into it.

Joe's chuckle didn't last long as he met her heat with heat of his own. When she jumped up and wrapped her legs around him, he caught her against him and pressed her back against the shower wall.

When he lifted his head, the intent in his eyes made her smile as need slammed into her. "Again?"

"Absolutely."

The shower curtain opened and Colt stood there grinning. "So, we're both staying?"

Joe pulled her away from the wall and lowered her to her feet so Colt could climb in behind her. "I couldn't let Frank mess this up for us too."

Colt wrapped his arms around her from behind and covered her breasts with soapy hands, massaging gently. "Well, if we're going to stay with Dakota permanently, she needs to learn that she can't always have her way."

Joe chuckled and nodded. "I agree. I thought about it a lot today. Dakota likes to be the boss. We're going to have to teach her differently."

Dakota looked from one to the other, narrowing her eyes. "Dakota is standing right here, you know."

Colt slid his soapy hands down her body as Joe poured shampoo into his palm and began to message it into her hair. Colt's hands slid around her, one in front and one behind.

Dakota's breath caught and her head fell back against Colt's shoulder, as one slick finger slid into her pussy while the other pushed into her bottom. He spoke to Joe as if he hadn't heard her. "This should be a lot of fun. I say we start right away."

With his hands in her hair, Joe tilted her face up for his kiss as the first orgasm washed over her. "Agreed. Dakota needs to learn her place."

Colt's thumb flicked over her clit. "Yeah, right between us."

# Epilogue

Dakota moaned as Joe urged the horse faster. With her sundress bunched around her waist and impaled on Joe's cock, she held on tightly as they galloped toward the ridge. The hands at her back that held the reins also held her securely on his lap with her arms and legs wrapped around him.

The movement of the horse set the rhythm for his thrusts. The friction on her clit as it pressed against him drove her over the edge far too soon.

Her cries of release got muffled against his throat. She breathed deeply, loving the smell of him as she shuddered all around him.

His own groan and the pulsing inside her told her that he'd followed. His arms tightened around her, rocking her against him as he slowed their pace, drawing out their orgasms as long as possible. Finally, he came to a halt and lifted her face from his shoulder to look down at her. "Isn't this better than riding your own horse?"

Dakota lifted her face for his kiss and smiled, her happiness complete. "I may never ride again."

Colt chuckled from beside them. "You may never wear jeans again, either. I like those sundresses. I think we should buy more of them the next time we go to town."

Joe's lips twitched as his hands moved over her bare bottom, lifting her dress to expose her to Colt. "But no panties. She doesn't need them."

Dakota wrinkled her nose at him, while inside she thrilled at his playfulness. She'd set out to teach them to play and got more than she bargained for. "I only have three pairs of panties left. You two ripped all the other ones."

Joe lifted a brow. "Are you complaining? I'm telling you right now, if you put one of those panties on, I'm ripping them, too."

Dakota moaned again when he shifted her on his cock. They'd come a long way in the last several months. Both men still brooded occasionally, but she could usually snap them out of it. They'd taken over all the physical work on the ranch, telling her that they wanted her energy reserved for them. How could she complain? She'd never considered herself such a sexual being before, but with them she thought of little else. She happily submitted to their desires, especially since they mirrored her own.

Not that she'd had much choice. They'd taken over her body in ways that sometimes overwhelmed her, sometimes shook her, but always thrilled her. They'd given her more pleasure than she'd ever known, and not just physical.

Little by little they'd loosened up with her, although they never talked about their time in prison. The people in town had learned to give them a wide berth when they had those hard looks on their faces, and smiled indulgently when they saw how much both Joe and Colt adored her. Just as she adored them. She'd fallen head over heels in love with both of them and didn't care who knew it.

Jill had been thrilled to learn of Dakota, Joe and Colt's relationship. Joe and Colt both treated Jill as they would a sister and watched out for her, much to the amusement of both women.

Ben had left for another assignment and Dakota still missed him, but knew she could never be the woman for him.

She'd made her peace with the town, and no one said a word about Dakota living on the ranch with two men. Not that it would have mattered. She was happier than she'd ever dreamed she could be and wouldn't let anything get in her way.

Her eyes closed, and she slumped against Joe as they rode to the top of the ridge, his arms like hot bands around her.

Ed had gone to prison, and Joe and Colt's records had been wiped clean. Colt's parents had both passed away while he'd been in prison, along with Joe's dad, but Joe had spoken to his mom and his sister, and the three of them would be driving to see them next month.

At the top of the ridge, they stopped. Dakota opened her eyes and lifted her head to look down at the acres of land spread out below them.

Joe ran a hand up her back. "Everything we see belongs to us."

Dakota turned to face him to find both men looking at her. She reached out her hand to Colt. "Yes, it does."

Colt chuckled. "You, too. But I think Joe was also talking about the land."

Dakota grinned up at him. "Not quite all. Our ranch only goes to that fence."

"Not anymore."

Dakota frowned and looked up at Joe. "What do you mean?"

Colt reached into his pocket and pulled out a piece of paper, unfolding it and handing it to her.

Dakota looked down at it, hardly believing what she saw. "What? I don't understand. How—"

Joe smiled and kissed her forehead, lifting her from his cock. "Between the settlement the lawyer got us for being locked up all those years and the proof that Frank used the money from the insurance from Colt's parent's house, we managed to get the property and stock that Frank had."

Dakota knew her eyes had to be huge as she stared from one to the other. "I didn't know you were doing this. How could I have not known you were doing this?"

Colt ran a hand up her thigh as he brought his horse even closer. "We wanted to surprise you. Your name's on the deed, too. All of this belongs to all of us."

"Holy hell," Dakota breathed.

Colt chuckled. "We've already started hiring hands."

Stunned and elated, Dakota laughed. "I can't believe it. It's really true?"

Both men grinned, making her heart skip a beat. Colt leaned over to slide his lips over her, running his tongue over her bottom lip. "It's true, baby. We have more than we could have ever dreamed of. Once we get you pregnant, we'll have it all."

Dakota's heart leapt to her throat and she couldn't resist teasing. "Cocky, aren't you?"

Colt laughed. "You should know. In fact…"

Joe's hand tangled in her hair, tugging until she turned her face up to him. His mouth covered hers, his tongue sweeping erotically as he pulled her tightly against him.

Her senses spun out of control at the possessiveness in his kiss, in his hold. She thrilled at the way both men openly showed their love and need for her. She felt his cock harden against her stomach and squirmed against it. When he lifted his head, he kept a tight hold on her hair to keep her from following. "Fuck. I've got to get my dick back in my jeans and that's not going to help."

"Put her across your lap," Colt told him.

Dakota's head whipped around at that to see Colt squirt lube onto his finger. Her bottom clenched in anticipation as she stared at him incredulously. "You brought lube on a horseback ride?"

His cock had already been freed and he stroked it, working a generous amount of lube onto it. His eyes glittered as they met hers before he squirted more lube onto his fingers. "Around you, it pays to be prepared. You're riding back down the ridge with me. Care to guess where my cock's gonna be?"

Before she had time to react, she'd been lifted and placed over Joe's lap, his hard hand at her back keeping her in place and holding her dress up so her bottom remained exposed. She groaned when the cheeks of her bottom were spread and the cool lube worked into her.

Looking down at the ground, she couldn't see either of them and couldn't believe how vulnerable and exposed she felt. On a horse, for God's sake!

They never failed to surprise her. Not knowing what they would do to her from one minute to the next kept her constantly filled with anticipation. Their mischievous behavior got more erotic every day.

And they never disappointed her.

"I can't believe the things you do to me," she moaned.

Colt shoved a finger deep. "You love what we do to you, darlin'. You're soaking wet again. Now come to me so I can get inside that tight ass."

"Oh God."

Knowing they could hold her, she allowed Joe to pass her to Colt, trembling as Colt bent her over his arm facing away from him. Looking over, she watched Joe stroke his cock as he watched Colt begin to enter her bottom.

The forbidden feeling always surprised her as Colt began to work his cock into her. Once he pressed the head of his thick shaft past the ring of muscle, she groaned, shivers racing through her as he began to fill her.

"Damn if that's not fucking beautiful," Joe murmured as the strokes on his cock increased in speed. Dakota couldn't look away.

Colt's arms wrapped around her and slowly pulled her back against him and fully onto his cock. "Fucking incredible. We're going to go slow and take the long way back."

Dakota groaned loudly as he filled her completely, the burn of her anus being stretched already causing warning tingles throughout her body.

One hand held the reins while he held her in place with the other. His hand covered her abdomen, his fingers skimming over her throbbing clit.

Lost in sensation, Dakota leaned back against him, watching as Joe came, his seed spurting as he threw back his head and groaned. The sight of her lover pleasuring himself made Dakota even hotter and she gripped Colt's thighs as her body began to tighten.

They waited as Joe finally managed to zip his jeans and turn to smile at them. "Ready to go home, baby?"

Dakota moaned as the cock in her ass jumped. "I'll never survive it."

Colt's chuckle ended in a groan when she clenched on him. "Let's ride, cowgirl."

Dakota squeezed her eyes closed at the naughty and unbelievably erotic feel of riding back to the ranch in her lover's arms with a thick cock filling her ass. The horse started to move, slowly at first then slightly faster. Before they'd gotten off the ridge Dakota's scream of release filled the air.

Before they got back to the stable, another orgasm hit her and she screamed again.

But this time she took her cowboy with her.

# THE END

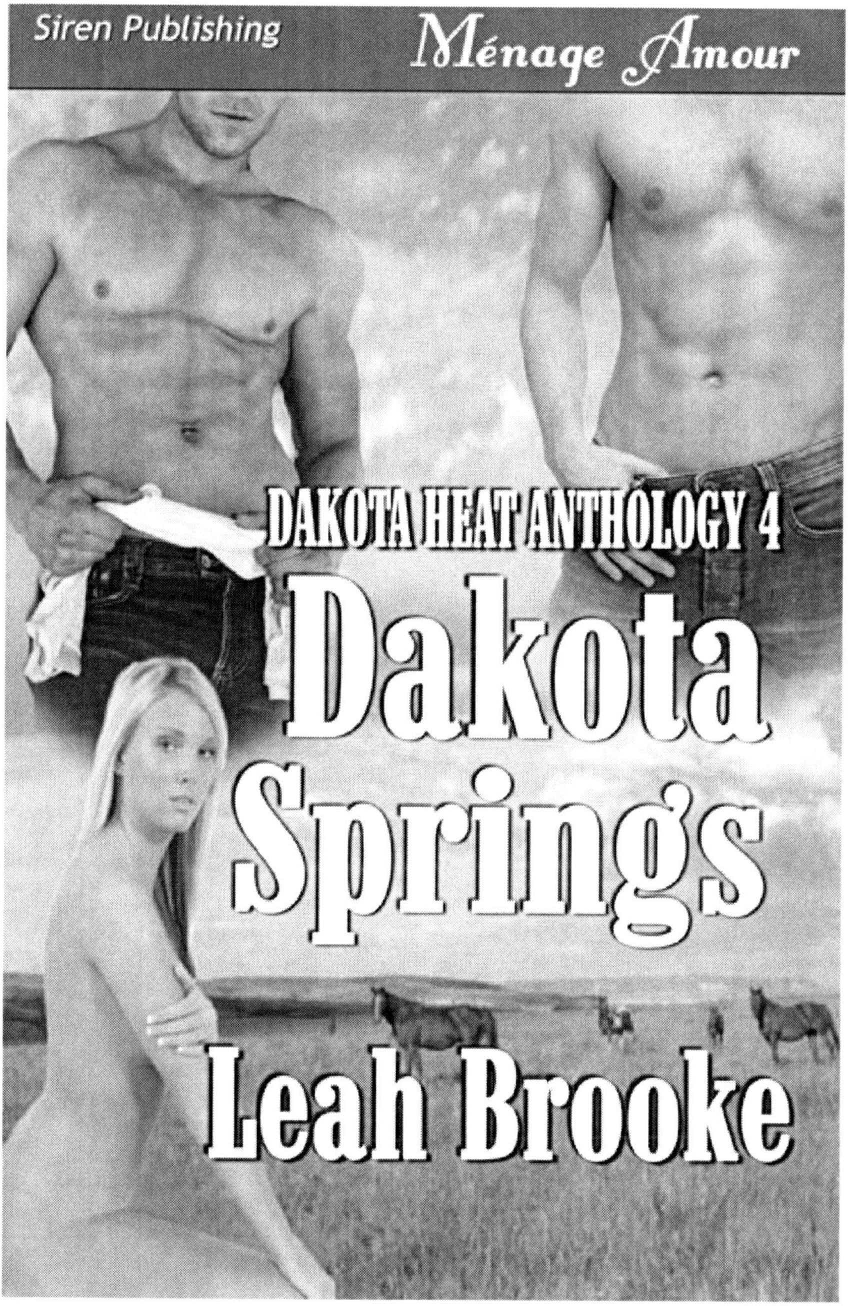
Siren Publishing
Ménage Amour
DAKOTA HEAT ANTHOLOGY 4
Dakota Springs
Leah Brooke

# DAKOTA SPRINGS

## *Dakota Heat Anthology 4*

## LEAH BROOKE
Copyright © 2010

## Chapter One

Elizabeth Reed gripped the receiver tightly, her gaze automatically flying to where her daughter played on the floor. "Hayden?"

"Of course it's me! Your mother just told us that your divorce is final. Pack your things. I'm coming to get you."

Holding the receiver away from her ear, she stared at it, dumbfounded.

After all these years, why the hell would Hayden call her now? Not wanting Angie to hear, she moved to the kitchen.

His icy tone finally broke through as she warily lifted the receiver again. "—get there I'm going to beat the hell out of him and beat your ass raw."

With her heart beating frantically, her legs wobbled, forcing her to grip the kitchen counter for support. She kept her tone firm, not about to let him hear any kind of weakness. "This is none of your business, Hayden, and I certainly don't need you to come and get me. I've grown up, just like you wanted, and I can get home all by myself."

"Push me on this, Lizzy, and you'll be sorry. You never should have married him. If I had known about it beforehand, I would have stopped you."

Shock and anger rendered her nearly speechless. He'd always been arrogant, but she'd never really had it directed at her before. If he thought she would just take it like one of his ranch hands, he was in for a surprise. "Listen, you son of a bitch—"

"No! You listen! Get your shit packed. I'll be there in the morning."

"I won't be here!" Elizabeth pushed the button to end the call and hurriedly tossed the phone onto the kitchen table as if it burned her. Backing away on legs that felt like jelly, she jolted when the phone rang again. And again. She took a step back with each ring, her heart racing. She had to get out of there. She couldn't deal with him right now.

Why the hell had he called?

Each ring grated on her nerves until the answering machine finally picked up.

"Lizzy, honey, it's Chandler. Pick up the phone and talk to me, baby. Come on." After a few seconds of silence, his voice took on an edge. "I know you're there. If you don't pick up the phone right now, we're getting the next flight and coming up there. And we won't be happy. If you pick up and let me know you're okay, we'll wait for you to come home, if that's what you want."

"Mommy, the phone ringed. A man's talkin' in the 'chine."

Spinning, Elizabeth took a deep breath and forced a smile for her three-year-old daughter. "I know, sweetheart. I'm going to talk to him now. Go back to your dolls, darling."

Watching her daughter walk back into the living room, Elizabeth picked up the phone, taking a deep breath before she pushed the button to talk. "Chandler, I have no idea why you and Hayden are calling, but I don't want to talk to either one of you. We have absolutely nothing to say to each other. Promise me you won't come here."

"Calm down, darlin'. I don't want you takin' off. We just wanted to come up and help you."

Elizabeth winced as Hayden yelled something in the background. "Chandler, I haven't talked to either you or Hayden since…"

"Since we called you when we heard you got married."

Elizabeth still wanted to cry every time she thought about that call and the defeat in their voices. But they'd already turned her away. "Look, I don't know what's gotten into either one of you. I'm coming home at the end of the week. I want to start over. I want Angie to be raised in the same small town that I was raised in. Don't worry, I'm not coming back to bother either one of you again."

Chandler sighed. "You've never been a bother to either one of us."

"I remember it differently."

There was a long silence, followed by a muffled sound as if Chandler had his hand over the receiver. When he came back on the phone, his frustration came through loud and clear. "We won't come up there. But this isn't over. We'll talk to you when you get home."

"We have nothing to talk about. You'll really stay away? Both of you?"

"Yes."

Elizabeth had trouble believing that. "You're lying."

Chandler's voice dropped so low she had to struggle to hear him. "I've only lied to you once in my life, Lizzy, and my life has been hell ever since. We'll wait. But you're supposed to come home this weekend. If you don't, we're coming to get you. By force, if necessary."

Tears rolled down her face, but she fought to keep them out of her voice. "Goodbye, Chandler." She hung up and reached for a tissue to wipe away her tears before Angie saw them.

Eight years ago, Hayden and Chandler had wanted her to leave them alone. What the hell did they want from her now?

\* \* \* \*

Elizabeth drew a deep breath, wiping her hands on her skirt as the airport came into view. In just a few minutes, they would be on the ground. In an hour they would be back in Dakota Springs.

Home.

She found it hard to believe that it had been almost eight years since she left Dakota Springs and everything she'd ever loved. Her life had changed so much since then.

"Mommy? Will Grandma and Grandpa be at the 'port?"

Elizabeth smiled down at the biggest change in her life. "Airport, sweetie. And yes, they'll be there."

Angie had been excited about this move ever since Elizabeth had told her that they would be living in the same town as her grandparents.

Unfortunately, Hayden and Chandler Scott lived there, too.

The last time she'd seen either one of them had been the night of her eighteenth birthday, a night she wanted to forget. She'd been in love with them forever and that night she'd been happier than she'd ever been in her life, believing that they'd just been waiting for her to turn eighteen to tell her that they loved her.

She could still remember their sardonic laughter and her own mortification as her dreams of a future with them shattered.

"Mommy? Will I like 'Kota Springs?"

Elizabeth smiled and took her daughter's tiny hand in hers. "Da-ko-ta Springs, sweetie. You'll love Dakota Springs. I did when I was a little girl. You'll start school there soon and make lots of friends. And there's a park right down the street from Grandma and Grandpa's house."

"You said there's horses. I telled Becky."

"You *told* Becky," she corrected absently. Memories of Hayden and Chandler teaching her to ride flashed through her mind. It had been the happiest time in her life, and she'd fallen a little more in love with them every day. In her naiveté she'd seen nothing wrong with it and wanted them both, dreaming that they would all live happily ever after.

Even now her face burned when she remembered how incredibly stupid she'd been.

She had no idea why the hell Hayden and Chandler suddenly seemed interested in what she did, but if either one of them thought they could try to run her life, they could think again. She'd mistaken their interest in her life before for caring. She wouldn't make that mistake again.

She'd grown up, and she'd be damned if she'd let them treat her like a child.

Until the other night, she hadn't spoken to either one of them since she got married, but she'd kept up with their lives through her parents. Anxious for any bit of news, she'd casually questioned her parents when she spoke to them, carefully keeping her feelings hidden.

For some reason, Hayden and Chandler had started fighting with each other several years ago. Mr. and Mrs. Scott had apparently had enough of it and sold the ranch to their sons and started travelling the way they'd always wanted to.

Since then, the Double S had become even more successful.

Angie bounced in her seat as the plane rolled to a stop at the gate, more animated than she'd been in a long time. She hadn't slept on the flight, as Elizabeth had hoped. She was too excited to start a new adventure.

Just watching her made Elizabeth even more tired. She hadn't slept much in the last several weeks. She'd been busy selling off the furniture Richard didn't want and packing and sending their belongings home.

The last of their belongings had been stuffed into the carry-on she now slung over her shoulder and, with them, the information that had been her ticket to freedom.

With Angie in her arms, she stood, anxious to see her parents again and start a new chapter in their lives.

A chapter that started with getting over Hayden and Chandler.

\* \* \* \*

With his stomach tied in knots that felt more like boulders, Hayden Scott stared at the gate, willing Elizabeth to appear. He could hardly believe that their Lizzy had finally come home.

It was about fucking time.

He'd spent the last four years believing that this day would never come and the last three months marking days off of his calendar. The last twenty-four hours had been spent watching the clock.

He felt alive in a way he hadn't in years.

They'd made the biggest mistake of their lives on Elizabeth's eighteenth birthday, and not a day had gone by since then that he hadn't regretted it. Every single day since she'd gone had only reinforced his conviction that he would never love anyone else.

They had a second chance with her and were determined that nothing get in the way of them having her.

Chandler stopped pacing to look back out the window, a tense stillness coming over him as the plane rolled to a stop. "I've never been so scared in my entire life. What if she can't handle what we want from her?"

Hayden drew a breath, fear tightening his own gut. "That's Lizzy you're talking about. That hard-headed brat can handle anything. I swear I'm never letting that woman out of my sight again." He tightened his hold, crushing the stuffed bear they'd bought for Angelina, unsurprised that his hands trembled. Carefully loosening his grip, he fluffed out the fur where he'd smashed it, wanting it to look perfect.

Would they be able to convince her to give them another chance?

They had to. He couldn't bear to think of the alternative. They'd done all they could to ease the way. They'd spent the last six months letting everyone know just what they felt for her and making sure her parents and the town accepted it.

He could still remember his panic and frustration when the letter he sent to her college dorm shortly before graduation came back unopened.

He and Chandler had purposely not contacted her while she attended school. They'd wanted to give her a chance to be on her own until they told her how they felt.

Her father had been furious, and it had taken months to get him to accept that they both loved Lizzy. They'd explained how they'd arrived at their decision to share her and answered all of his concerns.

They'd been stunned to learn of her marriage and even more so to learn that she carried her husband's child. They'd both spent the next several months growling at anyone who spoke to them, drinking too much, and going through women at an alarming rate in their hope of forgetting her.

Nothing had worked. They hadn't even made love to her yet and she'd ruined them for anyone else.

They'd tried to go on with their lives, but there was a hole where Lizzy should have been. Once they learned that she was getting divorced, they'd started living again, making plans, and setting things in motion for her return.

The waiting had finally ended, and the slippery minx would be with them again in a matter of minutes. Hayden kept his eyes glued to where she would appear. He and Chandler had every intention of spoiling both her and her daughter rotten and giving them all the love they could handle.

They'd tie Lizzy to them so tightly she would never be able to escape them again.

* * * *

Holding her daughter close, Elizabeth slowly made her way out of the plane, following the line of people moving into the airport.

Shifting Angie to her other hip, she adjusted the carry-on that had started to dig into her shoulder.

"Mommy, my shoe!"

With a sigh, Elizabeth stopped, moved to the side, and looked down at her daughter's tiny, bare foot, automatically reaching down to cradle it in her hand. "Where did you—never mind. I see it." The small pink sandal lay on the floor several feet back. By the time Elizabeth got through the crowd of passengers, picked it up, and checked to make sure Angie still wore the other one, she found herself at the end of the line.

Slipping the sandal onto Angie's foot, she tightened her grip on her and hurried into the airport. "Let's go find Grandma and Grandpa, sweetie." Searching the crowd for her parents, she stopped dead, her eyes going wide at the sight that greeted her.

Hayden and Chandler strode toward her, head and shoulders above the people around them, both looking more than a little anxious. They'd both matured in the years since she'd last seen them, looking colder and more formidable than ever. Their eyes glittered fiercely as their long legs quickly covered the distance between them.

They'd always been good-looking, but the years had added a few lines and honed the sharp edge of power and authority they'd always carried so easily. It turned them from handsome to striking.

Panic had her heart pounding furiously and kept her frozen in place as realization hit her. The men she'd loved for years had been replaced by two men who possessed an aura of danger that had never been there before and a desperate look in their eyes that she didn't remember.

Why had they come? Had something happened to her parents?

Hayden reached her first, his long strides eating up the ground, reaching out to grab her arm when she would have stepped back. "It's about damned time."

Elizabeth barely had time to blink before he pulled her against him and bent his head to take her mouth with his. Her senses soared as he deepened the kiss, his lips moving over hers hungrily, his big arms wrapped around both her and Angie. She never knew coffee and mint could taste so darkly erotic. She automatically met his ardor with heat of her own.

Everything around her faded away. She heard nothing but his breathing and her own heartbeat, felt nothing but the heat of his body surrounding hers as he took her mouth repeatedly, one long drugging kiss moving into another.

Home.

He tasted like home and heaven, need and strength, the very essence of what a kiss with a lover should be. The sharp edge of danger in his kiss made it even more powerful and compelling, weakening her knees.

Liquid heat flowed through her like honey, thick and sweet, intoxicating her and stripping away all of her defenses in a heartbeat.

She's always known it would be good, but nothing in her life had prepared her for this.

Holding her as though he would never let her go, Hayden explored her mouth, taking it thoroughly as though starving for the taste of her.

Her own hunger fueled the fire, making it burn even hotter. The stroke of his tongue led her on an erotic dance that stirred to life the need inside her that had lain dormant for years.

Her nipples beaded as they brushed against his hard chest, the sharp pinpricks of pleasure stoking the fire.

He swallowed her moan, his lips warm and firm as he tightened his hold, preventing her instinctive retreat. His kiss made demands, demands she couldn't refuse.

Her head spun and a kaleidoscope of colors whirled behind her eyes. Grabbing his shirt front, she pressed even closer, close to weeping in delight. Leaning into his solidness and warmth, she absorbed as much of it as she could.

Had she ever felt so safe and warm?

"Mommy!"

The sound of her daughter's frantic cry startled her. It apparently had the same effect on Hayden as he hurriedly broke off the kiss, his breathing uneven. Lifting his head, he kept an arm around both of them, his eyes nearly black.

Angie frowned and pushed at him, wrapping her arms around Elizabeth's neck possessively.

His lips twitched as he stared down at Angie, his eyes twinkling with amusement. "I can't blame her for being possessive of you, especially when I feel the same way. She's beautiful, just like her momma."

Elizabeth rubbed Angie's back when her daughter buried her face in her neck. "It's okay, sweetheart. They're friends."

Chandler stepped forward. "Much more than that, I hope. We've missed you very much, Lizzy. It's good to have you home." The intent in his eyes as he stared at her lips, still warm and swollen from Hayden's kiss, made them tingle with anticipation. He picked up the bag at her feet that she hadn't even remembered dropping.

Elizabeth stepped back, anxious now. "Are my parents okay? Did something happen to them?"

Chandler shook his head, his lips curving as he winked at Angie. "No. They're fine. We asked if it would be all right if we came to pick you up."

Angie lifted her head. "Mommy? Where's Grandma and Grandpa?"

Chandler smiled tenderly and bent to Angie's level. "Hello. My name's Chandler. You must be Angelina. You're even prettier than your pictures."

Angie hid her face again, tightening her arms around Elizabeth's neck.

Elizabeth smiled apologetically. "I'm sorry. She's shy with strangers."

Hayden's eyes hardened briefly, before warming again. "Don't apologize for her. She doesn't know us yet, and she's skittish." He shot her a pointed glance. "Just like her momma. Don't worry, we won't be strangers for long."

Chandler moved to her other side. "Do you have any other baggage?"

Elizabeth adjusted Angie to hold her more comfortably. She was so tired, and her arms wouldn't be able to hold her daughter for much longer. "No. I sent everything else ahead. All we have is that bag."

Hayden nodded, his arm heavy on her shoulder as he steered her toward the exit. "Good. Then we can get the hell out of here. You look like you're about to collapse."

Angie lifted her head, her eyes wide as she whispered, "Mommy, that man said a bad word."

Hayden stopped short, keeping Elizabeth beside him. Bending, he looked into Angie's face. "You're right. I did and I'm not supposed to. With you around, it's a habit I'm going to have to break. My name is Hayden. Whenever you hear me say a bad word, you tell me. It's not nice, and I'll try not to do it again. Okay?"

Angie nodded warily, biting her bottom lip and tucking her head beneath Elizabeth's chin. "'Kay."

Hayden smiled and handed her the big stuffed bear he carried. "This is for you. He's really soft so you can cuddle with him. He can be your friend until you make friends here. You have to give him a good name, okay?"

Angie lifted her head and reached out to touch the bear, her eyes wide as she looked at her mother.

Elizabeth smiled and nodded. "Go ahead, sweetie. You may have it. What do you say?"

Angie accepted the bear, wrapping her arms around it as she leaned back against Elizabeth. "Tank you."

Hayden's eyes twinkled. "You're very welcome. Now, let's get out of here."

Both men stayed close, flanking her as they walked through the airport. Their size and the aura of power they exuded so effortlessly had people moving out of the way as if by magic.

Although they'd slowed their steps for her, Elizabeth struggled to keep up. The sleepless nights had finally caught up with her, making it difficult just to put one foot in front of the other. She shifted Angie's weight again as her hold weakened.

Hayden took her arm to pull her aside. "Angelina? Would it be okay if I carry you and your bear to the truck? Your momma's getting tired."

Angie buried her face in Elizabeth's neck again and shook her head.

Elizabeth rubbed her back. "It's okay, sweetie." She looked up at Hayden. "I'm sorry, she's just not used to—Hayden!"

Hayden bent and lifted them both, holding them securely against his chest as he started for the door.

Surprised at his move, Elizabeth gripped Angie tighter. "Hayden, you can't carry us through the airport."

People around them stared, smiling indulgently.

Angie giggled. "Mommy, the big man's carrying us."

Hayden smiled down at Angie. "You two don't weigh anything. And what's this 'big man'? Don't you remember my name?"

Angie giggled again, turning pink and looking up at him through her lashes. "Hayden."

Chandler chuckled and bent to whisper in Elizabeth's ear. "Your daughter's a flirt."

Elizabeth's face burned at the attention they drew. Trembling at being held against Hayden this way, especially after the kiss they'd just shared, she avoided his gaze. "Hayden, please put us down. People are staring."

Hayden never broke his stride. "Who cares? You're nothing but skin and bones, and you have dark circles under your eyes. You're having a hard time carrying her. She's not willing to let me carry her yet, so this is the only alternative. We're almost there anyway, so just relax."

Resigned to being carried, Elizabeth couldn't help but smile at Angie as Hayden carried them out to the parking lot. Safe in her mother's arms, Angie giggled, obviously enjoying this immensely.

Once they got to the truck, Hayden carefully set her on her feet, lifting Angie against him as Chandler opened the door for her.

Surprised to see a seat for Angie, Elizabeth looked up at Hayden. "Is that the seat my mother has for her?"

Hayden settled Angie into the child seat before she had a chance to object, and began buckling her in. "No. Since you'll both be spending time with us, we wanted our own. The lady at the store assured us that this was the best."

Elizabeth kept her tone cool. "I really don't think we'll be seeing that much of each other." She started to walk away to get into the other side, only making it as far as the back of the truck before Chandler grabbed her, pinning her against it.

With an arm on either side of her, caging her in, he leaned over her until their noses nearly touched. "Oh, darlin', we'll be seeing a lot of each other. We've finally got you back, and we're not letting you get away from us again." His eyes darkened becoming the color of dark chocolate. "You're ours, Lizzy. Get used to it." His gaze held hers as he slowly lowered his head.

Mesmerized, she watched him move closer, knowing she should push him away. She also knew she couldn't. Her eyes fluttered closed as need swirled inside her.

Where Hayden demanded, Chandler coerced, gently seducing her into the heat. His hands moved to her waist, squeezing gently and sending need racing through her.

Her breath caught as his hands moved higher. Her breasts swelled, her nipples tightening almost painfully in anticipation. Moaning into his mouth, she grabbed fistfuls of his dark, silky hair to pull him closer. When his hands stopped right below her breasts, she groaned in frustration and leaned into him, needing more. Shifting restlessly as the heat from his hands burned the underside of her breast, she gasped against his lips as the evidence of his desire pressed insistently against her stomach.

Lifting his head, he stared down at her hungrily. "You've put us through hell."

Dazed, it took Elizabeth a few seconds to make sense of his words. When she did, she pushed him away furiously. "*I* put *you* through hell? Listen, you son of a bitch, I left because of you and that Neanderthal you call a brother." Damn it, she hadn't meant to say that. Even she'd heard the bitterness and hurt in her tone, something she hadn't wanted to reveal to either one of them. Taking a calming breath, she tried to ignore his knowing smile and carefully kept her tone cool. "But all that's in the past. I'm a different person now. I've grown up."

Chandler's smile turned cold. "Don't kid yourself, Lizzy. It'll never be finished between us. Let's go. Angie is calling for you."

Turning away, Elizabeth hurried to get into the truck, where she immediately began to settle a tired and cranky Angie, almost glad for the distraction.

Five minutes into the ride, Angie fell asleep.

No longer having Angie as a buffer, Elizabeth stared out the window as the tense silence lengthened. Searching frantically for a safe topic to break it, she cleared her throat. "How are your parents? I understand they're travelling."

Chandler turned in his seat to face her. "Mom and Dad are having a great time. They're on a cruise right now. They can't wait to see you again, and they're dying to meet Angie."

Elizabeth blinked. "They know I'm home?"

Chandler frowned. "Of course they know. They know we've been waiting for you. We've had some changes made at the ranch as soon as we heard about the divorce."

Elizabeth gaped at him, aware of Hayden's rapt attention to the conversation. "I don't understand either one of you at all. Before I left, you made it clear what you thought of my feelings for both of you." Just thinking about it made her face burn. "You were right. I was childish and selfish. I've grown up since then. All I care about now is what's best for Angie."

In the rear view mirror, Hayden shot a glance at Angie, before looking at her. "We were young and confused then, too, Lizzy. If you hadn't taken off in a huff, things would have worked out differently. But make no mistake, sweetheart, your fate has already been sealed."

Gritting her teeth, she tamped down her anger, not wanting to yell and wake Angie. "I know you've always felt obligated to take care of me because our parents are friends." It had taken her several months after she'd started college to realize the truth. "But I came home to raise my daughter close to my parents. I'm a big girl now and have been taking care of myself and Angie for a long time. Just butt out of my life. You have no right to plan my future."

Hayden's cold smile made her more than a little apprehensive. "Your future, Lizzy, is already set in stone. Believe me, you don't want to talk to me about our *rights* concerning you right now."

Before she could formulate a response, Hayden came to a red light and turned in his seat to face her and gestured toward Angie. "She should have been ours. Make no mistake, the next one will be."

# Chapter Two

After finally getting her daughter to sleep, Elizabeth tiptoed out of Angie's bedroom, quietly closing the door behind her. Her movements were lethargic as she walked out to the living room. She wanted nothing more than to go to bed, but she needed to talk to her parents while Angie slept.

Her mother greeted her with a cup of chamomile tea. "Drink this and go to bed, sweetheart. I told you we shouldn't have unpacked all of those boxes today."

Elizabeth accepted the mug and sat on the sofa, tucking her legs under her. "I want to talk to both of you while Angie's asleep."

"What's wrong?"

Elizabeth smiled as her father came into the room. "I know both of you were upset that I didn't want you to come to see me in New Jersey when I was going through the divorce, and I owe you an explanation."

Jeb Reed narrowed his eyes. "What have you been keepin' from us? Spill it, girl."

Wincing at his tone, Elizabeth took a sip of her tea. "I handled it, Dad. I just didn't want you and Mom in the middle." Setting her tea aside, she faced them both. "Richard's been cheating on me from the beginning. I found out about it within the first six months."

Paula Reed shot to her feet. "What? He's been cheating the whole time? I thought you divorced him because you'd just learned he was having an affair."

Elizabeth shook her head. "No. Our marriage was over before Angie was born, but we had to put on a show because of Richard's father."

Jeb scowled. "The senator? Did he know about it?"

Elizabeth laughed humorlessly. "Oh, he knew about it. He and his son sometimes saw the same women. But Richard wouldn't agree to a divorce because it would hurt his father's image. Richard Sr. told me that if I tried to divorce his son, he would see to it that I lost Angie."

Jeb plunked his coffee mug on the coffee table, some of the contents sloshing over the sides. "That bastard! And you kept all of this from us?"

Picking up her own mug, she sighed. "There was nothing you could do. The senator's a powerful man. They would have taken Angie. Richard and I have had separate rooms for years. When you came to stay with us, he slept on the floor."

Her mother and father looked at each other before turning back to her. Her mother's lips firmed. "I can't believe you kept this from us."

Even though Elizabeth had long since reached the age of consent, her stomach knotted at the look on her father's face. "I didn't want you to worry."

Her father jumped up from his chair, his tone furious. "Didn't want us to worry?" Glancing toward the direction Angie slept, he scrubbed a hand over his face and lowered his voice. "We're your parents. We should have known. I can't believe you didn't come to us with this. At least Hayden and Chandler had the courage to talk to us when they figured out how they felt about you."

Elizabeth felt all the blood drain from her face. "Hayden and Chandler *told* you?"

Jeb frowned at her. "Of course they told us. As soon as they found out you were getting a divorce, they came to us and told us how they felt about you and that they both wanted you."

Speechless, Elizabeth looked down into her tea, her face burning. "I can't believe they told you that." Shaking her head, she set her tea aside again. "It doesn't matter what they said. You don't have to worry. I would never do something like that to you or Mom. I had a crush on both of them when I was younger, but I see now that it's totally unrealistic. I just want to get a job and make a life for myself and Angie."

Her mother sat back, smiling, and shot a glance at her husband. "You didn't even ask what your father said when they approached him."

More than a little uncomfortable with this topic, Elizabeth grimaced. "I can only imagine."

Her father picked up his coffee again. "I was furious, as they knew I would be, but they still had the guts to come and talk to me. Over time I had a change of heart."

Elizabeth gaped at him. "You did?"

Her mother laughed softly. "Did you think we didn't know how crazy you were about them? Did you think we didn't see how you were always so careful when you talked about them when we came to visit? Didn't you think I figured out that you only married Richard because you were pregnant?"

Elizabeth shrugged, trying to cover her embarrassment. "The senator insisted. Richard's mother, Vivian, was furious. She said she didn't want the scandal of the senator having an illegitimate grandchild."

Her mother's lips thinned. "And they didn't want you to divorce him because of the senator's career either, right? What would have happened if the senator and his son got caught cheating on their wives? I guess that wouldn't have hurt his career either, right?"

Elizabeth smiled bitterly. "I don't think they thought they'd ever get caught."

Her mother got up and moved to sit with her on the sofa. "So what made them finally agree to a divorce?"

"They didn't have any choice. Richard had been giving me extra money, thinking that would keep me satisfied. I used the money to hire a private investigator and to get proof of his affairs and the senator's. Once I had that, they had to agree."

Her father shook his head. "And to think I kept Hayden and Chandler from going up there. If I'd have known, I would have turned them both loose on Richard and his father."

Elizabeth shifted uncomfortably. "About Hayden and Chandler—"

Her father lifted a brow. "What about them?"

"What did you say to them?"

Her father regarded her steadily before answering. "I told you I was mad as hell at first. But then when I saw how unhappy you were, I started to listen. I knew they'd always watched over you when you were growing up, but I didn't figure they felt that way about you. They made me see that they would do a better job of making you happy than Richard had."

Elizabeth started to get an uneasy feeling about this, making her almost afraid to ask. But she had to know. "Did Hayden and Chandler know that I wasn't happy before they came to you?"

Her mother shrugged and looked away. "I didn't say anything to them, but I told Beverly."

Elizabeth finished her tea and stood. "And Beverly Scott told her sons." Smiling sadly, she stared down into her empty cup. "Hayden and Chandler don't really want me. They're just trying to take care of me like they always have. They probably figured that it would be easier and give them both more free time if they shared the responsibility."

Her mother stood. "No, they really—"

Elizabeth waved a hand. "If you don't mind listening for Angie, I think I'll go outside for a bit before I go to bed."

Her mother sighed. "Of course we don't mind, but I think you're wrong."

Ignoring the look that passed between her parents, she smiled sadly. "I won't be long."

She headed to the kitchen and placed her empty mug in the sink before heading out the back door as her father turned on the news.

Her mind racing, she walked down the steps to stand in the backyard and stared thoughtfully out into the darkness.

Memories of the night of her eighteenth birthday assailed her, refusing to be held at bay any longer. Although it had been years ago, the events of that night had been branded into her mind, and she could remember every detail as though it happened yesterday.

It had been a warm, humid night, much like tonight. She could still remember the butterflies that fluttered in her stomach and the smell of burgers grilling and mingling with the scent of her mother's honeysuckle.

Her father had painstakingly hung hundreds and hundreds of Christmas lights which turned their backyard into a magical wonderland.

She'd deliberated over what to wear for days. She had finally gone shopping with her friends and bought a red tank top and the shortest white shorts she could find. Both had earned disapproving looks from her father, but she hadn't cared.

All that had mattered was that she looked good for Hayden and Chandler and showed them that she was no longer a child. If she dressed like the girls they dated, they had to notice her. They'd resisted all of her attempts to make them see her as something more than the daughter of a friend they felt obligated to look out for.

She'd flirted outrageously, started wearing make-up, and did her best to spend as much time at the ranch as possible.

They'd continued to treat her like a child, but they'd both started paying more attention to her, giving her advice, and acting possessive. They'd monitored her dates and tried to keep the boys in town away from her.

She'd been so excited, thinking they finally saw her as a woman and had been jealous.

When they'd arrived late to her birthday party, she'd done her best to look only mildly interested, while inside she'd become a bundle of nerves. Watching them mingle with the others, she'd been so excited she could hardly stay still. No one else had existed for her that night. She'd waited impatiently for them to separate themselves from the crowd before approaching them.

She'd given them her brightest smile and sauntered up to them in a practiced move. "Hi, Hayden. Hi, Chandler. Thanks for coming to my party."

Hayden's smile had sent her heart racing. "We wouldn't miss your birthday party for the world." His smile quickly disappeared as his eyes raked her figure. "Don't you think those shorts are a little short?"

Elated that he'd noticed, she cocked her hip, smiling flirtatiously and using her eyes the way she'd practiced in the mirror. "Do you like them?"

Chandler's scowl had made her feel even better. "What the hell are you doing dressing like that? Every guy here is imagining you naked."

"Including you?"

Chandler, then twenty-eight, had kept looking at the way her nipples poked at the front of her tank top. He looked away suddenly as though embarrassed, his jaw clenched. "No. I prefer grown-ups."

She'd walked up to Hayden, putting her hands on his chest. "I'm eighteen now. You don't have to push me away any more."

Hayden's eyes had gone cold. "You're a spoiled brat who can't even decide which one of us she wants. What kind of girl throws herself at two men?"

Even now, thinking about it made her eyes sting.

She'd tried again, breathing through the indescribable pain and unable to believe he would say such a thing to her and really mean it. "Hayden, it's not like that. I'm not playing games. I love both of you so much. I really do."

As long as she lived, she'd never forget the look of disgust on their faces.

Opening her eyes, she ruthlessly pushed the image away.

The question that Hayden had asked her that night had gone

through her mind a thousand times since then.

What kind of woman could love two men so completely?

She couldn't believe how incredibly naïve she'd been. She'd grown up in a hurry that night and clung to her dignity by a thread for the rest of the party.

Hearing laughter, she came back to the present and turned her head toward the street. Saturday night had always been the night that everyone came out in Dakota Springs. Her parents' house sat right on Main Street, enabling her to easily see and hear the couples as they strolled by. The sounds of their laughter and low conversation as they walked by in pairs only made her more aware of her own loneliness.

After the couples passed and silence reigned again, even the sounds of the crickets singing sounded sad to her and made her feel even more isolated.

She wasn't alone. She had her daughter and her parents, but she wanted more. She ached to have a man who would hold her in the night, one who would love her and would speak softly to her in the dark. They would plan their future and talk about their dreams and their love for each other.

A slight breeze, like a warm breath, blew the tendrils of hair at her nape but did nothing to relieve the oppressive heaviness of the warm, humid night. She really should go back inside and into the air conditioned house, but she couldn't. Not yet. Tired, but still too unsettled to sleep, she couldn't stop thinking about what had happened at the airport.

And ask herself yet again the question that had plagued her for years.

*What kind of woman could love two men the way she loved Hayden and Chandler?*

It didn't seem to matter how much time had passed. She'd known at eighteen that she'd always love them and in the eight years since she'd last seen them, nothing had changed. If anything, she loved them even more, and the last eight years proved to her just how rare her feelings for them were.

Why the hell couldn't she get over them? If she did, maybe she could fall in love with *one* man and have a chance for some happiness.

Looking back over the dark yard again, she wondered what Hayden and Chandler had tried to prove at the airport. If it had been a test to see if she wanted one of them over the other she'd failed miserably. Again.

Hard arms slid around her from behind, surprising a gasp from her as they pulled her back against a wall of heat. Warm lips grazed her ear. "You look so sad, baby. What are you thinking about?"

The dark timber of Hayden's voice washed over her, making her yearn for things she'd been trying to forget for eight years. He'd never used an endearment with her before.

She'd never heard that silky cadence in his voice directed at her before.

Together they combined into something totally irresistible.

She tried to pull away, but he didn't let her. "I was thinking about how selfish and naïve I was at eighteen. I'm glad I finally grew out of it."

Chandler moved to stand in front of her, his eyes gentle in the dim light. "We were just as naïve." Reaching out, he caressed her cheek. "We made a huge mistake with you, but at the time we couldn't handle what you offered so sweetly."

She blinked back the tears that threatened, swallowing the lump in her throat. There hadn't been a day in the last eight years she hadn't thought about them, missed them, or loved them. Hearing him say that now both saddened and angered her. "Neither one of you ever even called me. I know I disgusted you. I saw it on your faces."

Hayden's hand covered her stomach, gently caressing. "Never. It was an act. You've never disgusted us. If anything we were disgusted with ourselves." With his other hand, he cupped her jaw, turning her to face him. "We promised ourselves we wouldn't contact you until you came home from school. When you didn't come home, we came to see your dad and ask him what the hell was taking you so long." His voice lowered. "Your father told us that you were married and had a baby on the way." His hand tightened on her waist. "I could have cheerfully strangled you that day, Lizzy. Why the hell did you marry him? Why didn't you come home where you belong?"

Elizabeth laughed humorlessly. "Where I belong? I didn't belong here, Hayden. Not then. I was young and stupid and acted recklessly. What was I supposed to do, come home pregnant so you could think even worse of me?"

Chandler took both of her hands in his, and she cursed the fact that shivers went up her arm at the contact. His eyes glittered now. "We regret everything we said to you that night, Lizzy. We've regretted it every day since then." He sighed heavily and bent to kiss her forehead. "You scared the hell out of us, and we didn't know what the hell to do with you. We didn't figure it out for a long time."

Elizabeth pushed him away. "What to *do* with me? You don't have to worry about what to do with me, either one of you. I'm not the same child that left here eight years ago. I won't put you in any uncomfortable situations like that ever again." She wouldn't start the next chapter of her life making the same mistake she'd made in the past. "Let go of me."

Grateful that they released her, she moved away, glancing over her shoulder to find both of them staring at her. Turning her back, she took several more shaky steps away from them and looked out into the faintly-lit yard, stiffening when Hayden moved in behind her.

He leaned close, his lips brushing her shoulder. "We both wanted you. Badly. But we didn't know what to do about it. We knew you wanted both of us. A child's want. What we need from you now is a woman's love."

Having no idea what had come over them, or what kind of game they were playing with her now, she struggled to hide the urge to turn and throw herself in his arms. "You can't have it. Like I said, I was young and stupid. You were right in what you both said back then. I was a little girl playing at being a grown-up. I was confused about what I felt. I'm not that little girl anymore."

Hayden turned her in his arms, lifting her chin. "No, you're not. You're a woman now, and we're not about to let you slip through our fingers again."

More than anything, Elizabeth wanted to believe him, but the last time she'd thought they'd cared for her, she'd been wrong. She wouldn't be able to survive it if she was wrong again, and now she had a daughter to think of. Over the last eight years she'd finally come to realize just how impossible such a relationship would be. Taking a deep breath, she kept her voice cool, not looking at either one of them. "It's impossible. Please go away. And don't ever come back again. Excuse me, I have to check on Angie."

Chandler grabbed her arm when she would have walked away. "What's wrong with you? Angie's fine. She's sound asleep and your mom and dad are watching a movie. They can hear her. Stop trying to avoid us. Talk to us, Lizzy. I don't want any more misunderstandings between us. They've cost us too much already."

Elizabeth snapped at him. "Do you even hear what you're saying? I have a daughter to think about now, and what you're proposing is impossible. I won't have her ridiculed. Plus, I don't believe you. A long time ago, I mistook your caring for something more. You took it upon yourselves to watch out for me because our parents are friends. I won't make that mistake again."

Hayden gripped her other arm and pulled her against him, the anger in his eyes unmistakable even in the faint light. "Do you really think I would ever let anyone hurt you or Angie? We've spent a long time figuring out all of this. Just trust us."

Elizabeth smiled bitterly. "Now that I'm a single parent with a failed marriage behind me, I suppose you think I need to be taken care of. That's what all of this is about, Hayden. Don't try to pretend otherwise. I've got news for you. I know how to take care of myself and Angie just fine."

Hayden ran a hand over her hair. "Of course we want to take care of both you and Angie. If we have our way, we'll spoil both of you rotten. But that's not what this is all about and you know it."

With her hands on her hips, Elizabeth shook her head. "Nope. Not buying it. Did your mother put you up to this? Small town, divorced woman…no, she would have known that the town would never accept me being with both of you—"

Chandler swore under his breath. "You are the most exasperating woman on God's green earth! Our parents have nothing to do with this. You know damned well what this is about. You love us. *Both of us.* Stop playing these damned games. We want you to live with us. Bear our children. We'll be good fathers to Angie and to any other children who come along. We'll be good husbands to you."

Elizabeth shook her head, wondering if either one of them noticed that neither claimed to love her. "Husbands? I'm supposed to have two husbands in a town like Dakota Springs?" God, if it could happen, she would be the happiest woman alive. But not with men who considered her little more than an obligation.

Chandler laid a hand on her back, gently caressing. "We've already taken care of everything, Lizzy. The town already accepts it."

Incredulous, she gaped at him. "You told everybody? Of course you did. Well, I don't accept it. What's gotten into you? We've never even dated. We've kissed once."

Hayden grabbed her shoulders and pulled her against him, his mouth hovering just above hers. "We'll just have to fix that then, won't we? Give me another taste of what I had at the airport. I've been hungry for you for too long."

Her arm lifted of its own volition to Hayden's shoulder, kneading the thick muscle there as his mouth covered hers. In this, she could never fight either one of them.

Hayden wrapped his hand around her ponytail and tilted her head back as his tongue pushed inside. Sweeping her mouth with his, he devoured her, setting off wild sparks throughout her body. He nipped her lips gently, making them sting, before sweeping her mouth again.

Her lips felt swollen and ultra-sensitive as she tangled her tongue with his, reveling in the erotic taste of him.

When he finally lifted his head his eyes appeared lit from within as he stared down at her. "You're beautiful. You're passionate. You're ours."

Elizabeth swallowed heavily, trying to fight the arousal he'd ignited with so little effort. "No."

Chandler's hands came around from behind to her to cover her breasts, pulling her back against him. He bent his head to nibble at her neck as Hayden watched, his eyes hooded.

Her head fell back against Chandler's shoulder as need clawed its way to the surface. She couldn't tear her gaze away from Hayden as he watched her every reaction.

Chandler massaged her breasts gently, cupping them and moving his thumbs over her nipples, each flick over them causing her pussy to clench.

Her stomach tightened, the muscles quivering as Hayden's hand covered it. Tightening her thighs against the throbbing of her clit, she arched, pushing her breasts more firmly into Chandler's hands.

Hayden's lips twitched as he touched her, his hand moving in slow circles over her abdomen. "Your lips say one thing, but your body says another. You like having both of us touch you this way, don't you, baby?"

A moan ripped from her throat as he began to gather the material of her dress, raising it, inch by torturous inch. "It's just chemistry. Lust. It can't work."

Chandler lightly bit her earlobe as punishment. "Bullshit. You're not the kind of woman who can react this way with someone you don't care about." He lightly pinched a nipple through the material, making her cry out. "And it can work. You like that. Let's see what else you like. Hayden and I have a lot to explore, don't we, darlin'?"

Chandler tugged her nipples again, surprising another cry from her and making her ache to feel his hands on her bare flesh.

Gripping Chandler's sinewy forearms, she squeezed her eyes closed. God, she'd never imagined anything could ever feel as good as having both of them touch her this way. Liquid heat pooled between her thighs as her clit throbbed steadily. Her body, hypersensitive to every touch, shimmered with need. She could no longer tell the difference between their warm breath caressing her or the warm breeze. Blending together, they surrounded her, touching her everywhere. Dazed and weakened by the little burst of pleasure wherever they touched, Elizabeth arched into their hands, needing more.

Never in her life had she felt so needy, so desired.

Having both of the men she'd loved forever touching her this way was something out of her wildest fantasies. Her eyes flew open when Hayden's callused hand skimmed her bare thigh. Alarmed that he'd been able to raise the front of her dress completely out of the way without her even realizing it, she shuddered.

His big body stood between her and the street, blocking hers from anyone who might be walking by. Somehow they'd maneuvered her closer to the house so that she couldn't be seen from the windows. She could see Hayden's eyes more clearly as he slipped his hand inside her panties. "Nice and wet, huh, baby?" He bent, covering her mouth with his and swallowing her gasp as his finger slid over her clit.

Chandler released her breasts to grab her around the waist when her knees buckled. Holding her up, he buried his face in her neck. "That's it, darlin'. Let go. I've got you."

Elizabeth's body gathered as Hayden stroked her clit insistently, his mouth moving over hers to muffle her cries.

There was nothing teasing about his touch. He stroked her steadily, driving her relentlessly to the peak, and she'd been hungry for them too long to resist.

Her body sizzled, every nerve ending screaming with ecstasy as she came, trembling helplessly at the strength of her orgasm. Her body tightened and jerked as her pussy clenched desperately, her juices coating Hayden's fingers. Her clit burned where he stroked her, pulsing in time to her rapid heartbeat.

He swallowed her whimpered cries, his touch gentle now as he raised his head, raw possession glittering in his eyes. "So beautiful." Removing his hand from her panties, he allowed her dress to fall back into place.

Chandler turned her in his arms. "I can't wait to get you naked and explore every delicious inch of you."

She closed her eyes against the wave of longing, only to snap them back open again. Pushing against them, she moved several feet away, wrapping her arms around herself as a chill went through her. "I can't do this. Don't do this to me. I know you both well enough to know this won't work."

Both regarded her steadily for several long seconds before sharing a look. Hayden nodded, reaching out a hand to her, only to flinch when she took a step back. "You're tired. We'll leave you alone tonight. Get some sleep. We'll be back tomorrow."

Elizabeth took another step back. "Don't bother."

Chandler grabbed her arm before she could avoid him. Leaning close, he brushed his lips against hers. "Oh, it's no bother, darlin'. You'll be seeing us quite a bit."

Hayden ran a finger over a still pebbled nipple. "If you're trying to get rid of us, you've got a hell of a fight on your hands, baby."

Eight years ago, Elizabeth would have given anything to hear those words. Now they filled her with sadness. She could never be that woman again. "You're wasting your time."

Chandler cupped her jaw. "The last eight years of our lives have been a waste of time, Lizzy. It's time to start living again. We want you and Angie in our lives."

Hayden ran a hand over her hair. "We'll do whatever it takes to get you back."

Surrounded by all that raw masculinity, Elizabeth struggled to keep her voice cool, while inside she wanted nothing more than to believe them. Raising a brow, she backed away from them for her own sanity. "Get me back? You never had me."

Hayden's eyes hardened. "Don't kid yourself, Lizzy. You've always been ours."

# Chapter Three

Elizabeth sighed, rubbing her head where an ache had settled right between her eyes. Angie's grouchiness made it throb even worse.

"I don't wannum!"

Elizabeth shared a look with her mother and tried again. "Angie, you have to eat something. You like scrambled eggs. Finish them and we'll go for a walk."

She wanted to walk around Dakota Springs today, to familiarize herself with all the changes that had been made since she'd gone. She also wanted to check for help wanted signs, and she needed to pick up a few things.

It appeared Angie had other ideas.

Crossing her arms over her chest, Angie pouted belligerently, sticking her bottom lip out as far as she could. "No. Wanna see the horses."

Her mother hid a smile as she shook out two aspirin. "She sure does love horses, doesn't she?"

Elizabeth sighed again, smiling her thanks as she accepted the tablets. "She's never even seen one in person, but all of a sudden she's obsessed with them."

Angie glared at Elizabeth before turning to her grandmother. "Becky told me that I have to ride a horse or nobody's gonna like me."

Elizabeth sighed tiredly. She'd slept very little the night before and found herself struggling for patience. "Becky's wrong. People will like you if you don't ride. Not everyone in Dakota Springs rides horses. Look at Grandma and Grandpa. They don't ride, and everyone loves them." Spotting the local paper her father had pushed aside, she picked it up and began searching the help wanted ads. Grabbing a pen, she started reading, hoping that Angie would eat her breakfast.

"I wanna ride a horse now!"

Elizabeth went back to the paper and downed two aspirin with her coffee. A few of the jobs listed were within walking distance. "Not today, Angie. We'll see the horses another day."

Several families kept horses, but none on the scale of Hayden and Chandler's spread. They bred and trained horses and were considered the best.

Angie would love the ranch, but after what happened last night, Elizabeth couldn't go near it. Or them.

"You pwomised."

Elizabeth sighed again. "I said that we would see the horses one day but not today. Come on, sweetie. Mommy has a lot of things to do today. Wouldn't you like to go see the park?"

"Is there horses there?"

Scooping up a forkful of eggs, she offered them to her daughter. "No, baby. The park doesn't have any horses. But if you're not going to be a good girl, we're not going to go see any at all."

Petulantly, Angie pushed the fork away and turned her face.

Grateful that a knock at the door interrupted what might have turned into a full-fledged temper tantrum, Elizabeth went back to the paper as her father went to answer it.

"Hayden, Chandler. Good morning. What a surprise." Her father's tone implied it was anything but.

Elizabeth stiffened, her insides fluttering. Her face burned as memories of what they'd done to her last night made her clit tingle even now.

Her father grinned and gestured toward the table. "I'm having breakfast with my girls. Would you like to join us?"

Hayden's pained smile made Elizabeth's heart lurch. "You're a lucky man."

Both Hayden and Chandler wore faded denims, white t-shirts lovingly molded to their muscular frames, and their good cowboy boots. The strenuous work they did on a daily basis showed. Not an ounce of fat could be seen anywhere. Those bodies didn't come from a gym, like her ex-husband's had. Roped with hard muscle, Hayden and Chandler's bodies had been sculpted over time by years of backbreaking work and were built for strength.

Hayden lifted a brow at her continued silence, making her face burn as she realized she'd been staring. "Good morning, Lizzy."

Elizabeth looked away. "Good morning. What brings the two of you by this morning?"

Chandler looked down at Angie, frowning at her belligerent pose.

Angie put her head down, not meeting his eyes, and crossing her arms over her chest again.

Kneeling beside her, Chandler tapped a finger under her chin. "What's wrong, Angel?"

Angie lifted her eyes. "My name's not Angel. It's Angie."

Chandler lifted a brow and took a seat next to her, accepting a cup of coffee from her mother. "I know, but you look like an angel to me."

Elizabeth grimaced. "She may look like an angel, but she's not being very angelic this morning. Have you two eaten?" Good manners dictated that she ask, but she couldn't imagine sitting with them long enough for them to eat. The kitchen felt much smaller since they'd entered. Their presence was overwhelming, making it feel as though they'd sucked all of the air out of the room.

Hayden accepted his own cup with a smile and sat down next to Elizabeth, smiling at Angie who sat on Elizabeth's other side. "Hours ago. What's the problem?"

Elizabeth picked up her own coffee. "Angie doesn't want to finish her breakfast unless I agree to take her to see horses today."

Paula looked at the clock. "You father and I have to get to the garage. We'll see you at dinner."

Hayden smiled up at her, a warmer smile than usual. "We wanted to invite Lizzy and Angie to the ranch for dinner if that's all right with you."

Elizabeth's head shot up. "But I—"

"I think that's a wonderful idea." Her mother quickly gathered her things, kissing Angie on the cheek before turning to Elizabeth. "If you can't get your errands done today, give me a call, and I'll pick up what you need."

Elizabeth jumped out of her chair as soon as the door closed behind them. Sitting so close to Hayden played hell with her nerves. "Angie, please eat your breakfast so we can go."

Chandler sipped his coffee, eyeing Angie. "Why don't you want your breakfast? Don't you like eggs?"

Angie pushed the eggs around on her plate but wouldn't answer.

Elizabeth went to the kitchen sink and began washing the breakfast dishes. "She loves scrambled eggs, but she's mad at me because she wants to see horses. Now. Her friend back home, Becky, told her that when she moved here she would have to learn to ride or no one would like her. She refuses to do anything until she gets to ride a horse."

Chandler hid a smile and nodded. "Oh. Well, I guess we should be going then. We just came out to see if Angie wanted to see the puppies, but if she won't mind her momma—"

"Puppies?"

With her back to the table, Elizabeth couldn't see her daughter's face, but heard the excitement in her voice. "Maybe another time. Angie's grouchy today and we have a lot of errands to do."

"Mommy! I wanna see the puppies."

Elizabeth turned around to tell her 'no', automatically snapping her mouth shut when Hayden lifted a hand. Irritated that she'd reacted automatically to his authority, she glared at him.

Ignoring her, Hayden sat back, shaking his head at Angie. "Only good girls get to see the puppies. Maybe if you finish your breakfast and be a good girl while your momma does what she needs to do, we can go see the puppies and horses later."

Angie's eyes went wide. "You have puppies *and* horses?"

Chandler's soft chuckle sent a wave of longing through Elizabeth, and she turned back to her chore to hide it. "Yes. We have a *lot* of horses. Your momma used to ride them all the time. Eat your breakfast so we can get going."

Elizabeth turned slightly, determined to keep them from planning her day. "We don't have the time to go out to your ranch today. Maybe another time."

Angie stopped shoveling in eggs to protest. "Mommy, I wanna see the puppies and the horses. I'll be good."

With a tender smile, Hayden wiped away the egg that dribbled out of her mouth.

Trying to harden her heart against that smile, Elizabeth shook her head. She needed to come to grips with her feelings before she spent any more time with them. "Angie—"

Chandler interrupted her. "Your momma's the boss. Why don't you finish your breakfast and get your shoes? Maybe if you're a good girl while we do what your momma has to do, we can go to the ranch later. The puppies and horses will still be there."

"'Kay."

Angry now that he'd more or less promised Angie a trip to the ranch, Elizabeth started to turn to tell him 'no' when Chandler's hard body pressed against her back, pinning her to the sink. She automatically started to lean back against him before she caught herself. Her nipples beaded, pushing against her lacy bra as an ache settled low in her abdomen. Accepting the empty cup from him, she shuddered, hoping he hadn't noticed. "You can't promise her things like that without asking me. I have no intention of going out to the Double S today."

Chandler's lips brushed her ear, sending a shiver racing through her. It brought to mind the havoc they'd created in her so effortlessly the night before. A pool of lust swam languorously through her system, melting everything in its path. His hands settled on her waist, pulling her more firmly back against him. "All's fair, darlin'."

Elizabeth smothered a moan, frantically trying to maintain her composure. "I didn't realize we were at war." She absently heard Hayden speaking softly to Angie but couldn't focus on their conversation.

Chandler's hands slid up to cover her breasts, startling a gasp from her and making her nipples tingle. "It's not war, darlin'."

"Mommy, I'm done!"

Elizabeth jolted in Chandler's arms, grateful that he released her. She went to gather her daughter's dishes, unsurprised that her hands shook as she fought to regulate her breathing.

Out of Angie's view, Chandler slid a hand over Elizabeth's hip. "Come on, Angie. Let's go find your shoes."

With her face burning, Elizabeth turned back to the sink to wash the rest of the dishes, stiffening when she heard the scrape of Hayden's chair.

He moved in close behind her as Chandler had done, dropping his cup into the dishwater and sliding his arms around her. "Do you have any idea what it does to me to be anywhere near you?" His hands moved up to cover her breasts and began to massage gently. "Why the hell did you have to get married? You were supposed to come back here after you graduated. Christ, I've missed you like hell." Burying his face in her neck, he breathed deeply. "No one else smells like you."

Fighting the urge to lean back against him, Elizabeth grabbed his hands with her wet, soapy ones and pushed them away. Unnerved at the ache that settled low in her abdomen, she snapped at him. "Why the hell would I have come back here? You and Chandler both made your feelings for me plain enough. I've already made enough mistakes. I'm not about to make any more."

Hayden massaged her shoulders. "When we get some time alone,

Chandler and I are going to explain what happened eight years ago." He froze, tightening his grip and spun her around to face him. "Mistakes? Why does it sound like you're talking about more than just marrying the wrong man?"

Cursing herself for lowering her guard, Elizabeth reached for a towel. "It doesn't matter. Get out of my way." Drying her hands, she started past him, but Hayden pulled her up short.

"Explain."

Elizabeth shoved at him, wondering why she even bothered when he didn't move so much as an inch. "No. Look, I came back here to start over. I want Angie to be raised in a small town and for both of us to live close to my parents. The people in this town are old-fashioned. You know as well as I do they'd never accept what you're proposing." Gritting her teeth, she glared up at him. "Damn it, you've got me talking about it as if it could happen. It won't, Hayden. Ever. After what you and Chandler did to me and what I put up with from that jerk I married, I'm never tying myself to a man again."

Hayden pulled her close in an unbreakable grip, his eyes hooded. "We're not going to allow you to stick your head in the sand and ignore this thing between us. You can't throw away the rest of your life just because your marriage didn't work out."

Elizabeth wanted nothing more than to lean into him, to feel his arms come around her as she cried for all the lost years. Instead she shoved him, her bitterness spewing. "I'm not throwing my life away. I'm living it without a man. Richard cheated on me from the start. You and Chandler only feel obligated to take care of me. How long do you think we'd be together before you two did the same thing?" Just the thought of it filled her with dread. She'd never survive it.

Hayden's jaw clenched. "Never. Why didn't you leave your husband when you found out he was cheating?"

Careful to keep her voice low, she glanced at the doorway, not wanting Angie to overhear. Maybe if he understood her bitterness he would back off. "Because of his father, the senator. Richard Sr. said a divorce would hurt his career. The senator, his wife, Vivian, and Richard threatened to take Angie away if I tried to get a divorce. I never slept with my husband again. My marriage was over from the beginning. If you and Chandler think I'm going to make the same mistake again, you're crazy."

A muscle worked in Hayden's jaw. "That son of a bitch." Grabbing her shoulders, he shook her once. "Why didn't you call me? I would have taken care of it."

Elizabeth pushed at his chest and broke free, but she knew it was only because he allowed it. "I grew up, remember? I wouldn't have called anyone for help, least of all you and your brother. Contrary to what both of you think, I can take care of myself." Lifting a brow, she smiled mockingly. "See? I don't need either one of you."

Hayden grabbed her, lifting her to her toes, his eyes hard and furious. "You're ours, Lizzy. Both of you. You might as well get that through that hard head of yours right now."

"You son of a—"

"Mommy! I putted my shoes."

Shaken, Elizabeth shoved at Hayden and moved to her daughter, not bothering to correct her. "Great, darling. Let me get my purse and we'll go. Say goodbye to Mr. Hayden and Mr. Chandler."

Hayden ignored her glare and smiled smugly. "That won't be necessary. We'll go with you to do your errands before we take you back to the ranch. That way you can see how the entire town has already accepted us." Looking at Angie, he grinned. "Then we can go see the puppies and the horses."

"Yay!"

Elizabeth glared at him again, having to raise her voice over Angie's excited squeals. "You haven't won, Hayden."

"We will. That's all that matters. Get your shoes and your purse so we can go."

\* \* \* \*

Hayden wanted to throttle her.

Watching her walk stiffly down the street a few feet in front of him, he couldn't keep his eyes away from her delectable ass in those skin tight jeans.

He knew it would take some time, but it pissed him off that she didn't even want to listen to them. She didn't believe they loved her even after all of the fights he and Chandler had had over her.

It had taken a lot of soul searching, the kind that was best accomplished when drunk, before he and Chandler had decided that the only way they could all be happy would be for *both* of them to have her. It seemed like a good idea, especially after several straight whiskeys.

To their immense surprise, the next day it had still made sense.

Sure, it was unconventional, but if they could be happy, he didn't give a damn what other people thought.

But he knew Lizzy would, and he cared for her parents very much.

So they'd ironed out rules and gathered all the information they could find on ménage relationships. He'd been surprised to learn that they were more prevalent than either one of them had ever suspected. They'd learned a hell of a lot, especially about themselves.

What they'd heard and read about taking a woman together kept him awake at night, hard as hell, aching for Lizzy.

All that had been put on hold when they'd learned she'd gotten married.

As soon as her parents had told them about the divorce, they'd immediately let it be known that they wanted her and that both of them loved her. At first there had been a lot of awkward silences but as the folks of Dakota Springs got used to it and saw how anxiously they both waited for her the awkwardness ended. Glad now that they'd done it in time for the shock to wear off, he watched Elizabeth now as old friends greeted her.

Watching her smile and laugh, he nearly burst with pride. His little Lizzy had grown up, and he was falling in love with her all over again.

# Chapter Four

Elizabeth wanted to scream.

Walking around town with Hayden and Chandler proved to be more nerve-wracking than she could have imagined. By staying close, they gave the image that the four of them had already become a family.

She was stopped often by people she'd known her entire life but hadn't seen in years. She did her best to ignore Hayden and Chandler as they stood by waiting patiently for her to finish her conversations. Sometimes they would join in, but often they just greeted the other person and stood next to her with a hand on her arm or shoulder and talked with Angie.

They made sure that everyone they came across, from the teller at the bank to the butcher, knew that she and Angie were with them.

Their possessive attitudes had her grinding her teeth.

She cut her errands short and headed toward the pharmacy to get a few items she would need and let the rest wait for another time.

Trying to concentrate on her purchases and not on Hayden trailing slightly behind her, she listened, reluctantly amused as Angie tried to convince Chandler to buy her some candy in the next aisle. She couldn't see either one of them, but from the tone of her daughter's voice, she knew the expression on Angie's face.

"But I been good. I like this kind. Mommy lets me have it. If you get it for me, I'll be good."

Hayden's lips touched Elizabeth's neck. "Angie's quite the little negotiator, isn't she? I'm going to put her in charge of sales."

Fighting her body's response to having him so close, Elizabeth turned away to reach for a bottle of baby shampoo to add to her basket. "Chandler's going to fall for it. I just hope he doesn't let her eat too much."

Hayden chuckled next to her ear. "Of course he's going to fall for it. We're both going to do our best to spoil both of you rotten. Don't worry. He won't let her have more than a piece or two. We have to take care of our girls. Speaking of taking care of you, are you on the pill?"

Looking around frantically to make sure no one had overheard him, she smacked him in the stomach. "Hayden!"

He rubbed his stomach absently as he reached for another bottle of the same baby shampoo. "Chandler and I have both had physicals. The doc has our permission to show the results to you whenever you want to see them. Do you or Angie have any health problems?"

Knowing what he was asking regarding her, her face burned. "No, we're both fine. I had myself checked regularly since the beginning of my marriage and one of the reasons I never slept with him again. I didn't want to catch anything. And Angie's always been healthy as a horse, thank God."

Turning, she continued down the aisle, a jolt of heat going through her when Hayden wrapped an arm around her from behind and bent to whisper in her ear. "Are you on the pill, baby?"

Elizabeth tried to pull away, but Hayden wouldn't let her. Already her nipples beaded, desperate for his touch, the underside of her breasts tingling where they rested on his forearms. "No. Okay. I'm not. Now let go of me."

"Be still. One more question. Do you want to get pregnant right away or would you rather wait a few months?"

Her stomach clenched as his hand covered her abdomen. Closing her eyes, she imagined what it would be like to be carrying their child. Her panties grew damper just picturing them in bed together, their heat wrapped around her, inside her. Oh, God. Pushing out of his arms, she took several shaky steps, needing to put some distance between them. Swallowing heavily, she struggled to keep her tone cool. "I have no intention of getting pregnant again."

Hayden inclined his head in that arrogant way he had of implying that he'd granted permission even though she hadn't asked for it. "All right, baby. We'll wait a few months, but Chandler and I are anxious to have more children and we're not getting any younger. It'll be better for Angie if the children are close in age. We'll take care of it."

Elizabeth opened her mouth to deliver a scathing comment she hadn't quite thought up yet, but Hayden had already walked away.

She went back to her shopping, wishing with all of her heart that she could truly believe she could have both of them. Even now they treated her like the girl she'd once been instead of the woman she'd become.

Hayden came back around the corner, smiling as he listened to Angie's chatter in the next aisle. He dropped several boxes of condoms in her basket before taking it from her. "What else do you need?"

Ignoring him, she dropped a children's pain reliever into the basket, frowning when he added another. "Hayden, why the hell are you adding another of every single thing I put in the basket? One is enough. I can always come back when I need more."

"One for your parent's house and one for the ranch. That way you and Angie will have what you need while you're there."

"Hayden—"

Come and get the rest of what you need. Martha will have lunch ready by now."

"Hayden, I still have something to do. I never agreed to have lunch with you today."

Chandler met them at the end of the aisle with Angie in his arms. "We'll do whatever you have to do and then we'll go out to the ranch. Right, Angie?"

Elizabeth watched in amazement as Angie giggled, tucking her head against Chandler's neck. "She doesn't let anyone but me or my parents hold her."

Chandler grinned, kissing Angie's hair. "And me. Are you about done? Angie's getting hungry."

Elizabeth gestured toward the pharmacist. "Mr. Wilbur has a 'Help Wanted' sign in the window. I need to talk to him about a job."

Chandler frowned. "Who the h—" He shot a glance at Angie. "Who's going to watch Angie while you're working?"

Hayden gripped her elbow and headed toward the counter. "You already have a job, taking care of Angie."

"Taking care of Angie doesn't pay the bills. Would you two mind watching her for a few minutes so I can talk to Mr. Wilbur?"

Hayden led her to the counter and started to unpack their purchases from the basket. "There's no need. We have a job for you at the ranch." He lifted a hand when she opened her mouth to speak. "We'll tell you all about it over lunch."

Elizabeth's face burned when he pulled out the boxes of condoms. Shooting a glance at Mr. Wilbur, she leaned close, whispering to Hayden. "Do you have to buy those now?"

Hayden's lips twitched. "We're gonna need 'em soon. Besides, it wouldn't matter if I bought them now or later. Mr. Wilbur's gonna know who they're for."

"Mommy, can I have a choc'late?"

Elizabeth smiled at her daughter who was held securely in Chandler's arms and wearing a smear of chocolate on her mouth. "It looks like you already have. Oops. I forgot to buy wipes." She went to get them and came back just as Mr. Wilbur had begun bagging their purchases. Opening the package, she pulled one out, setting the package on the counter. "Let's get you cleaned up."

"Hello, Elizabeth. Your daughter's a real beauty. She looks a lot like you did at that age."

Smiling, Elizabeth finished and turned to the pharmacist, who also happened to own the drugstore. "Thank you, Mr. Wilbur. It's nice to see you again. I see you have a sign in the window. I wanted to talk to you about—"

Hayden nudged her aside. "No. He's not hiring you. Nobody in town's going to hire you. Chandler, grab some more of those wipes."

Mr. Wilbur's hair had turned mostly gray in the years since she'd gone, but his eyes still twinkled. He smiled broadly as he finished ringing up their purchases. "How does it feel to be back home? These two have been bears since you left. When's the wedding?"

Elizabeth clenched her jaw. "There's not going to be—"

Hayden held out the money, putting a hand over hers to prevent her from opening her purse. "As soon as we can rope her in. She doesn't believe that we're both in love with her."

Chandler snuck Angie another small piece of chocolate that Elizabeth guessed she wasn't supposed to notice. "She doesn't believe the people in Dakota Springs will accept it. We're just going to have to convince her."

Mr. Wilbur chuckled. "She's giving you a hard time then?"

Hayden accepted the change, smiling down at her. "Sure is."

Elizabeth glared at Hayden. "She's standing right here, you know?"

Chandler grabbed another wipe to erase traces of the last piece of chocolate. "Grouchy, too. She must be hungry."

"I wanna see the horse and the puppies!"

Chandler lifted Angie high above his head. "You betcha, baby. Let's go."

Walking back to her parent's house, Elizabeth tried to pick Angie up, but she wanted to walk holding Chandler's hand.

Chandler's smug smile made her want to hit something.

She and Hayden strolled behind them. "Hayden, I don't have time to go to the ranch. I need to look for a job."

Hayden's wrapped an arm around her shoulders, pulling her close. "You're in luck. We're hiring."

"Damn it, Hayden."

Hayden put a finger over her lips, gesturing toward Angie.

"Watch your language. She's a tattletale."

Angie skipped ahead, not at all interested in the park they came to. "I wanna see the puppies and the horses."

Everyone they passed smiled indulgently at seeing the four of them together. Elizabeth found herself watching closely for any sign of disgust or censure. To her amazement, she saw none.

Hearing a squeal, Elizabeth turned and found herself nearly strangled by a very pregnant woman. "Patty?" Hugging her back, they both started talking at once. Patty Fisher, Patty Conner now, had been her best friend from kindergarten until Elizabeth left town eight years ago. They hadn't been in touch since right after Angie was born. They talked for several minutes, making arrangements to meet later in the week for lunch to catch up.

Patty sobered. "Elizabeth, we were all sorry to hear about your divorce, but I'm so glad that you decided to come home." She smiled, showing her dimples. "These two grouches have been driving everyone crazy waiting for you."

Chandler chuckled. "Lizzy doesn't believe that. You look beautiful, Patty. Only a few more weeks, huh? Give me your bags. I'll put them in the car for you."

Patty grinned and turned over her shopping bags. "Yes. I can't wait and neither can Brian." She turned to Elizabeth. "We had such a hard time getting pregnant. I had two miscarriages. We'll have trouble believing it until we have her in our arms."

Elizabeth jolted at Angie's frightened cry. She spun and started toward her, but Hayden got there faster. To Elizabeth's astonishment, her daughter flung herself at Hayden, wrapping her arms tightly around his neck as he straightened.

"He's gonna get me!"

Hayden lifted her high in his arms as a big dog ran up to them, his leash trailing behind. "It's okay, baby. He won't get you. I've got you. Shh."

Chandler raced up, placing himself between the dog and the

women. "Hey, Buster. It's okay, Angie. Buster gets loose from Charlie all the time." He bent to pet the large dog, grabbing his leash.

A little boy about ten years old came running up. "I'm sorry, Mr. Scott. Buster got away from me again." He looked up at Angie, who'd plastered herself to Hayden. "It's okay. He won't hurt you. I promise. You wanna pet him?"

Angie didn't answer. Instead, she tucked her face back into Hayden's neck.

Hayden rubbed her back, crooning softly to her as he held her securely against his chest. The play of emotion on his face as he held Angie close brought a lump to Elizabeth's throat.

Chandler handed Charlie the leash. "It's okay, Charlie. Angie isn't used to dogs. We're taking her out to the ranch to see the new puppies."

Charlie grinned. "I'll bet she's happy she gets the pick of the litter, huh?"

Bending, Chandler whispered. "She doesn't know."

The little boy turned red, shuffling his feet. "Sorry, Mr. Scott."

Chandler ruffled his hair. "No harm done. You'd better start eating more if you're going to be strong enough to hang on to Buster."

"Momma says I'm eating her out of house and home. Are you and Mr. Scott both really gonna be her daddies?"

Elizabeth's face burned, but none of the others seemed to see anything wrong with the question.

Chandler glanced at her and nodded. "Yes."

"Wow! Cool. Two dads. I have to go. My mom's waiting for me."

Elizabeth looked up to see a woman waving in the distance. She waved back as Hayden and Chandler each lifted a hand in acknowledgement.

Patty touched Elizabeth's arm. "There are times I wish I had another man around the house and times I want to kill the one I have. You're a braver woman than I am to take on these two. Don't forget our lunch date."

Elizabeth answered her, not quite sure what she said, but it must have been the right thing because Patty just smiled, nodded and walked away. She turned back to find both Hayden and Chandler watching her intently. "Are the two of you out of your minds?"

Chandler put an arm around her shoulder, nudging her along. "Come on. We're all hungry. We can talk all you want back at the ranch." Sobering, he slowed, allowing a little more distance between them, Hayden and Angie. "Did you have any problems when you were pregnant with Angie?"

"No, everything went perfectly."

Chandler smiled and picked up the pace. "She sure is a sweetheart. Was she close to your husband?"

Averting her eyes, she shook her head. "No." Smiling as Angie attempted to talk Hayden out of another piece of candy, she lowered her voice. "Don't believe that angelic face. She has her moments."

Chandler chuckled and bent to brush her lips with his, sending her heart racing. "All females do. That's what makes them so irresistible. We're already wrapped around her little finger and the stinker knows it. Didn't your husband feel the same way?"

"No." Not wanting to talk about it, she hurriedly changed the subject. "A good father has to learn to say no." Horrified at what she'd said, she looked away from his questioning look. "I meant in general, not you specifically." Damn, she hated when they made her so nervous her tongue ran away with her. She scrambled to find something else to talk about, but he had her too flustered to think. The hand caressing her waist moved to her hip, pulling her even closer.

"Hayden and I will be good fathers to Angie, Lizzy."

Elizabeth shook her head. "I told you I wouldn't get married again."

Chandler led her up the driveway to her parent's house to put her things away while Hayden took Angie and the other bag to the car. Once inside, Chandler pinned her against the wall and bent to kiss her deeply. "Of course you'll marry us. We've just got to convince you. Let's get to the ranch. I'm starving." Pressing against her mound, he nibbled at her lips. "And not just for lunch."

Uncomfortable and more than a little aroused, she pulled away and went to her bedroom. Something felt wrong and it took her a few minutes to discover what had happened. "That bastard!"

Chandler came rushing in, scanning the room. "What is it, Lizzy?"

Elizabeth looked around, opening the closet to look inside but she knew she wouldn't find it. Pointing to the window, she answered before she thought about the consequences. "That window was closed when I left. The air conditioner is on. And my bag is missing."

She knew damned well she'd left it on the chair beside the window, but continued to look for it until Chandler grabbed her arm. "Someone broke in here and stole your bag? Is anything else missing?"

After searching the house, they ended up back in the kitchen. "I don't think anything else is missing, but I'll have my mother check." Plopping into the kitchen chair, she ran a hand tiredly over her face. "I doubt if they would take anything else. They thought they had what they wanted."

What the hell could she do now? She couldn't very well allow anyone to break into her parents' home, but if she called the sheriff, she'd have to tell him the truth. How would she keep Angie safe when they discovered they hadn't gotten what they were after and come back?

She should have known better.

"Damn it, Lizzy. What's this all about? What was in the bag?"

Chandler's harsh tone finally penetrated.

Trying to remember what she hadn't yet put away, she frowned. "Uh, just a couple of sweaters and some toiletries."

"What did you mean, they thought they had what they wanted? What did they think was in the bag? Who the hell are *they* anyway?"

Seeing Hayden approach the back door, she stood. "I have to go shut the window and call my mother."

"To hell with that. We're calling the sheriff."

"I can't, Chandler."

Hayden looked in before opening the back door, keeping Angie from seeing inside. "What's taking so long? You two better not have started something—"

Chandler opened the door. Smiling at Angie, he took her from Hayden's arms. "We have a minor situation here." He quickly explained everything to Hayden, keeping his voice low as he occupied Angie with a cookie.

Hayden kept glancing at her, his face becoming more granite-like with each passing minute. Finally he nodded, approaching Lizzy. "Let's go into the other room for a minute."

Resigned, she allowed him to lead her into the living room. Chandler followed, picking up one of Angie's dolls to keep her entertained while they talked.

Shooting a glance at her daughter, Elizabeth leaned forward. "Look, I don't want you involved in this. Just trust me that I can't call the sheriff."

Hayden sat back, his expression cold. "Tell us everything right now or I'm calling your parents and the sheriff and I'll paddle your ass in front of both of them until you tell me the truth."

Damn. He meant it.

Sighing, she glanced at Angie meaningfully. "In order to escape the situation I found myself in, I used funds meant to keep me silent to hire someone to document certain immoral actions. I needed this proof to get out of my situation. I got proof of more than one person conducting immoral activities. A powerful man had to let me have my way, knowing I would use this material to gain my freedom."

Hayden groaned. "So you still have the potential to use it and it's making him nervous."

"Apparently. I can't think of any other reason for someone to break in here and take the bag I'd been keeping it in."

Hayden and Chandler exchanged a troubled look.

Chandler adjusted Angie on his lap. "And where is this information now?"

Glancing at her purse, she smiled. "I keep it with me at all times."

Neither man looked impressed with what she'd managed to do. In fact they both looked downright furious. Hayden stood and picked up her purse and began to rummage through it.

Jumping up, she tried to reach around him for it, but he kept her away until he found a thick manila envelope and pulled it out. "We'll hold onto this. Call your mother and tell her what happened. I want her to check to see if anything else is missing as soon as she gets home. Tell your dad we'll bring you back in time to check the house out more thoroughly and with something to rig the windows."

Elizabeth nodded, watching as Chandler left the room with Angie. When the back door closed, Hayden grabbed her arm.

"I can't believe you would do something like this. Do you have any idea how much danger you could be in?"

Tugging her arm, she slapped at him. "Damn you. I did what I had to do. I told you the senator only cared about his career."

"Well when we go outside, I'm keeping this in plain view. I want everyone to know that I have it now. Hurry up and call your mother so we can go."

Eyeing him, she reached for the phone. She glanced up at him several times while dialing, disconcerted by his anger. "Hayden, I told you that I can handle this."

"Yeah, you're doing a good job of it. What would have happened if you and Angie would have been here alone while this asshole broke in? *We'll* handle this from now on. You just do as you're told."

"Damn it, Hayden. I'm not a child." Her mother answered just then, keeping her from arguing further. As she told her mother what happened, she watched Hayden leave the room.

Damn it. The last thing she wanted was for Hayden and Chandler to think they had to solve all of her problems for her.

She heard her bedroom window close and lock again before he reappeared just as she hung up the phone.

"Let's get to the ranch. I'm going to put this envelope in my safe. Then we'll talk about the job you insist on having. You'll work at the ranch or you'll work nowhere."

"Damn it, Hayden—"

"Shut up, Lizzy. I'm so furious right now, you're lucky I don't turn you over my knee. Get your stuff and let's go." Pulling out his cell phone, he punched in numbers as he walked outside, glaring at her through the screen.

Elizabeth gathered her purse and keys and started outside, feeling like a child who'd been admonished, and she didn't like it one bit.

# Chapter Five

At the ranch, Elizabeth met Martha, the older woman who took care of the house for them. Sally, the woman who'd worked for their parents had retired a few years ago.

Her face wreathed in smiles, Martha greeted them warmly. "Well now, you were right. She is a beauty. And the little one! My, my, she does look like an angel, doesn't she?" After putting out cold cuts and fresh potato salad, Martha gathered her purse and keys. "I'll be going now. I'll see you tomorrow morning." She paused at Elizabeth's chair. "Everything's ready. If there's anything that needs to be changed, you just let me know."

Elizabeth blinked, turning to Chandler when Martha left. "Ready? Changed? What's she talking about?"

Chandler handed her two slices of bread and started making a peanut butter and jelly sandwich for Angie. "I'll show you after we eat."

Hayden excused himself to put the envelope in the safe, glaring at her when he came back. "I still can't believe you kept that from us." His lips twitching, he took his seat. "But it's just like you. I'm sure neither one of them knew what hit him."

Beaming, Elizabeth warmed inside. "Yeah, the senator looked a little surprised."

Thankfully Angie talked through lunch, basking in Hayden and Chandler's attention. She chatted happily as she told them all about her best friend, Becky.

Elizabeth's eyes stung, her heart melting at the way Hayden and Chandler appeared to be completely enthralled by everything Angie did or said.

Richard had never given Angie any attention at all.

"I wanna see the puppies!"

Hayden finished his second sandwich and smiled. "Of course you do. Come on then, angel. Let's go see the puppies and the horses while Chandler shows some things to your momma." He stood, lifting Angie from her seat and turned toward the door. Halfway there, he looked over his shoulder to stare at Elizabeth. His eyes darkened as they moved over her, settling on her breasts. "I'm sure you surprised the heck out of them."

Elizabeth, who'd already come to her feet to clear up the remains of their lunch, froze, her nipples warming and pebbling under his stare as if he'd actually stroked them.

When he lifted his gaze to hers, the heat in his eyes sent a wave of longing through her, tightening her insides and making her ache with need for him.

She took a step toward him before she could stop herself, coming to a halt as his eyes flared, the promise of future satisfaction gleaming in them. Staring at his back as he walked out the door, she jumped as Chandler touched her arm.

He grabbed the bag from the drugstore and, holding her hand with his other, led her back through the foyer and up the stairs. "Let me show you some of the changes we've made."

Elizabeth found herself pulled up the stairs and down a hallway. "Damn it, Chandler. I'm not letting you pressure me into moving in here."

Chandler took her past several rooms until he got to the one at the end. Pushing the door open, he hauled her inside before closing and locking it behind him. Opening the bag, he tossed one of the boxes of condoms toward the headboard and dropped the bag on the floor. "I'm not trying to pressure you, Lizzy, but I'll be damned if I'll let you put up road blocks where there are none."

Seeing the intention in his eyes, Elizabeth took a step back, fighting the urge to leap at him. "We're different people now, Chandler. We don't even know each other anymore."

Chandler's grin flashed. "Then let's get reacquainted, darlin'." Moving in quickly, he wrapped an arm around her waist and pulled her close, his lips hovering over hers. "We know each other, Lizzy. Some things never change and this thing between us is never gonna go away. You know that as well as I do."

At the touch of his lips on hers, she melted. Plastered against him, her curves fitted against his hard muscular frame, Elizabeth felt alive, desired as only Chandler and Hayden could make her feel.

His kiss sent her soaring, her lust for him quickly burning out of control. Panicked, she pushed at him, instinctively trying to keep him from taking more of her than she was ready to give.

Chandler surprised her by raising his head, his eyes glittering as he smiled down at her. "I won't do anything you don't want me to do, Lizzy, but I'm not gonna let you hold back from me."

Gulping in air, she curled her hands in his shirt, not letting him pull away. She needed him. She'd needed him too long to deny it any longer. "Damn you, Chandler." Grabbing fistfuls of his thick hair, she pulled his head back down.

Moaning into his mouth, she pushed herself closer, trembling when his arms tightened around her. She'd dreamed of being in his arms this way thousands of times but hadn't been prepared for the reality of it, especially when she knew where it would lead. Her nipples tingled where they rubbed against his chest, making her desperate to feel his naked flesh against hers.

As though reading her mind, he began to undress her. After tossing her shirt aside, he quickly divested her of her bra. Breaking off his kiss, he held her slightly away from him, his thumbs brushing back and forth over her nipples. "Look at you. You are the most beautiful thing I've ever seen in my life." He lifted his gaze, no longer smiling. "I've got to see the rest of you, darlin'."

Holding onto his shoulders for support, she arched her breasts in offering. She would die if he didn't touch them soon. Her breath hitched as he reached for the fastening of her jeans.

He knelt in front of her, lowering them slowly, his fingers tracing over every inch of skin he revealed.

When they hit the floor, she quickly stepped out of them, gasping as Chandler licked her belly. Holding him against her, she shuddered as he started to lower her damp panties.

"I gotta taste you, darlin'."

His lips scorched her stomach, his hands firm as he stripped her of her last remaining item of clothing. When she hurriedly stepped out of her panties, he nudged her to keep going as his mouth moved lower. Her mind reeling, she obediently took another step back and felt the edge of the mattress against her thighs. Another nudge toppled her onto it.

Chandler took immediate advantage, edging her thighs apart and shouldering his way between them. Holding them high and wide, he draped them over his shoulders.

Elizabeth grabbed fistfuls of the thick quilt beneath her, her mind going blank as Chandler swiped his tongue through her slit. She bit her lip to silence her cries as he slid his tongue repeatedly over her folds and into her. It felt too intimate and too intense as he used his mouth on her and held her spread wide. Her clit burned, throbbing for attention, feeling as though it had doubled in size.

She fought his hold, the pleasure too intense to remain still. It aroused her even more when he held firm. Something about being held this way, forced to endure the incredible pleasure excited the hell out of her. No longer able to hold back her cries, she twisted as much as Chandler's hold allowed, moaning and crying out as he took her higher and higher.

Lifting his head, his warm breath wafted over her folds. "Come for me."

Elizabeth couldn't have done anything else as Chandler focused his attention on her clit, sucking it into his mouth and stroking it with his tongue. Her body stiffened in shock as bursts of electricity burst from her clit and spread outward. "Chandler! Oh God, Chandler." Her throat wouldn't work right making her voice came out as a series of harsh croaks.

Swallowing heavily, she gulped in air as the bed dipped. Hearing the rustle of clothing, she looked down, getting her first look at his naked body. Sitting up on her elbows, she smiled her appreciation. "Holy hell, Chandler."

His cocky smile sent her heart racing again. "All for you, darlin'." He wrapped a fist around his thick cock and began stroking.

She couldn't look away from it, her hands itching to touch him. Sitting up, she pushed Chandler's hands away to take him into her own. Kneeling in front of him, she began running her hands over him, touching her lips to a chest corded with muscle. Working her way down his body, she bent and touched the tip of his cock with her tongue, closing her eyes as she savored his taste.

A groan rumbled deep in his chest, the raw sound of it adding to the erotic atmosphere. His hands tightened in her hair as she took his cock into her mouth. "Jesus, Lizzy." The sounds he made told her she must be doing something right.

Sucking gently, scared to death of hurting him, she slid her hands around him to knead his tight buns. Stroking the underside of his cock with her tongue, she smiled inwardly as the hands in her hair tightened even more.

"Damn, Lizzy. Stop. No more. No more." He pulled her away from his cock and tumbled her back onto the mattress before grabbing the box of condoms. He ripped the box open, sending condoms flying everywhere.

Elizabeth laughed as he cursed and finally managed to rip the foil and don one of them.

Chandler poised the tip of his cock at her slick opening. "So you think this is funny?" Pressing just the head of his cock inside, he paused. "Let's see how long you're laughing."

Elizabeth's laughter died as he began to fill her.

Chandler worked his length into her, an inch at a time. "You're not laughing now, are you, darlin'?"

Amazed that this was finally really happening, Elizabeth wrapped her legs around him as he pressed deep, filling her completely. She trembled with excitement as he surrounded her with his heat, both inside and out.

His big hand tangled in her hair, tilting her head back to nuzzle her jaw as his other hand slid under her, lifting her into his slow, smooth, strokes. "Nothing in my life has ever felt as good as being inside you." His voice, raw and needy, rumbled in her ear, exciting her even more.

Digging her heels into his tight buttocks, she lifted into his thrusts, her pussy clenching desperately at his cock as it slid over delicate tissue. She couldn't believe how good it felt to have him finally inside her after all the years of wanting. Her body gathered and sparks of pleasure shot from her slit outward with each deliberate stroke. Grabbing his shoulders, she arched her neck as he nibbled at a particularly sensitive spot. "Chandler. Oh, God. It's so good." Tears leaked from the corners of her eyes as the tingles grew stronger. "No, Chandler. Don't let it end."

Chandler moved faster, his strokes taking his cock impossibly deep. He nibbled his way to her lips. "It's only the beginning, darlin'. We've got a life full of lovin' ahead of us."

She tightened on him as his strokes came faster, the pleasure of his thick cock rubbing against too sensitive tissue sent her quickly into another orgasm. Holding onto him tightly, she cried out, aware that he stiffened above her, his low groan against her neck telling her he'd found his own release.

Holding himself deep, his leanly muscled body shuddered in her arms as his own arms tightened around her. After several long minutes of caresses and dizzying kisses, Chandler lifted his head and stared down at her, his eyes searching hers. Apparently pleased with what he saw, he smiled. "Welcome home, darlin'."

Elizabeth smiled back, still shaken by their lovemaking. Even with her inexperience she knew what had just happened had been extraordinary. Limp as a wet noodle, she reached up to smooth a lock of hair from his forehead. A sense of vulnerability had her blurting out her thoughts before she could censor them. "Chandler, you do know how much I care for you, don't you?"

Chandler smiled tenderly, kissing her deeply before lifting his head to stare at her again. "Yes, but do you?"

"Chandler—"

"Come on, darlin'. Angie and Hayden are probably waiting for us." Withdrawing, he dropped another hard kiss on her lips before standing and reaching for her.

"Damn." The reminder had Elizabeth scrambling from the bed and into her clothes. "Damn it, Chandler. I have to get back to Angie. What's Hayden going to think about this? He's going to know what we just did."

Chandler chuckled and pulled her against him, nuzzling her jaw again. Laughing softly, he held her despite her struggles. "Of course he knows what we've been doing. He's going to be anxious to be alone with you." Pulling the panties she'd just slipped on back down again, he slapped her ass lightly. "You'll get used to it, Lizzy."

Elizabeth glared at his back as he went into the adjoining bathroom to rid himself of the condom. She had no intention of getting used to it. She knew if she did, they'd break her heart for sure. Scrambling into her clothes, she hurried to get back to Angie.

\* \* \* \*

Hayden sat at the table to hide the fact that his cock had gotten hard again.

He couldn't take his eyes from Lizzy as she moved around the kitchen, pouring milk and getting Angie some of the cookies Martha had made earlier.

Elizabeth moved gracefully around the kitchen, pouring coffee for the three of them, her face an adorable pink. Her swollen lips and tousled hair added to the appearance that she'd just been well-fucked.

He couldn't wait to wake up to that tousled, dazed look every day.

Her gaze slid to his several times before she looked guiltily away, her face coloring even more.

He didn't care for that part a bit. Every time she did it, it made him even angrier and made his cock jump with the need to take her.

He'd expected that there would be times when jealousy would rear its ugly head, but there'd be no place for it in a relationship like the one they wanted with her.

That didn't keep it from happening.

He couldn't wait to spend some time alone with her. Intimate time. Only then would she look at both of them that way. He waited until she finally sat down, facing him. "How did you like the master bedroom?"

If possible, Elizabeth's face got even redder. "It's nice."

"Nice? Is there something you don't like about it?"

Staring down into her coffee, Elizabeth shook her head. "No, it's fine."

"Do you like the bed?" He hid a smile at her sharp intake of breath.

"Yes, it's nice."

"Do you like the color of the room?"

Sipping her coffee, Elizabeth wouldn't meet his eyes. "The color's fine."

Sitting back, he shared a smile with Chandler and took a sip of his coffee. Putting the cup down, he leaned forward. "What color is it, Lizzy?"

Her eyes flew to his, before she hurriedly looked away again. "White."

Hayden smiled. "Nope."

Jumping to her feet, Elizabeth wiped Angie's mouth and started to gather the remnants of her snack. "We should get home. It's time for Angie's nap."

"Mommy! I wanna ride da horses."

Elizabeth put her daughter's glass in the sink and turned back. "Another day, Angie. You're too tired today."

"No, I not!"

Chandler shared a look with Hayden, not even bothering to hide his grin. "Why don't you let me take her out to see the horses and then she can take a nap here? When she wakes up, we can take her for a ride."

Angie stuck her bottom lip out and kicked her feet. "I wanna ride now."

Hayden shook his head. "After you take a nap you can go for a ride. No nap. No ride." He smothered a grin when Angie looked up at him through her lashes, her bottom lip pushed out even more. "But, Mr. Hayden, I wanna ride. I been good. I take a nap after I ride."

Chandler coughed and stood, moving to the sink to stare out the window, his shoulders shaking.

Hayden somehow managed to keep his expression stern, but it wasn't easy. He wanted to be a good father to Angie. To do that, he would have to learn to put his foot down. With her, he could see that would be a difficult thing to do. She would prove to be just as hard to resist as her mother. Shaking his head, he pushed his coffee aside. "No deal, angel. You can go see the horses, but you can't ride until after your nap. If you don't want to do that, we can take you back to your grandma and grandpa's house and forget the whole thing."

Angie's lip went back in, and she appeared to mull it over. But the little negotiator hadn't finished. "After I take a nap, can I have a puppy?"

Hayden coughed to cover his own laugh and stood to refill his cup. "The puppy is up to your momma. But you can't have one yet. They have to stay with their momma a little bit longer. They're just babies and need their momma."

Angie looked at Elizabeth before turning back and nodding. "'Kay. Where's da puppy's daddy?"

Hayden took his seat again, enjoying her immensely. "Their daddy's name is Sam, and he's out there somewhere."

Angie's face fell and she nodded sadly. "He don't like 'em. My daddy don't like me, too."

Elizabeth gasped, her face draining of all color. "Angie, that's not true. Your father loves you very much."

Angie shrugged and yawned. "My puppy's name's Fluffy."

Elizabeth's shaky smile twisted his gut as she knelt down beside Angie's chair. "Is it? We'll have to talk about a puppy later. Honey, you know how much Mommy loves you, don't you?"

Angie wrapped her arms around Elizabeth's neck and yawned. "I yuv you, too, Mommy. I like 'Kota Springs."

Hayden could see that Angie had just about run out of steam and how upset Elizabeth had become. He shot a glance at his brother, wanting to spend some time alone with Elizabeth and find out more about her ex-husband.

Chandler nodded and lifted a very sleepy Angie from her chair. "Come on, Angie. I'll show you some horses." He bent and kissed Elizabeth's forehead, looking at her worriedly.

Once they'd gone, Hayden leaned forward. "What the hell did your husband do to her?"

She paled even more. "He did nothing to her except ignore her as much as possible. I didn't think she even realized it. He never wanted either one of us, but I tried to keep her away from him as much as possible."

Incredulous, Hayden wrapped his arms around her, pulling her close and tucking her head under his chin. "Then he's an even bigger idiot than I gave him credit for." Holding her slightly away, he wiped the tears on her cheeks. "All those years wasted on a man who didn't deserve either one of you. If I had known, I would have dragged you back here years ago." Pulling her close, he rubbed her back, burying his face in her hair. "I promise you, baby, from now on, both you and Angie will know how much you're loved."

She shook her head and pushed away, frustrating the hell out of him. "Hayden, I'm not risking Angie's happiness, or mine, ever again. We both know the only reason you and Chandler are doing this is out of some sense of obligation. You care for me, but not the way I need, and I'm not going to pin Angie's future on a relationship that's doomed to fail."

Irritated that she wouldn't see what was right in front of her face, he grabbed her hand and tugged her out of the room. "Come here. I want to show you something."

"Hayden, I don't think this is a good idea."

Not answering her, he hid a smile as he paused beside a door as she continued toward the master bedroom. "Here we are."

She flushed again, looking so adorable he wanted to ravage her on the spot. "This isn't the master bedroom."

His cock swelled and hardened again, pushing uncomfortably against his zipper. "I never said we were going to the master bedroom. I want to see what you think of Angie's room."

"Angie's room? Hayden, I told you we're not moving in here."

"Of course you are, but not until we get married. Not with Angie in the picture. Anyway, tell me what you think. We had it painted light pink, but when we went to buy furniture, we didn't have any idea what Angie would like or need. I never knew what a shitload of furniture was out there for little girls. We liked one with a canopy, but didn't know if she would like it. We need you to come with us to pick it out." He watched her face anxiously as she looked around the room. "She likes pink." Hell, almost everything she wore had pink on it somewhere.

Elizabeth's eyes went wide as she looked around the room. "I can't believe you did this. It's beautiful. You even had new carpet installed. The window seat is wonderful! It's the perfect place for a little girl to play with her dolls. Did you buy that dollhouse?"

A rush of pride warmed him as she watched her inspect it. "Actually, Chandler and I made it. We started it when we heard you were getting divorced and coming home. It kept us busy at night. Do you think Angie will like it?"

She looked up, and averted her eyes. "She would love it, and you know it. Damn it, Hayden. I'm not going to be pushed into this."

Crossing to her, he gripped her chin, tilting her head up until she met his eyes. "I know what we want from you is unconventional, but you've seen for yourself that the town already accepts it. If you marry me and live with us, we'll have a home filled with love. Isn't that what you want for Angie?"

Elizabeth pushed away. "Love? Hayden, you and Chandler may love me as a friend, but not the kind of love I need. I remember how you were with all those women you two used to sleep with. And don't try to make me feel guilty by throwing Angie in the middle. She's living in a home where everyone loves her right now."

Hayden's temper frayed around the edges. "You're the one who keeps throwing Angie in the middle as though Chandler and I would be bad for her. You're hiding behind her to deny yourself and us a future together. I get that you're afraid, Lizzy. But, we've already promised to be good fathers to her and good husbands to you. You know damned well that neither one of us would do anything to hurt either one of you."

Fire flashed in Elizabeth's eyes. "How the hell do I know that, Hayden? I haven't seen or heard from you in years. You wanted nothing to do with me before, how the hell can I believe that you do now?"

Hayden's temper snapped. "Damn it, Lizzy. We explained all of this. We were confused and fought over you constantly. We had no idea what to do about it, but we knew that neither one of us could have a relationship with you then, feeling the way we both felt about you. The jealousy would have ruined everything."

Elizabeth looked up at him and smirked, making his hand itch to paddle her tight ass. "So there's no longer any jealousy and because you say so, we'll all live happily ever after. That is, until one of you decides you want a woman all to yourself or you come to your fucking senses and see that you don't love me the way a man should love a woman. Just curious, how did you and Chandler make the decision to share me?"

His gut churned when he thought back to that time. "The night you left, Chandler and I got drunk, really drunk. We talked about nothing but you. Somehow the idea came up that we should share you. I have no idea which one of us said it, but we both thought it made sense. The next day, after we recovered from our hangovers, we talked some more. And we kept talking."

Reaching out, he cupped her jaw. "It was the first time we'd talked to each other without fighting in a long time. If you chose one of us now, it would destroy the other."

Narrowing her eyes, she crossed her arms over her chest, rubbing them as if she'd gotten chilled. "So you made this decision when you were drunk and decided to share me so you wouldn't fight anymore? Well, excuse me for not falling in with your plans, but you don't even know me anymore. And it looks like I don't know you either."

Hayden shook her. "You know us and we know you. The years we've been apart haven't changed that." Leaning close, he smirked, knowing damned well it would piss her off. "And you still want both of us, baby. You wouldn't react the way you do with *both* of us if you didn't still want *both* of us."

"You son of a bitch!"

Smiling as she turned her back to him and moved to the window, Hayden came up behind her, covering her breasts with his palms. His cock jumped when she immediately leaned back against him, her nipples pebbling beneath his hands. "Your body doesn't lie even if you try to. You get aroused anytime either one of us touches you, and when we touch you together, you go up in flames."

She gripped his hands as if to push them away, but moaned as her head dropped against his shoulder. The mixed messages made him crazy to have her.

Sliding his hand under her shirt, he felt her shiver. Smiling against her neck, he undid her jeans and slid a hand inside, at the same time unsnapping the front closure of her bra. Her sharp intake of breath made his cock throb as he simultaneously slid a finger through her wet slit and stroked a nipple.

Although her hands covered his, she made no move to stop him. "Hayden, damn you."

"Shh, baby." He ran a finger through her slick folds, zeroing in on her clit. Closing his fingers over her nipple, he pinched lightly. "Your pussy's soaked. You gonna try to tell me again that I don't turn you on? You know you damned well that you love me."

"Bastard."

Holding her firmly, he chuckled against her neck as he doubled the speed of his strokes on her clit, groaning when she moaned and her body started jerking. "That's it, baby. See how fast I can get you hot? Think about spending the rest of your life with Chandler and me doing this to you all the time."

He pinched her nipple a little harder and almost came in his jeans at the sweet sounds she made as she stiffened in his arms and went over. Slowing his strokes, he drew out her orgasm, the rush of her juices over his fingers making him insane to have her.

Sliding his hand lower, he slid a finger into her hot, creamy cunt. The quiver of her inner muscles as she milked his finger almost had him coming in his jeans. "This is right for us, baby. And you know it." Going for broke, he slid his slick finger from her cunt and poised it at her bottom hole, holding onto her as she jerked.

* * * *

Elizabeth shivered, gripping his forearms tightly. "Wh-what are you doing?"

Hayden scraped his teeth over her neck as he applied pressure, pushing his finger through the tight ring of muscle and about an inch into her ass. "You're a smart girl. I'm sure you'll figure it out."

The pinch startled her as the most erotic sensations raced through her. She'd never felt such a thing! Never even imagined it. Hayden touched her more intimately than she'd ever been touched, making her mind go numb at the unbelievable naughtiness of it. Embarrassed because her bottom kept clenching on his finger, she struggled against his hold, only to freeze when it moved his finger in her ass.

He slid his foot between hers, pushing her jeans to the floor. "Step out of them and spread your legs."

Stunned, she did it without thinking. "Hayden, I've never—Oh God."

Applying more pressure, he stroked his finger in and out of her once, twice and then slid his finger deep into her anus.

Holding onto him when her knees buckled, Elizabeth gulped in air. Moisture coated her thighs as he began stroking her clit again with light, fleeting strokes that had her whimpering like a child. His finger in her ass felt huge, spearing her and making her anus burn. "Hayden, I can't…what are you…I'm gonna come."

"Not yet, you're not." Withdrawing his finger from her ass, he turned her to face him. Reaching into a pocket, he pulled out a condom, quickly lowering his jeans and putting it on. Wrapping an arm around her, he lifted her against his chest, holding her ass in one of his big hands. Holding her gaze he slid that thick finger back into her anus as he lowered her onto his waiting cock. "Now you're gonna come."

Embarrassment at having Hayden's finger in her ass had kept her from looking at him, but now she had no choice.

His features had hardened, a tortured look on his face that she'd never seen before. But his eyes…his eyes glittered, so dark and mesmerizing she couldn't look away. The emotion in them had her sliding her hands from his shoulders to his neck and then into his hair.

Holding onto him, she lifted herself to touch her lips to his jaw. "Oh, God. Hayden, you're inside me." She wished she could have had him naked, but it had happened so fast neither one of them had even gotten undressed.

Bending, he touched his lips to hers, moving her on his cock and holding his finger inside her bottom. "That I am, baby. I plan on being inside you a lot from now on."

The feeling of fullness amazed her, her pussy stretched as he moved her on his cock. Clenching on both his cock and his finger, she moaned as it intensified the sensation in both openings. Barely able to catch her breath, she held on as his strokes came faster. "I can't believe you're doing this to me."

Hayden's smile was pure evil, a look she expected from Chandler, but never from him. Already overwhelmed by having him inside her and the naughty, vulnerable feeling of having his finger stretching her anus, she couldn't resist that evil grin.

Those amazing tingles began, but this time they also sizzled around the finger pressing deep inside her, sending her over the edge so quickly it stunned her. She clamped down on him, her inner muscles milking him.

Hayden groaned. "You feel so fucking good, baby. I don't give a damn what you say. I'm never letting you go."

# Chapter Six

Sitting in Hayden and Chandler's office three days later, Elizabeth sat back, folding her arms across her chest. "I've been looking for a job in town for two days now. Not a single person will hire me. They smile, apologize, and give me one of these." Wadding the paper she held into a ball, she tossed it at Chandler.

Smiling, he unfolded it and scanned it briefly before passing it to his brother. "Yeah, we passed those flyers around town so we could find someone to handle our correspondence and a few other things. Are you here to apply for the job?"

Torn between laughter and the urge to smack him, she glanced over to where Angie played with one of her dolls. "And no one else applied for this job?"

Hayden wadded the flyer into a ball again and tossed it into the garbage can. "No. They all know the job is yours."

Eyeing them hungrily, Elizabeth hid a smile. She hadn't seen either one of them since they'd taken her home the other night.

She and Hayden had come downstairs to find Angie sound asleep on Chandler's chest as he reclined on the sofa. When Angie woke up, they went riding, with Angie riding on Chandler's lap. Afterward they'd had dinner, thankfully keeping the conversation light. By the time Hayden and Chandler had taken them home, Angie had started to fall asleep again. Several people had already been at her parents' house, installing new locks and deadbolts.

Hayden and Chandler had jumped in to help and stayed until everyone else left.

Since they left that night, they'd called several times, but had kept the conversations light as though they'd tried to give her some space.

It appeared her space had run out.

They'd showed up at her parents' house about a half hour earlier, and had hustled her and Angie out to the ranch before she had a chance to object.

Now, both of them watched her hungrily, smiles playing at their lips.

Tapping her fingers on the arm of the chair, she narrowed her eyes. "What, exactly, would I be doing for you?"

Hayden looked away from where Angie played and waved a hand toward the massive desk he sat behind. "Chandler and I are hardly ever in the house during the day. We're either busy with the horses or meeting with someone who wants to buy them. Martha does a great job of taking care of the house, but she's no spring chick and doesn't know a thing about computers. She can't keep running out if there's a message to relay, and she doesn't have the time to keep stopping to answer the phone."

Elizabeth eyed him warily. "If you needed someone to do all of this, why haven't you already hired someone?"

Chandler looked up from where he sat on the sofa close to Angie. "We used to take care of it at night. Now we want to keep our nights free. You need a job, and this way you can bring Angie to work with you. I don't want her going to any babysitter, and I want both of you here as much as possible so we can keep an eye on you. It works out well for all of us."

Elizabeth couldn't find any flaws in his logic. It would be nice to be able to make a living and still keep Angie with her. Glancing at Angie, she cursed the fact that her face burned. "No strings?"

Hayden's face hardened. "The job is yours regardless, but don't think for a minute that we're not going to pursue the rest."

Seeing no other option, she nodded. "Okay. Thank you. When do you—shoot. My cell phone. I'm sorry, but it might be Mom or Dad."

Hayden leaned back as she rummaged through her purse. "Take it,

Lizzy. We're not going anywhere."

Elizabeth finally found her phone and quickly answered, not even bothering to look at the display. "Hello."

* * * *

Chandler couldn't wipe the smile from his face as he watched Angie play with her doll. The fact that she talked to it, pretending to be its mother totally captivated him. When the doll's shoe came off, she struggled to put it back on until Hayden reached out a hand for it.

"Richard?"

Chandler's head shot up to see that Elizabeth's face had drained of all color. With a glance at Angie, who'd also looked up, he jumped to his feet, sharing a look with Hayden before grabbing Elizabeth and leading her out of the room.

Elizabeth looked up at him, her eyes panic stricken. "It's none of your business, Richard. You have no right to dictate how I live."

Cursing, Chandler grabbed the phone from her. "This is Chandler Scott. What the fuck do you want?" He wanted so badly to reach through the phone and grab the other guy by the throat, he shook with it.

"Well, well, well, if it isn't one of the men fucking my wife."

Chandler had to force himself to loosen his grip on the phone before he smashed it. "What I do with Elizabeth is none of your business. And in case you've forgotten, she's your *ex*-wife. You couldn't keep your dick in your pants, remember?" He had to hold out a hand to keep Lizzy from grabbing the phone from him. Putting a hand over her mouth so he could hear what the other man said, he winced, glaring at her when she bit him.

"It looks like one man's not enough for her. That's not a good atmosphere for my daughter to be raised in."

A cold knot of fear formed in his stomach, cooling the white-hot fury that raced through him. "Is that a threat?"

Elizabeth stilled beside him, her face pasty white.

Richard laughed coldly. "Not from me. I don't want the brat. But my mother's pissed off that I lost her only grandchild. She's causing a lot of trouble for my father and me. We don't need this. She's going to end up wrecking my father's career and she's threatening to cut me out of her will if I don't try to get Angie back for her."

Elizabeth must have heard him because her knees gave out.

Catching her around the waist, he led her to the kitchen and set her on the counter, standing between her legs. He held her gaze as he spoke to her ex-husband. "You think you're going to get Angie back?"

"No. I've done my research. I thought you and your brother were just poor ranchers, but I've checked you out. You're a lot more influential than I thought you'd be, which works out for me. I don't want Angie. I never wanted either one of them, but when Elizabeth got pregnant, I had to marry her or ruin my father's career. I couldn't even let her divorce me."

For the first time Chandler realized that the other man slurred his words. "But she did anyway."

Richard laughed, the sound grating on Chandler's nerves. "Only because I gave her the evidence she needed to get a divorce. She thought she was being so sneaky, using the money my father thought would appease her to hire a private investigator. But Elizabeth caught my father, too. He's worried. Now my mother's worried about what'll happen if word gets out that her grandchild's being raised in a house where her ex-daughter-in-law is fucking two men. But it's more than that. Both of them are scared of the information Elizabeth has. They're scared she'll use it."

Chandler stood close to Elizabeth, practically leaning over her, and Richard didn't even try to keep his voice low.

The frightened look in her eyes told Chandler she'd heard everything. Grabbing the phone from Chandler, Elizabeth sat up and snapped. "Richard, tell them I'll go to the newspapers with everything

I have if they try to take Angie."

Chandler yanked the phone from her before she said anything else. "Richard, thanks for the warning. But someone already broke into her parents' house and tried to steal the proof. Tell them she no longer has it. We do. If there are any further attempts to take Angie, or do anything to either one of them, we'll go to the press in a heartbeat with everything. Believe me, we have quite a few reporters in our pockets."

Laughter rang loud through the receiver. "Damn if you don't deserve each other."

"Thanks for giving her the evidence she needed."

"It took her long enough. I knew what she'd done and let her catch me. But she caught my father, too. Elizabeth used that information to blackmail us into letting her have her divorce. Now, my father's scared she'll use it, and my mother does whatever she can to please my father. She wants Angie, but having a kid cramps my style. Why don't one of you marry her? That way the senator and my mother wouldn't be able to touch Angie."

Chandler's eyes never left Elizabeth. "We're planning to, just as soon as we can arrange it." Knowing he should have left it at that, he nevertheless kept going. "She's not being very cooperative. She's worried about Angie."

Richard's voice went low. "If she wants to keep her, she'll do it. Put her back on the phone."

Reluctantly, Chandler handed Lizzy the phone just as Hayden walked into the kitchen.

"Angie's asleep. Martha's watching over her. What the hell's going on?"

Chandler watched Elizabeth as he gave his brother a brief rundown.

When she finally disconnected, she looked up at both of them and jumped down from the counter. "I guess I'll be accepting your proposal after all. That is, if it's still open."

Hayden nodded once. "It is."

"I still want the job. I want to earn my own money."

Hayden inclined his head. "You can still have the job. I want my nights free."

Elizabeth colored. "I'll start tomorrow."

Chandler grinned. "I'll teach you the program as soon as we pick out the furniture for Angie's room."

Opening her mouth to say something, she apparently thought better of it and nodded. "I'd better check on Angie."

Chandler watched her go. "You'd better arrange it quick. I want both of them living out here where we can watch them as soon as possible."

Hayden went to the window. "When Angie wakes up, make sure they get home okay. I'm going to go talk to the judge and the sheriff. I want to print out a couple of pictures of Lizzy's ex, the senator, and his wife."

Chandler frowned. "It's not how I wanted this to happen."

Hayden whipped his head around. "I'll take her any way I can get her. We'll make sure she's and Angie are safe and worry about the rest later."

* * * *

This isn't how she'd wanted it to happen.

Waving goodbye to her parents and the Scotts, Elizabeth held Angie's hand in hers as they walked across the restaurant parking lot to the truck for the ride home.

She and Hayden had gotten married only a few hours earlier in a ceremony that seemed more like a dream than reality.

Once they'd taken their vows, Chandler had come forward in front of everyone to take her hand in his. Sliding another gold band on her ring finger to rest against the one Hayden had just placed there, he smiled tenderly. "You belong to both of us now. I promise to be a good husband and a good father. I adore you, baby." He'd kissed her softly, his eyes dark with promise.

That look had disappeared as they settled Angie in the truck for the ride back to the ranch. She'd thrown a tantrum, not wanting her mommy to go back to the ranch without her. They'd promised her that after the wedding, the 'pink room' would be hers, and she didn't want to miss a single night in it.

Elizabeth rode in the front with Hayden while Chandler sat in the back listening to Angie talk about Fluffy. Leaning toward Hayden, Elizabeth whispered. "I'm really sorry about this. I know you didn't plan to have a three-year-old on your honeymoon." She loved her daughter dearly but hadn't spent any time alone with either one of them since the afternoon Richard had called.

Hayden reached for her hand, lifting it to brush his lips across her knuckles, his expression somber. "I didn't want to leave her anyway. I feel better having her at the ranch, at least until things get a chance to settle. I don't trust your ex-husband any more than I trust his parents. I can't believe you didn't call us when they were trying to force you into marriage." His look hardened. "Don't worry. We'll take care of it."

Elizabeth's stomach dropped. Careful to keep her voice low enough not to be overheard by her daughter, she clenched her fists on her lap. "Hayden, it's bad enough that we had to get married to keep them from trying to get Angie, but I can deal with them. I want you and Chandler to stay out of it."

"Stay out of it? Are you crazy?" Looking over his shoulder, he smiled at Angie's look of surprise. "It's okay, sweetheart. Tell Chandler what you named your new doll." He waited until Angie resumed her monologue, before pulling Elizabeth close. Keeping his voice low, he kept one eye on her and one on the road. "*You* will stay out of it and let us deal with it, which is what you should have done from the beginning."

With a sinking heart, she remained silent the rest of the way home. She'd married them to keep Angie safe, but she wanted this marriage to work. Arguing with either one of them was a waste of time. She'd deal with anything as it came up, but in the meantime would do her best to get her husbands to see her as a grown woman instead of someone who needed to be looked after.

She couldn't go through the rest of her life as an obligation.

# Chapter Seven

Elizabeth tiptoed out of Angie's room, her heart racing as she headed toward the master bedroom. The silk nightgown she'd bought for tonight slid sensuously over her legs as she walked, the friction of the lace bodice over her erect nipples sensitizing them even more. Wiping her palms on the matching robe, she reached for the doorknob, wondering which of them would be waiting inside for her.

Swinging the door open, she came to a halt, every erogenous zone tingling at the sight that greeted her.

Hayden, wearing nothing but unbuttoned jeans, rose from the chair by the window as Chandler, wearing jeans and a t-shirt reclined on the bed. Hayden quickly came forward, wrapping an arm around her waist and pulling her close. "Is Angie asleep?"

Elizabeth nodded. "Y—"

Hayden swooped before she finished, his mouth taking hers before she could even draw a breath. He released her long enough to slide the robe from her shoulders before pulling her against his body again and lifted her in his arms, his mouth not leaving hers until he placed her on the bed next to Chandler. Straightening, he shucked his jeans as Chandler began to undress her.

Chandler's fingers moved over every inch of skin he exposed, teasing her nipples as he slid the gown down her body.

Once naked, Hayden reclined on the bed next to her. "Keep going. I want to see all of her."

Trembling under their combined gazes, Elizabeth kept looking from one to the other. She should have expected this, but hadn't.

Both looked at her hungrily as they slid the gown from her,

touching her everywhere at once. Propped on their elbows, they both leaned over her, the low lights from both nightstands illuminating her body for their perusal.

It also let her see them better.

She couldn't take her eyes from Hayden's naked form. His cock rose toward his stomach and its amazing thickness made her shiver in anticipation. Rolling slightly toward him, she ran a hand down his chest, touching him the way she'd always dreamed of.

Taking her hand in his, he kissed her fingers, his eyes fierce on hers. "Touch me." Lowering her hand to his cock, he drew a quick breath, his eyes closing when she wrapped her fingers around it. "Jesus."

Chandler's arm came around her from behind to caress her stomach.

Her stomach muscles quivered beneath his touch, her pussy clenching with need. Breathless now, she couldn't tear her eyes away from Hayden's as his fingers traced their way up her body. She gasped as they skimmed the sensitive skin on the underside of her breast, her nipples burning with the need to be touched.

Still he denied her, his eyes flaring when she moaned in frustration.

Chandler chuckled and kissed her shoulder before sliding off the bed.

Hayden looked over her shoulder at Chandler briefly, nodding once before turning back to her and kissing her again.

Elizabeth arched into Hayden, needing a firmer touch, but he continued to tease her with fleeting caresses. Her senses on overload from being with both of them this way, she kissed Hayden back hungrily, sinking into him. Teasing him, she ran her fingers up and down the length of his cock, thrilling at the velvety texture covering the steel beneath it.

Hayden rolled her to her back, lifting his head. "Enough." His eyes stayed on hers, dark and glittering as he lifted her hand over her head.

Naked now, Chandler slid into bed on her other side, his slow smile somehow evil and tender. "Now we've got you right where we want you."

Having both of the men she'd dreamed about like this, their hard bodies surrounding hers, had to be the most erotic moment of her life. Every inch of her skin warmed from the heat their bodies gave off, tingling where their gazes caressed her. "I didn't know it would be this way. I never imagined…"

Hayden watched her indulgently as he continued to run his fingers lightly up and down her body, from shoulder to hip and back again. Lowering his head, he nuzzled her jaw. "You never imagined what, baby?"

Elizabeth gasped as Chandler bent to take a nipple into his mouth, sucking gently. "I didn't realize you would take me together."

Hayden's lips hovered over hers, his warm breath gentle on her face. "We'll take you together, separately, and one at a time. You're not quite ready for together yet, though."

Twisting restlessly, Elizabeth panted as Hayden's fingers slid lightly over her mound. "I'm ready, Hayden. Don't make me wait." She cried out when he parted her folds and slid a finger through her slick juices, barely skimming her clit. Rocking her hips, she tried to get him to touch her there again.

Hayden chuckled softly, sliding his finger lower and into her pussy. "You *are* ready, aren't you, Lizzy?" Bending again, he nibbled at her bottom lip. "We'll have to work on getting you ready to take both of us together."

Elizabeth barely heard him as Chandler ran a big hand over her stomach and down to her thigh.

Pulling it toward him, he hooked it over his, spreading her wider. "After all these years you're finally ours."

Hayden added another finger, smiling when she moaned. "That's it, baby." Running his hand through her hair, he curled the fingers inside her, pressing at a spot that had her catching her breath and making her tremble even harder.

Rocking her hips, she moaned again as Chandler raked his teeth over her nipple. "Damn it. I wanted to seduce you."

Hayden flicked a thumb over her clit. "You did that by walking into the room."

Elizabeth twisted restlessly, grabbing onto their shoulders, her cries growing in intensity. She'd had every intention of seducing first one, then the other, wanting to make them desire her as much as she did them. Every time she tried to reach for their cocks, they stopped her, teasing her with the feel of their thick lengths on each of her hips.

Cupping her jaw, Chandler turned her face toward him, taking her lips with his. "You seduce me by walking past me. You make me crazy when you twitch that ass at me." Smiling, he shot a glance at Hayden. "I want my mouth on her pussy when she comes."

Elizabeth's eyes went wide. "Oh, God. I can't believe the way you talk."

Chandler laughed softly. "I like to let the anticipation build. Isn't your clit throbbing, knowing my mouth is going to be on it real soon?"

Hayden withdrew his fingers, bringing them to his mouth to lick them clean. "She's sweet and juicy." His hand moved to cover a breast as Chandler positioned himself between her thighs.

Elizabeth shook as Chandler settled himself between her thighs and grabbed her ankles to pull her legs high and wide, smiling at her.

"Ready, baby?"

Elizabeth closed her eyes, unable to process all of the sensations racing through her. She never would have believed how exciting it would be for one of them to do such erotic things to her while the other watched her reaction to it.

It made the intimacy even more intense.

Chandler couldn't see her face as he parted her folds and swiped his tongue through her slit, but Hayden could and wouldn't allow her to hide her face against his chest or look away. After several licks of Chandler's tongue, she no longer cared. He held her open and ate at her, flicking his tongue over her clit just often enough to keep her arousal growing.

She trembled uncontrollable, jerking in Hayden's arms every time Candler touched her clit. "Please. I'm so close."

Chandler chuckled, easily holding her legs as she kicked at him, sliding his tongue inside her instead of giving the attention to her clit.

Hayden kissed her deeply, his tongue sweeping through her mouth repeatedly as his fingers moved over her breasts. An occasional flick of his thumb or a light pinch on her nipples had her crying out, the warning tingles of an approaching orgasm driving her mad.

With her nipples and clit throbbing, her pussy clenching frantically on Chandler's tongue each time he slid it into her, Elizabeth couldn't stand any more. This is not how she'd envisioned seducing them. They seduced her, taking over her body so completely, she could do nothing but hold onto them as her entire body went up in flames.

Hayden gripped a nipple, tugging it as he stared down at her. "Send her over."

Elizabeth's breath caught as Chandler closed his lips over her clit, his hands tightening on her thighs, holding her firmly as she bucked against such a raw sensation. Searing ribbons of bliss pulled her body taut, her scream of release muffled by Hayden's mouth as they drew out her orgasm. Layers upon layers of the most amazing pleasure washed over her until she lay spent and trembling.

Hayden lifted his head. "Beautiful." Running a possessive hand over her body, he kept her from closing her thighs as Chandler donned a condom.

Chandler lifted her ankles again, pushing them back to open her thighs wide. "Damn, if that ain't sexy as hell." Poising the blunt tip of his cock at her opening, he slid deep with one smooth stroke, groaning as he filled her. "Damn, you feel incredible."

Incredulous that her body came alive again, Elizabeth held onto Hayden, gripping him tighter with each of Chandler's smooth strokes.

Chandler leaned over her, hooking her under the knees and holding her wide as he began to thrust harder. "Damn, you feel good. So fucking good."

Hayden's hands slid over her breasts, his jaw clenching as he watched Chandler take her. "Damn, watching her this way is driving me crazy."

"Chandler, it feels so good. No, don't stop."

Chandler clenched his jaw, leaning down to kiss her, the move lifting her legs even higher. "Come for me, darlin'."

Holding onto him for dear life, Elizabeth thrashed, her hoarse cries getting louder as Chandler began to thrust into her faster. "Chandler, my God!" Her pussy milked him, her inner muscles quivering as he stroked deep. All of a sudden it hit her and she tightened, involuntarily pushing against Chandler's arms as her body stiffened and bowed.

Chandler growled his release, throwing his head back, his strength holding her in place and keeping her from straightening her legs. "That's it, baby. So fucking good." After several long seconds he released her legs with a groan to gather her close.

Burying her face against his shoulder, Elizabeth breathed him in, the delicious scent of him helping her to settle. She still trembled, her emotions raging as she held him desperately. God, she needed this. She needed to feel him this way, as close as a man and woman could get.

She hadn't realized until this moment how much she'd needed to feel them both here with her, the level of intimacy unequal to anything she'd ever experienced. The love and happiness on their faces as they looked down at her gave her hope for the first time that they could all find happiness together.

Chandler lifted his head, his eyes hooded as he stared down at her. Sliding his hands under her neck, he tilted her head back to kiss her deeply, his mouth loving hers gently. When he lifted his head again, his eyes shone with tenderness. "I love you so damned much."

Elizabeth smiled shakily, still feeling vulnerable. "I love you, too." The words came out shaky and breathless, not as confident as she felt them. Turning her head, she included Hayden in her smile. "Both of you." After several minutes of low murmurs and soothing caresses, Elizabeth pushed at Chandler's shoulder. "Did you even see my nightgown? I bought it to seduce you, and you didn't give me the chance."

Laughing, he dropped another kiss on her lips before rolling off of her. "Next time, baby."

Elizabeth smiled seductively as Hayden took his place. "Maybe I'll seduce you." With the intention of getting Hayden on his back, she pushed at him.

Hayden lifted her hands over her head, pressing her into the mattress. "Not this time, Lizzy. I'm too fucking hot for you."

Glancing over she saw Chandler head toward the bathroom and took a moment to ogle his gorgeous ass. Lifting her eyes to Hayden, she rubbed her breasts against his chest playfully, inspired by the heat in his hooded gaze. Lifting herself slightly, she nuzzled his jaw. "How hot are you?"

Narrowing his eyes, he tightened his grip on her hands. "You're playing with fire, baby." Releasing her hands, he tangled one hand in her hair to pull her head back while the other went around her to cup her buttocks. Making a space for himself between her thighs, he pressed his cock against her opening. "You're not ready to play with that kind of fire yet."

Pulling his head down, she ran her tongue over his bottom lip before she bit it. "You have no idea what I'm ready for."

Hayden's eyes flared. Lifting himself slightly off of her, he scraped his teeth over a nipple, smiling mischievously when she cried out. "Let's find out."

Elizabeth gasped as he flipped her to her stomach, quickly

covering her and pressing her into the mattress. "What are you doing?"

Hayden slid an arm under her hips as he kissed her shoulder and her neck before nibbling her earlobe. "Trust me." He moved so fast she didn't have time to react. Sliding off of her, he lifted her and placed pillows beneath her hips.

"Hayden?" Not sure what he would do, her voice came out shaky.

Running a hand over her hip, he bent and kissed the small of her back. "Shh. Trust me."

Elizabeth didn't trust that tone at all and got even more nervous when Chandler came back chuckling. She tried to lift up but Hayden's hand on her back held her in place as he spread her thighs wider and settled between them. With her bottom in the air, she felt exposed in a way she never had before, especially when she knew both of them were looking at her. She trembled, nervous even through the lust that raged inside her.

Hayden ran a hand over her bottom. "Do you remember what I did to you?"

Oh, God. How could she forget? "Hayden—"

Chandler reclined beside her, running a hand over her hair. "For both of us to take you together, Lizzy, one of us will take your pussy while the other's in that tight ass."

Elizabeth had never heard a more frightening or erotic statement in her life. Shaking, she met Chandler's eyes, lust and fear combining into something strong, powerful and…decadent. Oh God. Could she do this? What would happen if she couldn't? "Please. I don't know if I can."

Hayden ran his hands over her bottom and down to her slit. "We won't do anything you don't want, baby." Kissing her back, he slid a finger into her. "We'll have to stretch you first, honey. Don't be scared. Neither one of would hurt you for the world."

Chandler slid a hand under her to tug lightly at a nipple, grinning when she moaned. "We're going to make you want it so bad, you'll beg for it. Christ, I'm getting hard again just thinking about it."

Hayden ran his hands over her bottom again, moving them closer and closer to her crease. "You loved it when I pressed a finger inside you. When we stretch you enough to take a cock, you're going to come harder than ever." The thick finger stroking her pussy shoved all thoughts of protesting aside.

Elizabeth squirmed restlessly as his fingers withdrew to move over her clit. Her body, already sensitized, came to life once again. Hearing the rip of foil, she shuddered in anticipation.

Chandler ran a hand over her hair. "You're trembling. If you could see the look on Hayden's face, you'd shake like hell. He looks really hungry."

"Oh God."

Hayden poised the head of his cock at her opening, holding her hips tightly to control her squirming. He slid into her pussy slightly and froze, tightening his hold as the thick head of his cock stretched her opening. "Jesus." He groaned as he slid slowly into her, leaning over her and burying his face in her neck. "I don't know how I lived without you."

Chandler held her hands in his as Hayden began stroking, slow, smooth strokes that took her quickly to the edge again. The reality of being touched intimately by both of them at once while their low voices washed over her added yet another layer to the intimacy and erotic atmosphere.

Three voices whispering endearments. Three voices moaning with pleasure.

She couldn't imagine anything more decadent than being surrounded this way by the two men she'd always loved.

Hayden's thick cock stretched her, each sure stroke taking her higher, his firm grip on her hips holding her for the best penetration. In this position, his cock went deep, the feeling of vulnerability building inside her stronger than before. She arched her bottom higher as her orgasm loomed close, those warm, delicious tingles waking every nerve ending.

Hayden stopped moving, holding her in place when she began to struggle in frustration. His voice, sandpaper rough, washed over her. "She's fucking clenching. Damn it, stay still, Lizzy."

Elizabeth couldn't have stayed still if her life depended on it. So close she could actually feel the warning tingles begin to spread, she tried to rock her hips.

With a muffled curse, Chandler held her firmly, his lips moving over her shoulder. "Easy, baby. You can't come until Hayden works a finger into that ass."

Groaning, Elizabeth fought his hold. "I want to come. Now. Oh God, I'm so close." Kicking her feet, she moaned her pleasure as it moved Hayden's cock inside her. When something cold touched her bottom hole, she froze.

Hayden pushed against her vulnerable opening, the lube easing his way as he slowly pushed his thumb into her, his hand splayed over her bottom.

A whimpered cry escaped before she could prevent it. The pinch of his invasion quickly gave way to the burn and forbidden sensation of having her anus breached. The cold lube and the intimate burn made her lose all control. Her body took over, pushing back against him, demanding satisfaction as her orgasm rapidly approached. She was already on the edge, and it only took a few of Hayden's deep thrusts for her to go over.

Her cries drowned out whatever Chandler said. Only Hayden's deep groan of completion cut through the fog as she spread her thighs wider, arching into him even more. She came hard. Waves of release burned her pussy and anus and spread throughout her body, forcing her to clamp down on Hayden's dual invasion.

She arched, whimpering as Chandler touched her nipples again. The thumb in her bottom moved, sending her over again, the long swell of pleasure leaving her limp and breathless.

Collapsing on the bed, it registered that her hands hurt, forcing her to loosen her grip on the covers she hadn't known she'd been holding on to. Feeling hands move over her hair, she opened her eyes to find Chandler watching her, an indulgent smile curving his lips.

Smiling down at her, he smoothed a hand down her back. "I love watching you come."

Now that she'd settled some, she started to feel a little self-conscious about the thumb Hayden moved in her anus. Shivering, she moaned, burying her face in the covers.

Hayden chuckled. "You come hard when you have your ass filled. Once we get you loosened up a little, I think we can do better, don't you, Chandler?"

Chandler laughed, turning her to face him. "We'll just have to keep opening up her ass until she's ready."

When she groaned, Hayden took pity on her and withdrew from both openings, patting her bottom before covering her body with his. He nuzzled her neck and bit gently. "Let's get you cleaned up. Martha left us some snacks. You're going to need your energy when Chandler and I switch places and do this all over again."

# Chapter Eight

Elizabeth kissed Angie's head, tucking the light blanket around her shoulders against the chill of the air-conditioning. Sound asleep on the sofa in Hayden and Chandler's office, her daughter did indeed look like an angel.

With a last look at her, Elizabeth started for the kitchen. She smiled at Martha, who looked up from her meatloaf. "Martha, I hate to ask this, but I have to run to the post office, and Angie's asleep. Would you mind watching out for her until I get back? I should be back before she wakes up."

Martha smiled. "Absolutely. As soon as she wakes up, we're going to make cupcakes anyway. Go. Do what you need to do. There's no hurry."

Smiling her thanks, she gathered her things and headed out, wanting to be back before Angie woke up. Pulling up to the post office, she got out, turning to wave at one of the ranch hands who'd just come out of the feed store.

The other man, she couldn't remember his name, looked surprised to see her and hurriedly looked away. Shrugging it off, she rushed into the post office. It took her longer than she'd meant it to because she'd been stopped by several people welcoming her home and congratulating her on her marriage. No one seemed the least bit surprised that she now lived with two men, but it still made her a little uncomfortable to openly talk about it.

But she wouldn't have changed the way she lived for the world.

Smiling to herself, she walked back out to Hayden's truck. She really needed to get her own car, but that would have to wait. She came to a halt on the sidewalk, groaning when she saw that she had a flat tire.

Damn, had she run over a nail?

She pulled out her cell phone and paused. She didn't even want to begin trying to change the tire on Hayden's monstrosity. Hayden and Chandler were out and Martha was busy cooking and watching Angie.

She called her father.

Once she'd explained the situation to him, she saw the ranch hand she'd seen earlier stop his truck behind Hayden's. "Dad, never mind. One of the ranch hands is here. I'll talk to you later." Disconnecting, she dropped the phone in her purse and walked toward him. "Hi. I'm so glad to see you. Do you think you could give me a ride back to the ranch?"

He smiled nervously. "Sure. Hop in."

Knowing he had to be a little anxious at having his bosses' new wife riding with him, she smiled warmly as she got into the passenger's seat. "I appreciate this so much. I want to get back home to my daughter."

He nodded, looking straight ahead as he started to drive. "So your daughter's at the ranch?"

"Yes. She was sleeping, so Martha's watching her."

"It's a shame you don't have her with you."

A little confused by his tone, she turned to look at him when she saw movement in her peripheral vision. She started to turn just as a hand came around, holding a cloth to her face.

"You dumb son of a bitch! Couldn't you have just kept your mouth closed? Where's the envelope, bitch?"

She struggled, trying to push the other man's hand away, looking toward the ranch hand in fear and confusion as he grabbed her hand.

*Why didn't he help her?*

Her vision started to blur and her struggles became weaker. The last thing she saw was the apology in his eyes before everything went black.

\* \* \* \*

Hayden walked into the kitchen to the smell of cake and Angie's laughter.

"Do you think Mr. Hayden and Mr. Chandler will like 'em?"

Martha laughed softly. "Of course they will. All cupcakes should have chocolate chip smiley faces."

Hayden looked over his shoulder, grinning at his brother. "It looks like we're having cupcakes for dessert."

Chandler grinned back. "Later on I'm having Lizzy for dessert."

Hayden shook his head. "Nope. My turn." Walking into the kitchen, he came to a halt when Angie's smile fell. Shooting a look at Chandler, he knelt next to her. "What's the matter, sweetheart?"

Angie's bottom lip quivered. "I want my mommy."

Hayden picked her up, loving the way she wrapped her arms around his neck. "Well, let's go find her."

The look on Martha's face made him pause. "What is it?"

Chandler held out his arms for Angie. "Come here, angel. I want a kiss."

"Did you see the cupcakes I maded for you?"

Worry darkened Chandler's eyes as he cradled Angie against him. "They're beautiful."

Hayden moved closer to Martha, leading her away from Chandler and Angie. "What is it?"

Martha wrung her hands. "Mrs. Scott left to go to the post office. She said she wanted to get back before Angie woke up. That was over two hours ago."

Looking up at Chandler, he saw the same fear in his eyes that knotted his own stomach. He started back for his boots, whipping out his cell phone just as the doorbell rang. Changing direction, he went back through the kitchen as Chandler said something to Martha under his breath and set Angie back on her feet.

Hayden didn't wait for him, racing down the hall to the front door and flinging it open.

Jeb Reed stood on the front porch. "Hey, Hayden. How are you? I brought your truck so you didn't have to run to town for it."

Paula Reed pushed him aside as Angie came running out. "There's my baby."

"Grandma!"

The knot in Hayden's stomach tightened. Something must have shown on his face because Jeb frowned at him and started to say something but Hayden shook his head. "Paula, why don't you take Angie out to the kitchen? Angie, show grandma the cupcakes you and Martha made."

Trying to smile reassuringly at Paula's worried frown, Hayden led Jeb into their study.

Chandler closed the door behind them. "What the hell's going on?"

Hayden's hand shook as he dialed Lizzy's cell phone number.

Jeb looked back and forth between them. "Where's Elizabeth?"

Hayden's fear grew with every unanswered ring of the phone. "Martha said Lizzy went to the post office." Another ring. "That was over two hours ago." Another ring. "What the hell happened with the truck?"

Jeb's face paled. "She called me. When she came out of the post office she had a flat tire. She called me to come fix it for her. She saw one of your ranch hands and said forget it. She was going to get a ride with him and tell you two about the truck when you came in."

Hayden cursed when Elizabeth's phone went to voice mail. He hung up and immediately punched the number in again. "We just got in. Martha said she hasn't come home."

Chandler cursed. "Okay. Let's go out and find out who the hell she ran into in town."

They questioned every one of the ranch hands in the yard, leaving instructions for them to question everyone else. "One of the trucks is gone. I want to know who the hell is missing. Call my cell phone as soon as you find out. I want to get to the post office before they close."

Chandler scrubbed a hand over his face. "Where the fuck can she be? She never would have left Angie for so long. Why the hell didn't she call us?"

Hayden was already headed for one of the ranch trucks. All of them had the keys over the visor making it easy for anyone to use any one of them whenever they needed to. He wondered if he would come to regret that. His hands shook as he stuck the key in the ignition and took off toward town. "She's in trouble, Chandler. You know it as well as I do."

Chandler nodded grimly. "Someone took her. But who? The senator wouldn't dirty his hands personally, would he?"

Hayden clenched his jaw. "I doubt it."

Chandler hit the dashboard. "Damn it, where the fuck is she?"

Searching the sides of the road, Hayden tightened his hands on the wheel. "I don't know. Look out for her."

Chandler searched the landscape as they drove. "If someone did take her, we'll have to assume it was a professional."

Hayden had been thinking the same thing but hadn't wanted to voice it. "And whoever it is has someone from the ranch in their pocket."

"Fuck" Chandler pulled out his cell phone. "I'll call Bill. We can trust our foreman. Agreed?"

"Agreed. Bill would never do something like this. Call Jeb, too. Tell him to keep Martha there and to lock the house up tight. No one in or out until we get back."

Hayden pulled up to the post office and slammed on his brakes. God, he didn't know what he'd do if something happened to Lizzy. Racing inside with Chandler on his heels, he prayed like never before.

* * * *

Elizabeth woke gradually, feeling slightly nauseous, some instinct warning her to be quiet and still.

"Shut up and keep digging."

The unfamiliar voice brought everything back in a rush.

Carefully opening one eye, she saw the ranch hand digging a hole while another man held a gun on him.

The ranch hand wiped the back of his hand over his forehead. "You didn't say anything about hurting anyone. You said the senator just wanted his granddaughter back."

"Shut up. You told me the kid was always with her. You're a fucking loser. Now dig the damned hole. I've got to get rid of her before I can do anything else."

"You're really gonna kill her?"

"Of course I'm going to kill her! What did you think, I'd just let her go? Hurry up. I've still got to get the kid and the envelope she had." The man with the gun had obviously tried to blend in, wearing jeans and a t-shirt, but he had a city look about him.

Terrified for herself and Angie, Elizabeth looked around, relieved to see that she knew where she was. On the other side of the ridge lay a pond Hayden and Chandler used for fishing. When the man with the gun turned in her direction, Elizabeth hurriedly closed her eyes, pretending to still be unconscious. God, what had he given her? Her head spun dizzily as the sun nearly blinded her.

They'd left her in the passenger seat, leaning against the window. Opening her eyes to mere slits, she looked out again to see the man with the gun had looked away again, yelling at the ranch hand to hurry up.

She had to get out of here before they finished digging her grave. Turning her head slightly, she glanced at the ignition, her fear growing to find the keys gone. She had no idea how much longer they'd be, but when the ranch hand jumped down in the hole to finish digging, she knew she had to be running out of time.

She'd never be able to outrun them on foot, but she knew several hiding places. She'd used them more than once when she used to come out to spy on Hayden and Chandler as they fished.

Hayden and Chandler.

Oh God, they'd be worried sick. The thought of never seeing them again, never holding Angie again, never again being able to be with her parents again…

No, she couldn't think about that now. She had to concentrate on nothing more than escaping. Hayden and Chandler would know by now that something was wrong and they'd do everything in their power to keep Angie safe.

Impulsively, she reached over and pulled the visor down, tears of relief blurring her vision when the key fell to the seat.

God bless Hayden and Chandler's rules. Every one of their ranch hands had been trained for years to put the keys back above the visor before they got out of the truck. It had been ingrained in all of the men because of the number of times they'd lost keys on the ranch.

Moving quickly, she jumped into the other seat and started the truck, throwing it in gear.

Both men looked up and raced toward her as she hit the gas, kicking up dirt and grass as she floored it, turning the truck around. She easily corrected but fishtailed slightly. She hadn't driven on anything but asphalt roads in years, but she'd driven on dirt and grass often enough in the past that it came rushing back.

The back window shattered, startling a scream from her. Looking in side mirror, she blinked.

The man with the gun was shooting at her!

Crouching down, she headed toward the ranch. Hayden and Chandler would be worried sick, and she knew that she'd be safe once she got there.

Once she was far enough away that she could no longer see the two men in the mirror, she reached up to rub her shoulder where it burned. Feeling a sticky wetness, she looked down at her blood-covered hand in horror.

She'd been shot!

Now that she knew that the searing pain made itself known.

Her purse lay on the floor, and she couldn't reach it to get her phone unless she pulled over which was something she didn't want to do. She had to get to the ranch as soon as possible.

* * * *

Chandler disconnected, turning to Hayden. "Doug Stamper's missing. Everyone else is accounted for. Apparently he got a call earlier and said he had something to do. Bill's pissed at himself because he didn't know he'd taken a ranch truck."

Hayden's grim expression hadn't changed much in the last hour. "Where the fuck are they?"

Chandler's gut churned, and his fear for Elizabeth felt like a rock in his stomach. "Every hand is out looking for them. We won't stop until we find them."

"Damn it. I want her back. It'll be getting dark soon."

Chandler had been thinking the same thing. "It doesn't matter. We won't stop looking until we find her."

"How's Angie?"

"She's upset, but Jeb and Paula are watching a movie with her. Mom and Dad are on their way over." Constantly scanning the area, he narrowed his eyes when he saw what looked like a truck kicking up dust in the distance. "Look over there. Is that them?"

Accelerating, Hayden raced ahead. "It looks like they're headed right for us."

Chandler reached behind him for the binoculars. "She's gotta be okay. We just got her. We can't lose her now."

"We won't."

As the truck got closer, Chandler sat forward. "Holy hell. That's Lizzy! She's driving like a bat out of hell, and she's alone."

Hayden slowed. "Thank God!"

Chandler threw the binoculars into the back seat. "Stop. She's probably scared. Who knows what the hell's happened to her? Let her see it's us." As soon as Hayden stopped the truck, Chandler jumped out, waving his hands. "Lizzy!"

Thankfully she slowed instead of breezing right past them. When she got close enough, he saw the relief on her face as she brought the truck to a halt only feet away.

Chandler ran up to her, his only thought getting to her as soon as possible. Yanking open the door, he jerked her into his arms, burying his face in her hair. "Thank God." When she flinched, he released her with a curse, horrified at the blood that covered her. "Lizzy!"

Elizabeth looked down, her eyes going wide as Hayden pulled her short sleeve higher. "That bastard shot at me."

Chandler caught her, his eyes flying to Hayden's. "Hell."

Hayden stripped off his t-shirt and held it to the wound. "Let's get her to the hospital. She's lost a lot of blood. It looks like the bullet just nicked her but she's got a lot of cuts from flying glass."

They hurried to the truck, relief making Chandler almost giddy. Using Hayden's t-shirt, he brushed shards of broken glass off of her skin and as much blood as he could.

Lizzy grabbed his arm. "The senator hired someone to take Angie. He's at the pond with one of your ranch hands. I don't know his name. They were digging a grave for me. I was in the truck. Your truck had a flat tire. The other guy was in the back of the ranch truck. He put a cloth over my face."

Hayden patted her thigh, searching the horizon as he turned the truck and started back toward town. "Calm down, baby. You're safe now. Let's get you to the hospital and get you checked out."

Chandler threw the bloody shirt to the floor and pulled off his own to wrap it around the worst of the wounds. Pulling out his cell phone, he called the sheriff.

Lizzy turned to Hayden. "Give me your cell phone. I want to call

Martha and make sure Angie's okay."

Handing it to her, Hayden bent to kiss her, his eyes fierce. "We could have lost you. The senator is gonna pay big time for this."

Lizzy smiled for the first time. "I'm okay. I'm just worried about Angie."

Hayden nodded, holding onto her thigh as if he needed the contact. "Your parents are with her. Tell them to stay there until we get back. I don't want Angie to see you covered with all that blood. It'll only scare her."

Only then did Chandler realize that he held onto her, too. "I know it scares the hell out of me."

Lizzy leaned against him, holding Chandler's hand as she spoke into the phone.

Meeting Hayden's eyes over her head, seeing the relief and conviction on his brother's face that he knew had to be reflected on his own, Chandler nodded once, understanding completely.

They'd come far too close to losing her again, this time for good.

# Chapter Nine

They all sat around the kitchen table after finally getting Angie to sleep, each with a cup of coffee they barely touched. They all stared into them. Each person was preoccupied with his own thoughts. Her mom and dad's faces still looked a little pale to her, but having Hayden and Chandler's parents there seemed to help. The older Scotts had already been there when they got home from the hospital.

Elizabeth had spent the evening reassuring everyone that she was fine, and everyone else had spent the evening calming Angie. She'd also spoken to the sheriff and learned that the two men who'd taken her had been arrested.

Hayden and Chandler wore grim expressions all evening; their fury at the entire mess was obvious. They hid it pretty well until Angie went to bed, but now they made no attempt at all to do so.

Shortly after they'd arrived, she'd seen Hayden in what appeared to be a heated conversation with his foreman. Immediately afterward there'd been a lot of activity in the yard and since then men could be seen from every window.

"Are you sure you're all right?"

Elizabeth smiled reassuringly at Chandler to the question she'd answered at least a dozen times since this afternoon. "I'm fine. I'm just worried about Angie."

Wrapping an arm around her, Chandler pulled her chair closer. "We'll take care of it. The sheriff's trying to get the man who shot you to implicate the senator. In the meantime, neither one of you will be alone until this is settled."

Murmurs of approval sounded from the rest of them, but Hayden still looked grim.

Making a decision, Elizabeth looked back and forth between him and Chandler. "I'm calling the senator." Holding up her hand to stop the sharp objections, she stood. "The evidence I have that the senator has had a string of affairs helped me get my divorce. I'll use it again to keep Angie."

Hayden narrowed his eyes at her. "I've already taken care of it."

"Damn it, Hayden. I can handle this on my own."

Hayden started toward her, his eyes flashing. The ringing of the doorbell made him pause. "I told you I already handled it." He left to answer the door, fury in his long strides.

Elizabeth plopped back in her seat, glaring at Chandler. "What did he do?"

Chandler nodded grimly. "You'll see soon enough."

"Chandler, I want—" She broke off when Hayden appeared in the doorway, looking even more formidable than before.

"Lizzy, Chandler, come into the study."

Exchanging a look with Chandler, Elizabeth held onto his arm as she slowly got to her feet, wary now. "Hayden, what is it?"

His jaw clenched. "Your ex-husband wants to talk to us."

Elizabeth's jaw dropped. "Richard's here?"

Hayden nodded curtly. "He's waiting for us in the study."

Sharing a look with her parents, Elizabeth followed Hayden as he led the way back to his study, Chandler close behind her. She had no idea why Richard would ever show up here, but if he thought he could take Angie, she'd use those photos no matter what Hayden and Chandler said. Walking into the room, she glanced at Richard warily before taking a seat on the sofa.

He stood, coming forward. "Hello, Elizabeth. In spite of what happened today, you look wonderful." Nodding at Chandler, he extended his hand. "You must be Chandler. I'm Richard Forrester." As usual, he was impeccably dressed, his pants pressed to a razor sharp crease.

In contrast, both Hayden and Chandler wore the jeans and t-shirts they'd changed into as soon as they'd come home, not wanting Angie to see any blood on any of them. Their hair was mussed from running their hands through it repeatedly and their faces had become lined with tension.

They'd never looked better to her.

After greeting Chandler, Richard took his seat again, his eyes widening when he saw the way Hayden and Chandler surrounded her protectively, Chandler on the sofa next to her and Hayden standing directly behind her.

Elizabeth automatically adopted the relaxed pose she'd used with Richard for years in an effort to show his actions meant nothing to her. "What are you doing here, Richard? Isn't Dakota Springs a little out of your element? Hasn't your father done enough?"

Richard's smile was one she'd learned to detest years earlier. "You'll never be able to prove my father did anything. That's why I'm here."

Hayden cursed, his hand on her good shoulder tightening. "You son of a bitch. You know damned well your father hired him." Coming around the sofa, he grabbed Richard by his designer shirt and lifted him to his feet. "Lizzy could have been killed today. But that was the senator's plan all along, wasn't it?"

"With the help of one of *your* men!"

Seeing Hayden's face, Elizabeth jumped up and hurried toward him, clutching his arm before he could hit Richard.

Glancing at her, Hayden pushed Richard back into his chair and wrapped an arm around her.

Elizabeth leaned into him for both his solidness and warmth and also to keep him from going after Richard. Automatically rubbing her hand soothingly over his stomach, she looked up at him. "Hayden, what are you saying?"

Hayden's arm around her waist tightened. "With you dead, the senator wouldn't have to worry about you exposing him. Without a mother, the courts would most likely award Richard custody of Angie. All of their problems would be solved."

Incredulous, she turned slowly to Richard, already seeing the truth in his eyes. "Is it true?"

Richard ran a hand over his face, suddenly looking tired and stressed. "It wouldn't surprise me." Leaning forward, he sighed. "My father's a very ambitious man. He wants to be re-elected and he doesn't like having the threat of exposure hanging over his head. You'll never be able to prove it, though. The senator's too smart for that. Even if the man the sheriff's questioning admitted it, it would be his word against my father's."

She could barely take it in. Moving out of Hayden's arms, she moved slowly to the sofa and sank into it. "I can't believe it. The senator actually hired someone to kill me?" She'd known he was serious about his career, but she never would have dreamed him capable of something like this.

Richard's jaw clenched, something she hadn't seen since the first time she'd caught him having an affair. "I don't know for sure. My father would never confide in me, but I'd bet money on it."

Not quite trusting Richard, Elizabeth pushed out of Chandler's arms and sat forward. "So why are you here?"

Richard reached for his jacket draped over the adjoining chair, pulling an envelope out of an inside pocket. Tapping it against his knee, he met her eyes. "You and I should never have gotten married. I admit I treated you badly." Sighing, he continued to tap the envelope, looking unsure of himself for the first time since Elizabeth met him. "I'm not a good father to Angelina. To be honest, I have no desire to try. I'm too selfish."

Not sure what he was getting at, she glanced at Hayden to find him staring at Richard, his entire body tense.

Surprisingly, the hostile look on his face didn't appear to faze Richard at all. Leaning forward, Richard handed the envelope to her. "I had my attorney draw these up." Taking a deep breath, he let it out slowly. "I'm giving up all rights to Angelina. You have full custody." At her gasp, he gestured toward Hayden and Chandler. "Now one of them can adopt her. The senator wouldn't be able to do a fucking thing about it and could never get her." Looking away, he stared down at his hands. "Both of you will be safe from him."

Incredulous, Elizabeth glanced at both Hayden and Chandler, seeing the same surprise on their faces. Wiping away the tears that blurred her vision, she smiled tremulously. "You're wrong about one thing."

Richard snapped his head up, frowning. "What?"

"You are a good father and you're not as selfish as you think. You're risking the senator's wrath to make sure Angie's safe and happy." Impulsively, she knelt beside Richard's chair. "I'll never be able to thank you enough for this, Richard."

Looking more than a little uncomfortable, Richard smiled slightly and stood. "Just make sure my daughter's happy."

Hayden moved forward to shake Richard's hand. "That's a promise that's easy to make. We'll take good care of both of them."

Chandler helped Elizabeth to her feet, wrapping an arm around her waist. "With pleasure. Now are you going to tell the senator, or are we?"

Richard smiled, genuine amusement lighting his eyes. "Oh, allow me. You owe me that much." Folding his suit jacket over his arm, he started out.

Hayden smiled. "One other thing…"

Richard paused on his way to the door. "What?"

Hayden's grin was one she remembered from years earlier. "I've already sent everything Elizabeth had to the newspapers. She no longer has anything on him that the rest of the world won't know about in a few hours."

Stunned, Elizabeth could only gape at him. "You really did that?"

Hayden inclined his head in that sexy way he had. "I called the senator as soon as I put it in the safe and told him I'd use it if he ever threatened you or Angie. He did. I never bluff."

Richard laughed, a deep belly laugh she'd never heard from him before. "Oh God. I've got to get home. I can't wait to see the bastard's face."

Chandler shook his head. "You really hate your father so much?"

"Can't stand his fucking guts. He's interfered in my life too many times. We were never close, and he didn't want a damned thing to do with me until I was already grown. He and my mother deserve each other." Starting for the door again, he stopped, turning to Elizabeth. "When Angelina gets old enough to understand, do you think you could explain…?"

Nodding, Elizabeth realized she'd never really known Richard at all. "I will."

The joy she saw on Hayden's face before he turned to walk Richard out had her tears flowing freely. Wrapping her arms around Chandler's waist, she buried her face against his chest. "It's over."

Chandler lifted her chin, his own eyes misty as he kissed her lightly and wiped away her tears. "No, baby. It's only just begun."

# Chapter Ten

Flanked by Hayden and Chandler, Elizabeth stood on the front porch, waving goodbye. Angie had been beside herself with excitement all week, talking about little else but the trip to the circus with both sets of her grandparents. "Did you see your parents' faces when Angie called them grandma and grandpa?"

Chandler bent to kiss her hair. "I probably looked that way the first time she called me Daddy."

Hayden ran a hand over the shoulder that had healed, something he did often. "I have no idea how much she understands but thankfully she seems happy."

Elizabeth giggled, happier than she'd ever been. "She's thrilled. Neither one of us has ever been so happy, and she loves her two daddies like crazy."

Hayden smiled. "Her two daddies love her."

Chandler pinched her bottom. "How about her momma?"

Squealing, Elizabeth jerked away, turning to face both of them. Running her hands over Chandler's and then Hayden's chest, she smiled seductively, dancing away when Chandler reached for her. "Everyone's gone. Even Martha has the day off." Circling them, she ran a hand over their tight butts and the zippers of their worn jeans, smiling as the bulges grew under her caress. "How about if I show you?"

Whipping an arm out, Hayden snagged her around the waist, tossing her over his shoulder. "How about if you do?"

Chandler followed them into the house, running his hand over her bottom and thighs. "We're all alone, darlin'. You're in for it now."

Running her hands over Hayden's butt, she giggled, marveling at how lighthearted she felt now that the senator was no longer a threat.

The pictures of him with numerous women and the following interviews with the same women, who freely admitted to having slept with the senator, effectively ruined his career.

She pushed those thoughts of him away and turned her head to look up at Chandler. "Oh, you sweet talker. I'm all aquiver."

Running his hand over her bottom, he slid it between her legs. "Not yet, but you will be."

Hayden started up the stairs, his hand still on her bottom. "I'm taking this ass."

"Holy hell."

"I thought that might get your attention."

Elizabeth shuddered as Hayden carried her into the master bedroom and set her on her feet. Chandler followed them in, kicking the door closed behind him.

Hayden turned her, pulling her back against him, and burying his face in her hair. "You trust us, baby?"

Elizabeth moaned as his hands came up under her shirt to unsnap her bra and cover her breasts. "Yes."

Chandler reached for the snap of her shorts. "You'd better." Bending, he kissed her, nibbling at her lips as Hayden ran his fingers over her nipples. "Soon you're gonna be taken like never before."

Just thinking about what they would do to her had her insides clenching. They'd touched her there several times in the last few weeks, each time exciting her more than the last. The dark promises they'd made, telling her how incredibly full she'd be, excited the hell out of her.

It had driven her crazy with anticipation for weeks. It looked like today her waiting had come to an end. They quickly stripped her of her clothes, leaving her naked between them.

Fisting his hand in her hair, Hayden tilted her head back to take her mouth with his, using his other hand to manipulate her nipples.

The feel of his denim-covered cock pressing into the small of her back had her arching against him, gasping into his mouth when Chandler knelt in front of her and spread her folds. Not being able to see him somehow aroused her even more. No matter how many times they did things like this, it never failed to excite her. His bare thighs spread hers making her tremble when she realized he'd already undressed.

Leaning back against Hayden, she gripped his forearms tightly as Chandler ran his tongue through her slit.

Chandler's breath felt warm on her thigh. "Nice and wet as always, baby."

Hayden lifted his head, looking over her shoulder, but keeping her from turning to see Chandler. "Hmm, Chandler looks like he's enjoying himself." He smiled at her as he pinched a nipple.

The jolt of heat went straight to her clit, which throbbed under Chandler's attention, burning more with each mind-numbing stroke. Her nipples ached, needing a firmer touch, which Hayden denied her.

Her clit burned hotter, her body gathering when suddenly Chandler stopped. Groaning in frustration, she gripped Chandler's shoulders as he stood and lifted her against his chest.

Chandler's mouth covered hers, giving her the taste of herself as he moved toward the bed. Raising his head, he eyed her mouth hungrily. "I want to feel that mouth on my cock."

Rubbing against him, Elizabeth caught his bottom lip between her teeth and tugged. "I want to feel your cock in my mouth. Hard and thick and hot."

Setting her on her feet, he ran a hand down her bottom. "And then in your pussy."

Hayden, now naked, moved in from behind. "And your ass."

Watching Chandler eagerly as he positioned himself on the bed, Elizabeth crawled up between his legs, eyeing the way he stroked his cock, the drop of moisture on the tip making her mouth water. "Why don't you let me do that?"

Chandler released his cock and leaned back on his elbows. "Mouth only. Keep your hands right where they are."

Licking the plum-sized head, she smiled around it, her eyes fluttering closed as Hayden ran a hand down her back and to her slit. Keeping her hands on either side of Chandler's hips, she took him into her mouth, running her tongue over his cock, savoring the taste of him. It soon became hard to concentrate on what she was doing, her mind and senses taken over by Hayden's touch.

He spread her thighs even wider, stroking her pussy, his talented fingers driving her quickly toward the edge.

Elizabeth shuddered with both pleasure and emotion, still amazed that both men were really hers. Even knowing what they were about to do, she trusted them completely, knowing that neither one of them would ever hurt her.

If anything, they still babied her too much.

She wanted to see if she could make them want her so much they could forget about all of that, at least temporarily. She sucked Chandler deep to her throat, tilting her bottom higher, determined to make them wild for her.

"Fuck, Lizzy. Stop. Now."

Ignoring Chandler, she ran her tongue over the underside, digging her nails into his thighs, moaning when Hayden withdrew his fingers and began stroking her clit.

Chandler gripped her hair, pulling her away from his cock with a harsh groan. "Damn, I'm too fucking hot, just thinking about it. Let go, baby."

Hayden withdrew from her and slapped her lightly on the bottom.

With a firm grip, Chandler pulled her over his chest. "I like you right where you are."

She heard a drawer open and shut before two condoms landed on the bed beside her. "I like where I am, too." She closed her eyes again, rubbing her stomach against the hard cock that pressed into it, moaning when Chandler's hands went to her breasts.

Shivers racked her body as Hayden parted her wide again, positioning her legs outside of Chandler's. Wiggling against Chandler, she froze when a cold, lube-coated finger touched her bottom hole. Even though they'd done this several times, she could never quite become accustomed to having her anus invaded.

Hayden separated the cheeks of her bottom, spreading the lube liberally before pressing a finger into her, his hand on her bottom tightening when she shuddered. "Nice and easy, Lizzy."

Chandler seemed to know she needed more and slid his hand under her, his callused fingers resting on her clit, unmoving.

She rocked her hips, needing the friction, which also moved her on Hayden's finger. But she couldn't stop.

"That's it, Lizzy. Fuck yourself on my finger."

Shocked by the way he talked to her, she stilled. "Oh, God." Catching her breath, she held onto Chandler as she began moving again, unable to remain motionless.

"Two fingers now, Lizzy."

Unable to believe how her bottom opened to the relentless pressure of his fingers, she whimpered as the tight ring of muscle gave way. The burn, as always, surprised her, making her anus tingle in a way that seemed to take over her completely. It made her clit burn hotter, her pussy clench tighter, and her nipples ache to be touched.

Chandler removed his hand from between her legs. "No more of that. You're gonna come too soon." Wrapping an arm around her, he held her immobile against him.

"Damn it, Chandler. Oh!"

Hayden withdrew from her, leaving her empty and needy. "Christ, with the way she's clamping down on my fingers, I can only imagine what she's gonna feel like on my cock. Just a little more lube, darlin'."

With her face buried against Chandler's chest Elizabeth's arousal grew. The trepidation about what would soon happen only added to it.

Chandler held onto her thighs, keeping them parted with her knees on the bed, her bottom high, which also kept her from rubbing her clit against him.

The entire area from her clit to her anus burned, her body automatically arching her bottom higher, exposing herself completely to Hayden's ministrations. Needing his touch, she pushed back, offering herself to him completely. Her thighs had long since become coated with her juices, the addition of the lube making her slick along her entire slit. As Hayden worked even more of that lube into her, her anus gripped at him, desperate now to be filled as whimpered cries continued to erupt from her throat.

She never would have believed she would not only allow, but actually *need* something there. When Hayden leaned forward and wrapped an arm around her waist to pull her back against him, she gasped at the feel of his cock bobbing against her. Her body had become so sensitized that every touch enflamed her, and she burned everywhere as she watched Chandler clumsily don a condom. The fact that his hands shook make her feel even better.

"Ready, baby?"

Reaching up, she grabbed Hayden's shoulders, arching her neck to give him better access. "God, yes." She trembled when the muscles under her hands bunched and shifted as he lifted her slightly, positioning her over Chandler's waiting cock.

Inch by inch, Chandler filled her, his slow possession making her squirm.

Once his cock was seated to the hilt inside her, she rocked her hips helplessly. "Oh God. I'm going to come."

Chandler tugged once at her nipples, making her cry out as the warning tingles from her slit spread. "No. You're not coming until we're both inside you. Be still." He took her from his brother, wrapping his arms around her to pull her tightly against his chest. "Don't move. Fuck. Those hard little nipples are poking into me. Wait 'til I get my mouth on them again. Stop wiggling, damn it. Hayden, would you hurry the fuck up? I'm dying down here."

With a rip of foil, Hayden chuckled. "I'm enjoying the show. Do you know how fucking sexy it is to watch this lubed ass wiggling and know that I'm going to fuck it? Ready baby?"

Shaking with nerves and excitement, Elizabeth gripped Chandler tightly, moaning deeply when she felt the tip of Hayden's cock at her opening. "I want it so bad but I'm afraid."

With a hand on her back, Hayden held her steady. "Nice and slow, Lizzy." His low crooning came out ragged and deep, doing nothing at all to soothe her.

In fact it did just the opposite. Their hands gripped her more firmly than ever with a savageness that she'd never experienced in their lovemaking before.

But this is what she'd wanted, and she'd been damned if she let herself chicken out now.

Besides, she needed this, all her inhibitions fleeing as she pressed down against Chandler, tilting her bottom up for Hayden's possession. Squeezing her eyes closed, she groaned at the relentless press of his cock against her opening. When the tight ring of muscle gave way under Hayden's demand for entrance, she cried out, amazed at how much it burned. It felt nothing like his fingers, and just knowing it was his cock working steadily into her made her feel more vulnerable and helpless than she could ever have anticipated.

Each shallow stroke took him a little deeper, opening her up to his erotic possession. Chills racked her body as he continued, her cries and whimpers becoming louder and wilder with every stroke.

Hayden's hands tightened on her hips. "Too fucking tight." His voice sounded tortured, his breath coming out in groans.

Elizabeth felt as if her body no longer belonged to her. They'd taken it over completely. Each stroke of their hands, brush of their lips, or thrust of their cocks controlled her. Her anus burned, the indescribably full feeling stealing her breath. Taken completely, she could do nothing but hold on to Chandler as they stretched her in a way she'd never thought possible.

Hayden's voice, barely recognizable, rumbled close to her ear as his big body covered hers. "Fuck, Lizzy. You feel so good."

"Oh God. It's amazing." Her clit burned where it pressed against Chandler, and the friction on it as they moved her had her clenching on both of their cocks. Groaning harshly, they set up a rhythm, holding her securely for their deep thrusts, only to withdraw and thrust into her again. Her body jolted repeatedly as though touched by a live wire, and the erotic tingling of her pussy and anus combined with the sharp pleasure of the friction on her clit.

Filled to overflowing, her body gripped them both tightly, feeling every bump and ridge of their cocks as they slid over sensitive tissue. Suddenly it became too much. Holding onto Chandler's shoulders she came with long swells of sizzling heat that burned her pussy and anus and spread everywhere.

She tilted her head back, the cries erupting from her throat frightening her, sounding more animalistic than human.

Both men groaned hoarsely, Chandler's head thrown back as he rocked her on his cock, the pulsing of both cocks inside her prolonging her own orgasm.

Hayden's ragged groan sounded like nothing she'd ever heard before, and his hands, like vices, held her steady. His breathing sounded ragged in her ear. "If you don't think we want you after that…"

Elizabeth held onto Chandler's heaving chest, struggling to catch her breath. "Holy hell."

Chandler chuckled, the sound of it rumbling in his chest and comforting against her ear. "Now that we have that settled…"

Hayden kissed her shoulder and withdrew, smacking her bottom lightly before dropping a kiss on it. "I'm gonna take a shower. You want to wash my back?"

"I'm dead."

She yelped as Hayden lifted her off of Chandler's cock and into his arms. "Let's wake you up."

Curling into him, Elizabeth smiled. "Aren't you worn out?"

Lifting her, he dropped a quick kiss on her lips. "It seems with you, I have a never ending supply of energy for sex."

Burying her face in his shoulder, she blew out a shaky breath. "I can't believe we actually did that."

Hayden tightened his hold. "I never bluff, baby. You'd better remember that."

He entered the shower stall, turned the water on, and held her under the spray that hadn't yet warmed.

Elizabeth squealed. "Hayden, I'll get you for that!"

Hayden laughed and stuck his own head under the spray, kissing her deeply. Turning before they both drowned, he braced her against the wall. "Say it."

The tenseness in his body and on his face told her that this wasn't the time to tease. "I love you, Hayden Scott. I've loved you and Chandler since I was sixteen years old and not a day went by that I didn't miss you."

Groaning, he buried his face in her neck, a shudder wracking his body. "Christ, I felt like some sort of pervert for wanting you when you were still a teenager. Even my father saw it and told me to stay the hell away from you. When you went away…"

Alarmed when he shuddered again, Elizabeth gripped him tighter. "I'm back and I'm not a little girl anymore. I'm a woman who loves you."

The hand on her bottom tightened as he lifted her against him. "Show me."

\* \* \* \*

Lying on the bed, Chandler smiled.

He couldn't imagine life getting any better than this. Knowing how much Hayden needed this time alone with her, Chandler stayed where he was. His brother still paced the house at night, checking and double checking the windows. Not a night went by that he didn't get up at some point to check on Angie.

He couldn't help but grin every time he thought about the senator's fate. Richard had been the one to call to tell them that his father was now a broken man. The people he'd lied to and manipulated over the years turned against him. The senator's number of friends declined steadily until he'd had no choice but to resign and go with his wife to a property they owned by a lake somewhere.

Richard seemed thrilled with his life now and had actually proposed to his girlfriend, a woman his father couldn't stand.

Angie seemed more content and settled every day, and her laughter was often heard in the halls. She'd named every animal she came across and had already turned most of the ranch hands into her willing slaves.

Life was good.

Lizzy's squeal interrupted his musing.

Hayden's bark of laughter followed. It was a sound Chandler hadn't heard the entire time Lizzy had been gone but he heard frequently now. "But Lizzy, I'm just trying to help you wash off the lube."

"That's not how you wash it off. Hayden!"

Since it sounded like fun, Chandler stood and slipped into the steamy bathroom. Tossing his condom into the trash, he made his way through the steam. "Let me help you with that, Hayden."

Elizabeth squealed again through her laughter. "What on earth have I taken on?"

Chandler opened the shower door, his cock stirring as Hayden braced Elizabeth against the shower wall. "Two men who love you to death. Now about that lube…"

# THE END

www.leahbrooke.net

# ABOUT THE AUTHOR

When Leah Brooke isn't spending time with family or friends, she can be found working on her laptop creating new stories.

## *Also by Leah Brooke*

Desire, Oklahoma 1: *Desire for Three*
Desire, Oklahoma 2: *Blade's Desire*
Desire, Oklahoma 3: *Creation of Desire*
Desire, Oklahoma 4: *Rules of Desire*
Dakota Heat 1: *Her Dakota Men*
Dakota Heat 2: *Dakota Ranch Crude*
*Alphas' Mate*
Tasty Treats Anthology, Volume 2: *Back in Her Bed*

Available at
**BOOKSTRAND.COM**

**Siren Publishing, Inc.**
**www.SirenPublishing.com**

LaVergne, TN USA
09 January 2011
211724LV00009B/39/P